STRUM YOUR HEART OUT

CRYSTAL KASWELL

This is a work of fiction. Similarities to real people, places, or events are entirely coincidental.

STRUM YOUR HEART OUT
First edition. November 17, 2015.
Copyright © 2015 Crystal Kaswell.
Written by Crystal Kaswell.
Cover by Melody Jeffries.

Also by Crystal Kaswell

Sinful Serenade
Sing Your Heart Out - Miles
Strum Your Heart Out - Drew
Rock Your Heart Out - Tom
Play Your Heart Out - Pete
Sinful Ever After – series sequel
Just a Taste - Miles's POV

Dangerous Noise
Dangerous Kiss - Ethan
Dangerous Crush – Kit
Dangerous Rock – Joel
Dangerous Fling – Mal
Dangerous Encore - series sequel

Inked Hearts
Tempting - Brendon
Hooking Up - Walker
Pretend You're Mine - Ryan
Hating You, Loving You - Dean
Breaking the Rules - Hunter
Losing It - Wes
Accidental Husband - Griffin
The Baby Bargain - Chase

Inked Love

The Best Friend Bargain - Forest
The First Taste - Holden
The Roomie Rulebook - Oliver

Dirty Rich

Dirty Deal - Blake
Dirty Boss - Nick
Dirty Husband - Shep
Dirty Desires - Ian
Dirty Wedding - Ty
Dirty Secret - Cam

Pierce Family

Broken Beast - Adam
Playboy Prince - Liam
Ruthless Rival - Simon
Tempting Teacher - Max

Standalones

Broken - Trent & Delilah

Come Undone Trilogy

Come Undone
Come Apart
Come To Me

Sign up for the Crystal Kaswell mailing list

Chapter One

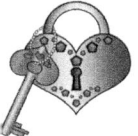

A buxom fan saunters in my direction. But she's not interested in me. I am invisible to her.

Her eyes are on Drew. She smiles. She shoves her hand in his face like I'm not here. "Oh my gosh. You must be Drew Denton. I'm such a big fan."

He shakes her hand, no signs of interest on his face. "I am."

She drags her fake red fingernails over Drew's forearm and thrusts her chest at him. "I love Sinful Serenade," she slurs. "You're sooooo good with your hands."

The worst thing about having a rock star guitarist for a best friend is hearing that line over and over and over.

Drew's lips curl into a smile. A smug expression creeps onto his face. "That's what I'm told."

And there's the second worst thing—hearing him give that same flirty response to every fan who is too rude to acknowledge the girl sitting next to him. Is it that obvious we're just friends or is she too desperate to care?

"Do you think... oh, gosh. Could you sign my, um..." She giggles. "My chest?"

His eyes dart to said chest. It's hard to blame him when her top is cut down to her belly button. No judgment. I've worn far sluttier things. Hell, my current getup could go toe to toe with this girl's in a *who is showing the most boob* competition.

A girl has to do what she can to get what she wants.

Apparently, this girl wants Drew's attention on her cans.

It's working. His eyes are wide. His mouth is open. He's staring like he's thinking about burying his face between her boobs.

Not that it bothers me or anything. Not like I want him to look at me that way. Not anything like that.

I adjust my bustier top for maximum cleavage potential and push myself up from my seat. Drew looks at me for a second, then his attention goes right back to the fangirl.

She drags those red fingernails up his biceps. "How do you stay so... fit on tour?"

He smiles. "On the floor."

She gasps like she's not at all familiar with the concept of push-ups. He smiles, all cocky and smug and totally cool.

He never flirts like this.

Never.

It shouldn't bother me. He's my friend and he can flirt with anyone he wants.

Doesn't mean I have to watch it.

I make my way to the dance floor, through the horde of twenty-something beautiful people here for the scene and not the music.

It's a pulsating, throbbing, electronic thing. Perfect. I step onto the vinyl. Eyes closed. Arms over my head. I shift my hips back and forth. No fancy moves. Just instinct.

The fangirl's hyena laugh cuts through the room. I

must be imagining things. There's no way she's louder than the music.

Drew is still talking to her. Not so much flirting but certainly staring at her cans.

This tension builds in between my shoulder blades. It's all wrong. My body is loose and free when I dance. Tension is not part of the equation. And Drew is my friend. He's flirting with a floozy. So what? He's a rock star. He probably flirts with lots of floozies.

He probably fucks them too.

My nostrils flare. I shake my head and press my eyelids together. No. I refuse to feel this right now. I refuse to feel anything except the music.

I throw myself into dancing. The world melts away, one piece at a time. The rest of the club. The hyena laugh. Drew's wide-eyed, lust-filled smile as the fangirl mauls him.

It's not even on my mind.

I move closer to the speakers. They drown out every other thought inside my brain. I'm only a vessel for the music. My hips move of their own accord. My chest shifts. My arms sway.

I'm free.

And then there are hands on my hips. Strong hands. A guy's hands. It's a normal part of clubbing. Usually one I enjoy.

But this feels off. I take a step forward to break free of the hands, so it's nothing but *me* and the music. Better. That tension between my shoulder blades relaxes. I drift into bliss...

The damn hands are back! I turn to face this guy. He's tall. Broad. He looks like a TV actor—handsome but not out-of-this-world hot. Any other night, I'd welcome him as a dance partner.

I throw my arms above my head and match his movements. He's a good dancer—perfectly in time with the rhythm. It's not all together awful.

He takes a step toward me, so he's pressed up against me. Those hands go to my hips again. No more bliss. I'm utterly on edge, tense and strained in all the wrong places.

"Excuse me." I make my way to the bar, some area free of guys with too few manners to ask permission.

The guy follows me. "Can I buy you a drink?"

"No thank you."

"Come on. It will be fun." He grabs my wrist. The left. Right above my silver watch.

I pull my hand into my chest. Manners be damned, next time he does that, I'm slapping him.

I offer my most polite smile and shake my head. "No thank you. I'm here with someone."

"Who?"

Fine. I hate using this line, but it's the only thing that works on guys like this. "My boyfriend."

The guy takes a long, hard look at me. At my cleavage, mostly. That awkward, awful tension builds between my shoulder blades again.

What the hell? This is supposed to feel good. A hot guy is checking me out. A hot guy wants to press his body up against mine in time with the music.

"Your boyfriend lets you go out like that?" he asks.

"Believe it or not, I have this funny thing called free will." I step backward. "And I don't let guys tell me what to wear."

"Your boyfriend sounds like a pussy."

"I'll let him know your feelings." Okay. The bar thing isn't working. Time for the nuclear option. I make my way to the women's restroom.

The guy follows. "I only want to talk."

"And I don't."

I take a quick step, but, even with my heels, I've got short legs and this guy is all kinds of tall. He's faster than I am.

He grabs my wrist. The right. I shake it off. No slapping necessary. Yet.

"You don't have to be so rude," he says.

Obviously, I do, because he's not taking the hint. I turn so I'm facing the asshole. Anger flares in my gut. I manage to hold my tongue. There are merits to telling this guy what he can do with that grabby hand, but it seems silly to cause a scene. It's easier to slip away with a careful excuse. No conflict necessary.

"Excuse me, ladies' room," I say.

He reaches for me again. Left wrist this time. Okay, that's it. I pull my hand free and go to slap him.

Someone stops me. His hand closes around my tricep. There's something right about it. Something magical.

It's Drew. Drew's hand is tight around my arm. Drew is touching me.

He looks at the asshole guy. "Can I help you?"

The guy looks at me with disbelief. "This is your boyfriend?"

I throw Drew a *please play along* look. "Yes. And we're very busy tonight."

"Is this guy bothering you?" Drew asks.

"It's fine."

"It doesn't look fine." Drew's eyes narrow. He stares down the guy. "You followed her across the dance floor."

He was watching me?

"We were having a conversation," the guy says.

"You grabbed her. Do it again and it will be the last time you ever touch anyone or anything beautiful," Drew says.

The guy holds Drew's stare. Trying out some kind of

intimidation and failing miserably. I almost feel bad for him. Idiot has no clue what he's in for.

The guy takes a step back. He mutters under his breath. "She's not even that hot."

"We both know that's not true." Drew slides his hand around my waist.

But the guy is still staring at us.

I turn to Drew. I slide my arm around his neck to sell the whole *we're clearly a couple* thing.

But the guy is still staring at me.

Drew stares back at him. "Either you leave in the next thirty seconds or we take this outside."

It does nothing to scare the guy off.

I grab Drew's arm and squeeze as hard as I can. No way I'm going to be responsible for the kind of fight that will get all three of us kicked out of the club.

Drew turns back to me. He takes my arm and places it around his shoulders. It's like he's promising this won't get out of hand.

His eyes find mine. He mouths, *You trust me?*

I nod. Yes. Of course.

His palm pressed into my lower back, pushing my body into his. He leans closer. His eyes close.

Mine do the same. Pure reflex. I rise to my tiptoes.

His lips brush against mine. A quick kiss to start. Then it's more. He sucks on my lower lip. He digs his other hand into my hair.

My heart picks up until it's going so fast I can't keep track. I'm aware of every inch of my body. The light feeling in my chest and stomach. The strain of my calves. The flutter building between my legs.

This is why I dance.

Drew releases me. He steps back and looks as if to check that the coast is clear. His demeanor shifts. No longer my fake boyfriend. Just my best friend. "You okay, Kara?"

"Yeah."

His arms goes back to his sides. His body moves away from mine. My heart is still racing. My chest is still light. I'm still acutely aware of every place that stretches, of every flutter or rush or buzz of electricity.

Drew kissed me.

For show, but still.

Drew kissed me and my entire body is still in overdrive.

Drew. Kissed. Me.

And, God I want him to kiss me again.

Chapter Two

Three Months Later...

"*Oh! Oh! Oh! Oh!*"

The bed upstairs squeaks like it's going out of style.

"*Miles! I'm almost... Oh... Oh... Oh...*"

"*Meg...*"

"*Uh...*"

Tom laughs. His messy brown hair falls over his eyes. "I never thought anyone would trump Pete."

"I do not sound like that," Pete says.

"*Oh... Oh... Oh...*"

Miles is a singer. It makes sense he's loud. The groans are not all that different from the ones he makes on Sinful Serenade tracks.

I can handle that.

But, dammit, I do not need to hear my best friend in the throes of orgasm.

Especially not with Drew on the other side of the couch.

"*Oh... Oh... Oh...*"

"*Mhmmm...*"

I press my eyes closed and open them. Nope. Not a dream. I'm still in Miles's house, listening to him have sex. He and Meg are all the way upstairs. How is it possible the sound is carrying like this?

Tom shoves his way onto the couch. The drummer is not shy about demanding his way. He pushes Drew over, so Drew's pressed up against me. His knee, his outer thigh, his shoulders—they're all pressed up against me.

There's this flutter just below my belly. I ignore it.

The groans run together into this strange mix of *oh yes, mhmm, oh, oh, OHHHHHHH*.

Tom laughs. "This is such sweet revenge."

Pete shakes his head. "Cindy and I are poetry." The bassist turns toward the noise with an amused smile. "That's pornographic."

"There's nothing poetic about *I'm coming in your mouth*." Tom nudges Drew to scoot over. He motions to me. "Give me some room. Sit on his lap or something."

Drew shoots him a death glare as he points to the empty love seat. "There's a couch right there."

MHMM!!!!!! UH!!!!!!!!!!

OH, OH OHHHHHHHHHHHHHH!!!!

The squeaking and groaning builds to a crescendo and it crashes into a somehow equally loud mix of sighs. I guess they came. Hopefully, Miles has a slow refractory period.

I put on my best happy face. The one everyone expects from me. "I will if you sit on Pete's lap."

"No way." Tom sticks his tongue out like he's disgusted.

Pete plops down on the love seat and pats his groin. "Are you afraid you'll like it?"

Tom jumps off the couch. "Forget it." He reaches for

Pete's phone and throws it to him. "Why don't you call Cindy so we can all have a round two, huh?"

"It's two a.m. in New York," Pete says.

"And that's stopped you before?" Tom asks.

There's more space on the couch—the left seat is totally empty—but Drew is still pressed against me.

That flutter shifts lower and lower. It's in full effect. It's ready to throw a tantrum to demand all of my attention.

I push myself off the couch with my best smile. "Excuse me."

Tom nods a goodbye of some kind. Drew turns ever so slightly toward me. I move to the kitchen so my back is to him, but I can still feel his eyes on me.

I pour a glass of water and drink it slowly. Pete and Tom are sparring about something. They're laughing and teasing, still oblivious to my discomfort.

The sliding door to the backyard is unlocked. I pull it open and step outside. It's mercifully quiet here. Cold, but mercifully quiet. Goosebumps spread on my legs.

I sit on the concrete, slide out of my shoes, and dip my feet in the water. The pool is cold but it warms up quickly.

The stars are shining brilliantly. No light pollution all the way in Malibu. Nothing around us except sky and ocean.

The sliding door opens. Footsteps move closer. I keep my eyes on the sky, but I don't need my eyes to know who it is.

My heart is racing. It must be Drew.

"You look comfortable." He sits on the concrete next to me.

I nod. My gaze turns toward him. His deep brown eyes are on me. Those are such gorgeous eyes and the rest of him is even better. Messy black hair. Strong jaw. Broad shoulders. His chest piece tattoo peeking out from his v-neck t-shirt.

I bring my gaze back to his eyes. My heart does nothing to slow down. It's still going rapid fire. Damn thing has no concern for my wishes.

"The water is nice," I say. "Once you get used to it."

"Is that right?" Drew kicks off his Converse sneakers and pulls off his socks in a smooth, seamless motion. His voice gets a little lower. "You don't have to stay and listen to that."

"It's fine," I say.

He raises an eyebrow. "You don't look fine."

"Well I am." I pull my arms over my ample chest. It barely fits into this dress. It barely fits into any dress. But that doesn't usually bother me.

Drew plants his hands on the edge of the concrete and leans toward me. "How much will you give me to skinny dip?"

"You're the one with money."

Drew laughs. "Okay. No bribery necessary." He glances toward the house where Tom and Pete are still going at it. "But you have to promise not to look."

My jaw drops ever so slightly. Drew naked. Drew naked. Drew naked. I cannot think about Drew naked.

"You don't have the balls," I say.

"The way you're talking, it sounds like you're going to look."

"No."

"I wouldn't blame you." He taps my shoulder with his. "After all that time in Asia, I'm pale enough to glow in the moonlight."

"You are not."

In the house, Tom screams something in our general direction. He and Pete wave goodbye.

"Don't be late to practice Monday!" he yells. "And don't forget to use protection."

Drew sends Tom another death glare. It only amuses the guy. By now, I'm well aware I'm a running joke. *Drew spends so much time with Kara. What the hell is he waiting for? A girl with tits like that... there must be something wrong with him.* The guys are not nearly as discreet as they think they are.

The front door opens and shuts. A car in the driveway turns on and pulls away. Tom and Pete are on their way home.

"Tom's an idiot," Drew says.

I kick my feet. There's so much drag in the pool. It's like moving in slow motion. "He's only kidding."

"He should learn to mind his own business." Drew shakes his head. "I can't wait to get my own place."

"Oh?"

His mood lightens. "You want to come apartment shopping with me?"

"That's a girlfriend task."

"You're a girl and you're my friend."

"This kind of thing is the reason why Tom teases you."

"I'll live." He nudges me playfully. "Come on. It will be no fun if I do it alone."

My heart is racing. Racing like a freight train. But I manage a calm expression. "Sure. My internship is done by six most nights, and I don't have class Friday."

"Perfect." He leans back and looks at the moon. "I'm going to do it."

"Move?"

"Skinny dip."

My face flushes red. Thank God he's not looking at me. "You won't."

"I will if you will."

Not happening. I don't swim and I certainly don't swim naked.

I try to respond but my mouth is not cooperating. Drew naked. Must not picture Drew naked. Must not picture Drew coming out of the pool naked and dripping wet.

I press my knees together. Not helping.

"It's freezing," I say.

"You'll warm up fast."

He stands and grabs the bottom of his t-shirt like he's going to pull it off. He makes eye contact and cocks an eyebrow. A grin spreads across his face.

He pulls the t-shirt up, exposing inches of taut abs. That flutter spreads to my belly and thighs. My body is responding to an attractive body. It's instinct. It's totally out of my control.

"Next time." Drew drops his t-shirt. His offers me his hand. "Let's go inside."

He pulls me to my feet. I stumble—the concrete is wet—and he throws his arms around my waist. He squeezes me for a split second and releases me.

"Thank you." I step to the side and grab my shoes.

There's a sound in the house. More footsteps. Miles and Meg step outside. Fully clothed, thank God.

"Having fun?" Miles asks.

"Not as much fun as you two," Drew says.

Meg blushes. Miles smirks.

"Thanks for inviting me." I shove my foot into my shoe. "But I should get home."

"I'll go with you," Meg says. "If you don't mind."

"Of course not," I say.

"You're supposed to stay the night." Miles slides his arm around her. "I'll drive you home in the morning."

"No," she says. "You'll distract me."

"I'm not staying if I have to hear that again," Drew says.

"I've been with you all week." Meg kisses Miles. "It's time to see my friend now."

"Stay," Miles says. "We'll watch *Star Wars*."

Drew objects. "Fuck no. I'm never watching *Star Wars* again." He turns to me. "They watched it a dozen times in four fucking weeks."

"We've tortured them enough," Meg says. "Kara and I are going home and no boys are allowed."

They kiss goodbye. It starts as a peck and slides into some serious necking.

Drew shoots me a *can you believe this* look. I shrug. They're in love. It's sweet.

Meg pulls from the kiss with a heavy sigh. She's panting like she's about to take Miles upstairs for round two.

Sweet only goes so far.

"That's my cue." I find my keys in my purse and motion *come here* to Meg. "See you guys later."

"Yeah, later." Miles blows Meg a kiss.

She mimes catching it with a giggle.

Drew stares at me. There's something in his eyes, but I can't place it. I wave goodbye and lead Meg to the car.

―――

MEG AND I SPEND THE NIGHT AT HER PLACE, EATING CEREAL and watching movies instead of sleeping. She's bursting at the seams with stories about her time on tour. It's nice to see her so happy, even if I was stuck here, taking winter quarter classes, unable to join in the fun.

It's just after ten when I leave. It should give me a few

hours in the common area before my roommate, Nadeen, wants the couch.

Only she's sitting on the couch with a concerned look on her face when I arrive at home.

"Listen, Kara." She folds her arms over her chest. "We have to talk."

Chapter Three

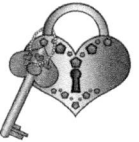

I run through a mental checklist of things that may have upset her, but nothing clicks. The bathroom is clean. There are no dishes in the sink. I haven't hogged the common area in weeks. I've mostly been in my room alone.

She watches me lock the door. I suppose I should ask her what it is that's wrong, but it's probably some minor thing from Nadeen's Big Book of Unacceptable Roommate Behavior.

She looks at the ground with a nervous expression. "Alex is moving in."

"There's no room for Alex here."

"I'm glad you agree." Her expression shifts. Not quite so nervous.

"Okay." I press my back against the door. I'm not sure where this is going, but I don't like it. "Well, as long as he's out of the way, it's fine with me."

"It's been fun living together and all, but Alex and I need to take our relationship to the next level."

"I'll wear headphones when I'm home." It's not like I'll

be the first college student to contend with her roommate having loud sex.

"See, he needs an extra room for his office."

"There are a lot of nice co-working spaces in Santa Monica."

"No. He wants to work from home."

She stares at me blankly. She wants me to put the pieces together. Nadeen's boyfriend needs an extra room. There are two rooms in this apartment. She's not about to give up her bedroom.

Shit.

Nadeen sighs. "We need you to leave by the end of the month."

"That's five days away."

"You can have your security deposit back."

"Gee, thanks so much." I press my palm flat against the door. Nadeen is kicking me out of my own apartment. Where the hell does she get the nerve? My breath kicks up. My heart races. I try to will myself to object, but it's not happening.

I'll only start a fight.

Her mind is made up. I'm screwed.

"Alex will help you move. His brother has a truck." She looks around the main room like she's taking inventory. "It's not like you have much stuff. Everything was here when you moved in. It was supposed to be temporary."

No. It was supposed to be this year. I was doing Nadeen a favor when her roommate bailed on her the week before classes started. I gave up a single in the dorms to live here. It made sense. The apartment was cheaper. Bigger. It came with two parking spaces.

"You could have told me earlier," I say.

"I'm sorry." Nadeen frowns. "I really feel bad. We're friends and you... you deserved more notice. Forgive me?"

Hell no. I run my hand through my hair. I step away from the door. "Yeah. Of course."

"Hey. Why don't you live with your boyfriend?" She asks.

"I don't have a boyfriend."

"No? But that guy is always over here. Um... what's his name? Does he have a job?"

"Drew. And he's in a band."

She scoffs. "Yeah. I see why that could be an issue. Maybe Meg has room in her place."

No. Meg has a tiny, tiny studio. She stays up until three a.m. studying every night. And her whole building smells like sushi.

Not that Nadeen cares. As long as she gets what she wants with as little friction as possible, she's happy.

As long as my wishes don't impose on hers, she's happy.

I fight the anger rising in my gut. "We agreed I would live here until school ended."

Nadeen frowns. "I'm so sorry, Kara. It was Alex's idea, but I really do want to live with him. And you'll be okay. I can help you find a new place."

"No thanks."

It's ten steps to my room and I'm away from Nadeen's desperate need to feel less guilty. I take them like it's no big deal. There really is no sense in starting a fight.

I step into my room and press the door closed. Finally, I can breathe properly.

This room isn't much, but it's been mine for the last six months. It's nice. It's comfortable.

This is a hassle, but it's not the end of the world.

I can figure it out.

Music. I need something to calm me down. I put my iTunes on shuffle and blast the volume. A rock song kicks on. It drowns out every bit of conscious thought in my brain.

I throw myself onto my bed and pull the covers over my head. It's calmer here. I'm alone. No one expects me to be their bubbly, supportive friend. No one expects me to take bad news without batting an eye. No one expects me to accept their bullshit half-hearted apologies.

The song changes. A familiar guitar riff fills the air. Damn. It's something off the last Sinful Serenade album.

That's Drew playing the guitar.

My stomach twists. I skip to the next track. I don't have time to deal with moving. Finance test tomorrow. Internship all day Tuesday. Essay due Wednesday.

My cell phone ring grabs my attention. I glance at the screen. Speak of the devil.

It's Drew.

I turn my music off and answer the call. Deep breath. Drew cannot, under any circumstance, know I'm upset.

"Hello." My voice is steady.

"You up for looking at apartments Tuesday around eight?" he asks.

"Yeah, sure. As long as I finish my essay." My voice cracks. Shit.

"Kara—"

"I have to study. I'll see you Tuesday. Just text me the address where we should meet."

"There's something in your voice."

"Remember how we talked about you minding your own business?" I ask.

"I'm afraid I don't recall."

A laugh breaks up the tension in my throat. He makes me feel so mixed up, but I have to keep up my *everything is okay* routine. Drew is so overprotective. He'll butt in and try to help, and I want to handle this on my own.

"I'll see you Tuesday." I hang up before he can respond.

My heart sinks. But that doesn't make any sense. It's not like I want to talk to Drew about this.

I turn my attention to my finance homework, but the uneasy feeling in my gut remains.

A KNOCK ON MY BEDROOM DOOR CUTS THROUGH THE music.

"Kara," Nadeen says. "Your boyfriend is here."

"I don't have a boyfriend," I yell back to her.

"Then what is he doing here?"

I push out of my chair and open the door. Nadeen is staring at me with an irritated look on her face. Almost like I'm the one trying to kick her out of her apartment.

I follow her into the main room.

Drew is here.

A lightness returns to my body.

"So, you know," Nadeen says. "You could ask him about moving in."

"He's not my boyfriend!"

Drew shoots me that *are you okay* look. I motion to my room. I'm not discussing anything in front of her.

He pushes past Nadeen like she isn't even there. "Come on." He grabs my hand, pulls me into the bedroom, and presses the door shut behind us.

"What's with her?" he asks.

I shrug like I don't know.

"You're so full of shit."

"Some people would consider that allegation rude," I say.

"Lucky for me you're not some people." He takes a few steps toward me. "You want to tell me why you're upset?"

"I'm not."

His eyes narrow. Not angry. Just serious. "You keep bullshitting me and I'll be the one who is upset."

"Good for you." On my computer, I pull up a PowerPoint presentation. It's Thursday's finance lecture.

I'm turned away from Drew, but I can feel him staring at me. His gaze is penetrating. It exposes something in me. Something I'd rather keep hidden.

I keep my eyes on the screen, like this is no big deal. "How can you care so much about other people minding their own business and be so willing to get in my business?"

"That's different."

"How?"

"I care about you. The guys are just creating gossip."

"They care about you too." Deep breath. My body is trying to react to this whole *I care about you* thing. It overreacts.

"It's not the same."

Okay. Body going into overdrive. My heart beat picks up. My mouth goes sticky. Does Drew even realize what he's doing to me? He must not. If he does, he's pure evil. There's no other plausible explanation.

He was sent from hell to rip my heart in pieces.

"I'm going to start guessing," he says.

"Okay. Fine. I'm going to keep studying. I have a test tomorrow."

"The second week of classes?" His voice is packed with doubt.

"It's a quiz. Does that settle things?"

"No." He takes another step toward me. "Something with Meg?"

"No." I drop my hands into my lap. "I'm not talking about it."

"Did you eat dinner?"

"I'm not hungry."

"It's almost eight. Don't make me drag you."

"You can't drag me. I'm too heavy."

He laughs. "You want to bet?"

My cheeks flush. Thank God he can't see them. I clear my throat. "No."

"You asked for this, Kendrick."

That flutter in my belly goes turbo. I'm melting over him calling me by my last name. I'm hopeless.

He leans over. His arms slide around my back. One slides all the way under my ass. It hooks around my thigh. I can feel the heat of his touch, even through my jeans.

His hand is so, so close.

Too close.

He lifts me from the chair with barely a grunt. He holds me against his chest like I'm a damsel in distress. There's no sign of tension on his face. He's not even strained.

Drew's lips curl into a smile and he tosses me on the bed. I land with the tiniest impact. He flops next to me. Right next to me.

"I bet you're still ticklish," he says.

Okay. Blush in full effect. Drew is trying to kill me. There is no other possible explanation.

I shake my head.

His smile widens. "You have two choices: tell me or suffer."

I shake my head again.

His eyes pass over my body. His hands hover over my stomach. Closer. Closer. Closer.

He tickles me. Oh God. Laughter rises from my belly to my throat. I kick my legs to contain the sensation. He was right. I am still ticklish. I'm unbearably ticklish.

Drew slides his hand under the edge of my top so it's

on the skin of my stomach. I can't do anything to contain the sensation. I kick and thrash and laugh until I can't take it anymore.

"Okay, okay. Mercy."

He doesn't relent. "Not until you admit you were upset."

"Okay, okay. I was upset."

He only tickles me harder. "And you admit why."

"Oh, God, stop."

I'm laughing so hard my stomach is aching and my cheeks are sore. I kick at his legs. I claw at his arms. He grabs one of my hands and pushes it over my head.

"Okay!" I scream. "It's Nadeen." A laugh escapes my throat. "She asked me to move out."

Everything in Drew's mood shifts. The happiness drains from his face. He's not having fun anymore. "Asked?"

I swallow hard. "I'll be okay. I'll find another place to live. It's not like Nadeen is a particularly good roommate." I shift toward the other edge of the bed. "I just have to find the time between class and my internship."

"Fuck that." He grabs my shoulder and turns me so we're face to face. "You're moving in with me."

"I can't."

"Why the hell not?" He doesn't wait for a response. "I'm getting a new place. You need a new place. It's perfect."

I play with the pockets of my jeans. "I don't want to impose."

"You don't."

"But you're so set to live alone."

He shifts toward me. His hand brushes against mine. "I'm set to live with someone who will respect my privacy." His eyes find mine. "I have absolute faith in you."

"Are you staying in LA that long?"

He nods. "It's home base now." His mood lightens. "It's a sweet deal. I'm on tour half the year but I pay my share of the rent every month. Place will be yours for three and a half months starting in April."

I nod. It would be a sweet deal with anyone but Drew.

Drew's hand closes around my right wrist. He looks me in the eyes. "Give me one good reason why not?"

How about the feeling coursing through my body, begging me to get back on that bed with him?

Drew doesn't see me that way. He's never going to see me that way. Being around him constantly...

It will drive me out of my damn mind.

"I have many reasons," I say.

He holds my stare. "So name one."

That's a bit more difficult.

Drew holds out his hand to shake. "We'll pick out a place together. Deal?"

Deal? I can't make a deal like this. Not if I want to live to graduate from college. Not if I want to keep breathing and sleeping and thinking.

I take a step backward. "Let me sleep on it."

"If you come to dinner with me."

"I have to study."

He slides his hand around my waist. "I'll throw you over my shoulder if I have to."

This time, I'm not challenging him.

I nod, and follow him to the car.

Truth is, I want to go to dinner with Drew. I want to live with Drew. I want everything with Drew. I've liked him since the day his family moved in to the house down the block and he invited me over to watch Batman cartoons.

I was eleven. He was one year older, already six inches taller than I was, already effortlessly cool. We were close until high school pushed us apart. By the time he went off to college, we weren't speaking. I figured I'd never see him again. Then he became a rock star, and I *knew* I'd never see him again.

I was wrong. About a year ago, he got back in touch. He wasn't a narcissistic fame whore who plowed through groupies. He was still Drew, that same caring, over-protective guy who could always see through me, who made me feel safe.

It was impossible to do anything but be his best friend.

Yes, I want him more than I want to breathe. I like him. More than that even.

But it's not worth risking our friendship. Sex will ruin things. It's better to be around him, even if he'll never be mine.

Drew is the most important person in my life.

I can't screw that up.

Chapter Four

I wake up to texts from Drew. The cross streets of a potential apartment and three low-resolution shots of it. He's so sure he'll get his way.

The place looks decent. I can see myself there. I can see us there, on a plush leather couch, watching one of Drew's favorite *Batman* movies. And I can feel the flutter building in my stomach as his hand skims my thigh. An accident. Means nothing. 'Cause we're only friends and we'll always be only friends.

I shove my phone into my backpack and promise myself I'll deal with this after class.

On my way out the door, I check the mailbox. No sign of my acceptance or rejection letter from the UCLA teaching program, but it's not due for another week.

My Finance 301 class is dull. My attention drifts to the browser open on my laptop. I can browse apartment listings and take notes at the same time.

That checks out.

There are about fifty rooms for rent in my neighborhood. Narrowing my price range knocks me down to a dozen options. Over half the available rooms come with a cat or dog. Those are out—I'm allergic to just about any animal with fur or feathers. Down to four. All of them use the words "open-minded roommate required" in the posting.

No way in hell that's happening.

Drew is my best option. Living with him is possible. So I'm attracted to him, so what? He's hotter than the molten center of the Earth. Of course my body reacts to his. And to his words and his voice and the way his cheeks crinkle when he smiles.

It's such a nice smile.

Okay. It's more than a crush. I'm fucking crazy about him. But I can't let that get in the way of a perfectly good living arrangement. Not when it's my best option.

I give myself until eleven p.m. to come up with another idea, but there isn't one. I'm going to live with Drew and I'm going to survive it.

I take a deep breath as I tap my reply.

Kara: Okay. Let's do it. Let's pick out an apartment together.

One minute later, my phone rings. Drew.

I pick up. "Why can't you text like a normal person?"

"You can't gloat in a text." His voice is cocky. "I'm glad you saw the light."

"It's not too late to change my mind."

"You won't."

"Goodnight, Drew."

His voice softens. "Sweet dreams."

I turn off my phone. It's just a crush. It's not going to kill me.

In theory.

Tuesday night, I go straight from my internship to the first potential apartment. Drew is leaning against the wall, picture perfect effortless rock star. His short, black hair is messy. His t-shirt hangs off his shoulders just so. Once again, it's cut just low enough to show a hint of ink.

What would it feel like to trace the lines of that tattoo?

Not that I want to touch him like that.

Not that I'm going insane thinking about touching him like that.

Not at all.

My blouse tugs against my chest. The top button threatens to come undone. I'm not sure what possessed me to buy a blouse with buttons. They never get along with my boobs.

I adjust the shoulders so the blouse rides a little higher, but that only sends the strain to the next button down.

We hug hello. His eyes pass over me. It's a quick thing, like he's taking in my outfit.

"I can't believe I've never seen you in professional mode," he says.

"One of us needs to class up the place.'

Drew nods to the apartment. I follow him up the stone staircase, to the second floor. Drew checks his phone and punches a code into a keybox. Success. He grabs a key and slides it into the lock.

He pushes the door open for me. "After you."

The room is nice but small. Beige carpet. Tiny rectangular windows. Cramped little kitchen.

Drew's hand brushes against my lower back. He nods to the one bedroom at the end of the tiny hallway.

"It's not bad." I say.

"It's a dump." He steps inside the bedroom. "But useful for comparisons."

"You're playing loose and fast with 'dump' for someone who lives on a tour bus."

"That bus is a dump," he says. "It's just for the road. We stay in hotels most nights."

"You're so fancy."

It *is* a small room. More carpet. Another rectangular window. A mirrored closet door.

He positions himself in front of the mirror and stares at his reflection. "I don't see it." He reaches for me and pulls me next to him, so we're both in the reflection. "I still don't see it."

He's too close. It feels too good.

I take a step back. "It's a little small."

He pulls his phone from his pocket and checks the time. "We're meeting another landlord in twenty minutes. Bigger place. Closer to UCLA."

It sounds perfect, but there's apprehension on his face.

"What's the problem?" I ask.

"Let's make a deal. You pay the same rent you were paying at your old place. I pay the rest."

"No way in hell. I'm paying half."

"Twice the rent you're paying gets you someplace like this." He nods to the peeling paint in the corner.

"You're not paying for me."

"Not for you. Just more than fifty percent. Consider it a fee for getting to make the final decision."

I throw him my best side-eye.

He cocks his eyebrow and folds his arms over his chest. "Kara."

"Yeah?"

"Your top button is undone." He smirks.

I look at my blouse. Dammit. He's right. I fix the button but it won't stay done.

Drew laughs. "I like it better that way."

I will not blush. I will not blush. Dammit, I will not blush! I clear my throat. "How much more than fifty percent are we talking?"

"It's not a lot of money to me." He takes a step toward me and brushes a stray hair behind my ear. "You'd be doing me a favor."

"You're so full of shit."

He grabs my wrist and moves toward the exit. "I'm going to get my way."

"You always do."

———

No way in hell.

This is not an apartment for a college student. The penthouse of a luxury condo is more appropriate for a movie star than a finance and literature double major.

This place must be two thousand square feet. Every wall is glass. The kitchen is stainless steel with quartz countertops. The balcony stretches on forever.

Drew looks at me. "There's a pool on the roof."

"No," I say.

"Should I prove it?"

"I can't live here. The rent probably costs more than my car."

"Your car is ancient."

I fold my arms.

Drew walks across the long living room. He opens a sliding door and steps onto the balcony. Even on this floor, it's loud. Wilshire is jammed and there's enough honking to prove it. The smell of gasoline and exhaust drifts into the room. Oh, Los Angeles, you really have a unique charm.

The wind whips Drew's hair and t-shirt. He turns and motions *come here*

I stay put. "This place is not us."

"What's us?"

"Don't you want to live in Hollywood?" I ask.

"So I can hit the clubs every night with Tom? No." His eyes find mine. "I want to live with you."

He steps inside, closing the door behind him. Instantly, the room is quiet. It's too quiet, actually. I can hear my racing heartbeat.

I clear my throat. "I hate Westwood."

"It's half a mile from UCLA."

"It's a clusterfuck. And all the people here are stuck up."

Drew raises an eyebrow. "You better watch yourself, Kendrick. Might offend someone."

"You're very down-to-earth. For a rock star." My blouse strains as I inhale. I adjust my purse so it's covering my chest. "Is there another option?"

Drew smiles. "Of course." He takes my hand. "And it's perfect."

———

THE LANDLORD LOOKS AT ME LIKE WE'RE CUT FROM THE SAME cloth. She's a lot like my mom—thin, impeccably groomed, wearing only the finest business casual attire. We shake hands. She says her name but it goes in one ear and out the other.

She turns to Drew with significantly less positivity. He's in skinny jeans and a t-shirt. I'm in my work getup. It looks like I'm the one with the job and the money and he's my handsome but useless trophy boyfriend.

"Aren't you a nice couple?" She smiles. "Will this be your first time living together?"

Drew nods. He doesn't correct her.

This place isn't an apartment at all. It's a single-family house. Cozy, but plenty of room for two.

We follow the landlord up a small stone path. The yard is all drought-tolerant plants—cacti and succulents surrounded by grey and white pebbles.

This place is at least twice the size of my current place. The main room stretches on forever. It has clean hardwood floors. The kitchen has an island. There's room for half a dozen mixing bowls and baking pans. There's room for fifteen coffee makers. I'm in love with the idea and I don't even drink coffee.

The landlord points to the stairs. "There are two bedrooms. You could use one room as an office. Or as a nursery. When the time comes."

Drew throws me a look. "Yeah, honey. It would make a nice nursery."

Two can play this game. "It's so nice that you want to be a stay-at-home dad, so my career can come first."

He raises his eyebrow *really?*

I nod. Sure, why not.

"Kara, sweetie, you know you always *come* first."

The landlord stares at us like we're crazy.

I press my palm against the sliding glass door to the backyard. There's a pool out there. It glows under the dark sky like a beacon of hope. It's practically screaming *this is the best place you will ever live and the only chance you'll ever have to go swimming without a panic attack.*

"Where do you work, Ms.—" she trails off.

"Kara is fine." I turn back to the rest of the house. It's huge. It's massive. It's perfect. "At Giffin Industries. I'm also a student."

"And you, Mr. Denton?"

He winks at me. "I'm in a band."

All that positivity falls right off her face. He's in a band. Talk about a loser who can't afford to pay the rent.

"We have to do a credit check. And we'll need some proof of employment. Our usual rule is that a couple needs to be making three times the rent before tax."

Drew cocks his eyebrows. He makes eye contact with me and smiles. It's like he's saying *watch this*.

He turns to her. "How about we skip all that and take a look at my Mint account."

He pulls his phone from his pocket. A few taps and he flashes the screen to the real estate agent. I can't see what's on display, but it must be a lot, because her frown turns right upside down.

Drew is no longer a penniless loser.

He has money now. He's worthy of her attention now. Never mind that he was always worthy of attention. Even before he was hotter than the sun. Even before he had enough money to rent a place like this.

I bite my lip. No reason to get upset with this woman for doing her job. It's not like she invented capitalism.

"I'd like to sign the lease now," he says. "Before my... Kara changes her mind about me."

The woman laughs like she doesn't consider this a possibility. After all, who changes her mind about the rich, hot rock star?

"I have a copy in my car," she says. "Feel free to look around the place."

Drew nods. He waits until she leaves to pull the sliding door open and step into the backyard.

"We never got the chance to go swimming at Miles's place," he says.

"And you're going to get naked, jump into the pool, and get dressed by the time she's back with the lease?"

Drew smirks. "She'll still approve us if I'm naked in the

pool." He turns back to me. "If anything, it will help our case."

My body buzzes. He offers his hand like he's beckoning me to follow him.

I shake my head.

"You used to be brave, Kendrick."

"Shove a sock in it." I move toward the stairs. "I'm checking out the bedrooms."

I turn so he won't see my face flush. Heat spreads through me. It calls all of my attention. It's like dancing. I'm acutely aware of every part of my body. Every sensation, every muscle, every stretch or strain.

Drew follows me up the stairs. He grabs my hand and jumps into the lead, pulling me into one of the upstairs bedrooms.

It's about average for Southern California. Cozy but not tiny. There's room for a bed, a desk, a dresser, and just enough empty space for floor work.

Drew takes in my expression. "You like it."

"Good thing since you already agreed to sign the lease."

He shrugs like he knew this would happen. His hand intertwines with mine and he leads me to the other bedroom.

The master bedroom. It's bigger and it has a mirrored closet door.

Drew stands next to me and stares at his reflection. We make a strange pair—me busting out of my blouse and skirt and him exuding effortless charisma in his perfectly fitted jeans and t-shirt. It's not that I don't hold up to him. It's just, right now, we look like opposites. My dark brown hair is in a tight bun. His black locks are hanging in his eyes. My outfit is light and neutral. His is dark and bold. I'm all soft, round curves. He's all hard lines.

Don't get me wrong. I'm decent looking. I may not be as thin as my mother is, but I'm just as good with my hair, makeup, and wardrobe. I work with what I've got. Cobalt eyeliner to bring out my brown eyes. A cinched waistline to play up my curvy frame. Three-inch heels to give me enough height to make eye contact without craning my neck.

But Drew is in a whole other tier. Even when he's trying to keep out of the spotlight, he stands out. Girls flock to him and he bats them away like it's nothing.

"How do you want to settle this?" he asks.

I shoot him a quizzical look.

"This is clearly the superior room. I'm willing to let you have it, but not without a fight."

"You can have it," I say. "Since you'll be paying—" I look around the room again. It looks outrageously expensive. "Ninety percent of the rent or something."

He frowns. "I don't want to hear anything like that again. We're equals here."

"But you're paying—"

"I don't care. Everything is even between us." He folds his arms across his chest. "Deal?"

I nod. "Okay, deal."

"How about we flip for it?"

"There must be a better way."

He pulls his wallet from his pocket and takes out a quarter. "Can you name one?"

Actually, I can't. I nod, okay, fine. We'll flip for it. "You flip. I'll call it in the air."

He nods. He places the coin over his thumb. Flip. It spins in the air.

"Head. Heads," I say.

And now my mind is right in the gutter.

Drew catches the coin in his palm. He makes eye

contact and raises an eyebrow. He looks down at the coin then holds his palm out so I can see it too. "*Head* it is."

I clear my throat. "Great."

"*Head* is great."

"Shut up."

He shrugs like he doesn't know what I'm talking about.

Chapter Five

Drew: Kendrick, I have a thought.

The buzz of my phone lulls me out of my finance class-induced boredom. I check to make sure the coast is clear. There are only twenty people and I'm right in the professor's eyeline.

I wait until he turns back to his PowerPoint presentation and tap a reply.

Kara: Don't leave me waiting in breathless suspense.

Drew: That's awfully poetic for a text.

Kara: Maybe I should be the one who writes Sinful Serenade's lyrics.

Drew: You better not let Miles hear that.

Kara: Miles should be more concerned about what he makes me hear.

Drew: You didn't like the free audio porn?

Kara: No.

Drew: We'll get him back eventually.

The person next to me clears her throat. And here I thought we all outgrew being the teacher's pet in third grade.

I drop my phone in my lap so it's out of view. It buzzes again.

Holy shit.

It's right between my legs. It's pressed up against my clit. That buzz is so...

I bite my lip so I won't react. This is so not the place. I try to grab the phone but it buzzes again.

The teacher's pet scowls at me. She shakes her head like she finds me distasteful. I mouth *sorry*. There. I shove the still buzzing phone in my purse.

The professor turns back to the class. He's looking right at me. I grab my pen and dutifully copy the notes from the slide. Eyes on the paper. I'm totally paying attention. I'm in college. Of course, I'm paying attention. It's not like I don't understand anything in my finance classes. It's not like I absolutely loathe my major and the plan my mom has set out for me: joining her company after I graduate.

I look around the room. The professor is lost in his dull lecture. The teacher's pet is lost in her obscenely neat notes.

Under my chair, my entire purse vibrates. I better turn the thing off. That story checks out. It's not like I'm grabbing it so I can reply to Drew's texts. Not at all.

Drew: What are you doing tonight?
Drew: I hope nothing, because we need to pick out furniture.
Drew: I'll pick you up at 7:30. Your place.

———

Drew plucks a vase from a wooden shelf. He stares at it like he can't understand its mystical and magical powers. It's a vase. It decorates and holds flowers. There's nothing to understand.

He moves to a tiny table. It only seats two and it looks

wobbly as all hell. He slides into one of the rickety wood laminate seats and picks up the plastic glass that's sitting on the table.

"Do you see yourself drinking coffee here?' he asks.

"I don't drink coffee."

He motions for me to take the other seat. I fight my desire to roll my eyes but I comply. There's something magnetic about Drew. I can't say no to him.

He presses his palms against the table and leans toward me. He's a foot away maybe and he's looking at me.

I clear my throat and lean back in the chair. "Are you really staying long enough to invest in furniture?"

"That's the plan."

"Not going to get sick of fame and quit the band?" I bring my attention to the floor. It's hardwood. Long, thin planks in this tan color. They're beaten and waxed to hell.

"Say I did. Where would I go?" He pushes himself up. "I have everything I want here."

"And what is that?"

"Sunshine. The beach." He stares right into my eyes. "I have this friend. But she's about to graduate college and move far, far away for some amazing opportunity."

"How do you know she's competent?"

"No clue. But if she shows up to an interview wearing the outfit I saw her in, she's a shoo-in."

Heat rushes through my body. There's no denying it. Drew is flirting with me. It's normal. Friends flirt with friends. It's not as if it means he likes me.

I shift out of my seat and study a bookshelf like my life depends on it. There is absolutely no reason why I'd buy this ugly bookshelf. Most of my novels and half of my textbooks are digital.

Drew moves on to a different part of the store. All casual like he wasn't flirting with me.

He runs his fingers over a wood table. This one is huge, big enough to sit eight people.

Drew turns to me and motions *come here*. I do.

I stare at the table the way he's staring at it. It's a pleasant cherry brown. It's thick. There is something awfully inviting about it. The perfect place to sit with a textbook and a cup of tea.

His fingertips slide over the curve of my hip. "Will you do me a favor?" He turns his head to the right then to the left, like he's checking to make sure no one is watching.

"What is it?"

"Agree first."

There's a mischievous look in his eyes. Okay, fine, I'll bite.

"Sure," I say.

His grip tightens around my hip. He grabs me and lifts me onto the table. I land hard on my ass. My legs part in a desperate attempt to maintain balance. Not enough. I lean back and plant my hands behind me.

Drew keeps one hand on my hip. The other slides down my leg, under my knee. He slings my legs around him. The same position we'd be in if we were fucking on this table.

My heart goes into freight train mode. I've got no clue what he's doing, but part of me doesn't care. He's so close. His crotch is pressed up against mine. If we weren't wearing all these clothes, we'd be steps away from something so perfect.

I take a deep breath. My body needs to calm the fuck down. "What are you doing?"

He grabs me by the knees and pulls me closer. "That's fairly obvious."

I lean all the way back, so I'm flat on the table. For

some crazy reason, I want to go along with this. "Should I even ask why?"

"I'm not about to get a table that's too tall or too short."

"Is this a regular problem?" I close my eyes so I won't look into his. That will send me straight into a frenzy.

He lowers my legs so they're hanging off the table. "It has been a problem before."

I push myself up and off the table. He keeps me pressed against it for a moment. His hands are at his sides. He's not even touching me and I'm ready to explode.

I shift to the side, so I'm not wedged between him and the hard edge of the table. It gives me no relief. Instead, I feel cold and empty.

I try to shake it off. I try to keep my voice even, like this whole flirting thing isn't getting to me. "And?"

"Perfect."

My eyes move to the floor again. Same hardwood. It's still beat up and waxed as hell. "You're not having sex on our dining room table."

"I'll clean up after."

"Still." I meet his gaze. "Are you even having sex?"

"Those are fighting words, Kendrick." He takes a step toward me. "Are *you* even having sex?"

"That's classified."

"That's a no."

"And how long has it been for you, Denton?"

The joy drops off his face. His expression steels. His gaze drifts to the window. He's somewhere else, somewhere far, far away.

I want him back. I have to say something to drag him back here. "That long?" I make it as playful as I can.

He snaps back. No joy yet, but he's not all serious. "I'll tell if you do."

"Only if you go first."

He shakes his head. "We do it on three. As many fingers as—"

"Years—"

He ignores me. "Months it's been."

I nod. I can do that. Only I don't have enough fingers. I've only been with two guys, two ex-boyfriends. And my last relationship ended a year ago.

Tension builds between my shoulder blades. He's going to get the wrong idea. To think I'm a prude or a loser.

"It's been a while," I say.

"Six months."

"More."

"A year?"

I shake my head. "Not since Jake."

"That asshole was the last person you fucked?"

I clear my throat. "And who was the last person you fucked?"

"A girl at a show."

I raise my eyebrow. "A groupie?"

"Not exactly."

"I thought you didn't sleep around on tour."

"I don't." He runs his hand through his hair. "It was a rough week. I needed something to take the edge off."

Something inside me flares. I snap without meaning to. "And so you fucked someone? Isn't that why man invented alcohol?"

"That would be much healthier."

"But..."

"We were keeping a dry tour. Because of Miles."

"No, I just mean..." I play with my hands. "That's not very fair to her."

His lips turn down. "We both got what we wanted out of it."

"So you were just staring out into space willing this poor girl's body to act as a distraction."

Drew raises his voice. "No. I was there. In that moment. Making sure she came."

That's so much worse. I can't chase away the image of Drew grabbing some other girl, throwing her on the table, and fucking her until she screamed the way Meg was screaming with Miles.

"Are you okay?" His voice is still serious.

"Just hungry." I look away so he won't see the expression forming on my face. Drew is my friend. I shouldn't care when he last had sex. It shouldn't hurt picturing him making sure some girl came.

He lifts my chin so we're eye to eye. He stares at me, through me, like he's absolutely not buying my story. "Was your ex-asshole at least a good lay?"

"Not exactly."

He stares at me like he's demanding an answer. "That why you ended things?"

"No, he broke up with me." I pull my purse into my chest. "We've talked about this before." Not in detail. We're never going to discuss it in detail.

"Did he at least try?" Drew asks.

"Why do you care if my ex-boyfriend was a good fuck?"

"'Cause I want the best for my best friend." He looks me in the eyes. "Was he at least good with his hands?"

"No," I say. "I don't know. I don't... do we have to talk about this?"

Drew is all steel and fire. He's dead set on hearing all the details so he can pick apart my intentions. God forbid I did something that wasn't in my best interests.

"Yes, we do." He grabs my hands. His voice gets

warmer. "How do you not know if your ex-asshole was good with his hands?"

This time, I stare at the ceiling. It's a very plain beige color. "Because he didn't use them."

"He didn't get you off manually?"

"Oh my God. I'm so not discussing this." I reach for my phone but there's no one to call. Meg is at work. And even if she wasn't, she doesn't have a car. She can't pick me up and drive me far away and I don't trust anyone else enough to discuss this.

"Okay, fine. Just answer yes or no," he says.

"Do I have to?"

"Yes," he says. "See. It's easy."

Drew drags his fingertip under my chin and tilts it so we're eye to eye. I try not to meet his gaze, but I can't help it. He has such piercing eyes. They make me melt.

"Did your ex-boyfriend use his hands—"

"No."

"His mouth?"

"No."

"And you allowed this because?"

"That's not a yes or no question." I take a step back.

"Why did you put up with that?"

"We both preferred it that way."

He stops dead in his tracks. "You don't... you're going to have to explain this to me."

"No, I'm not. It's none of your business, actually."

He stares at me with that same penetrating gaze. "If you don't explain it, I'm going to have to spend the entire night wondering."

"So spend the entire night wondering."

I turn and make for the exit. The mall is open for another half hour or so. I can disappear somewhere there, away from these questions that are so not Drew's business.

He catches up to me quickly. He grabs my wrist and pulls me back toward him. "Can I at least ask why?"

"No."

"Okay." He pulls me back into the store. He turns around so we're face to face. He stares at me like I'm a crazy person. "Have you ever?"

I bring my gaze to the floor in the hopes it will erase the feeling of being picked apart, but it doesn't work. I can still feel his gaze penetrating me. I can still feel the wheels in his head turning. He might as well just call me a freak and get it over with.

I pull my hands back to my sides. "It's complicated."

"It's not complicated. The guys you fuck don't finger you or eat you out."

Oh God... I take a deep breath. "Yes, and that is how I want it."

"How the hell could you possibly want that?"

"None of your business."

"How the hell do you talk someone out of that?" He takes another step toward me. So he's close enough to whisper.

"I move things along."

"And if he asks?"

"Do I need to reiterate how this is so not your business?"

"I'm just curious." He grabs my wrist. "Because I don't fuck a girl unless I get to feel her come on my face first."

A salesperson stares at us like he's watching a soap opera. He's within earshot and we're practically screaming.

We're screaming about oral sex in a furniture store. Who wouldn't stare?

I motion toward the sales guy. Drew shrugs like he doesn't care if the other guy can hear. He leans closer.

He brings his mouth to my ear. "You have no idea how

much I want to throw you on that table and show you what you've been missing."

Heat rushes through my body. I swallow hard. Drew wants to show me what I've been missing. He must mean that figuratively. It's not like he actually wants me to come on his face.

I grab onto the table next to me. Wow. The room is spinning. Funny, the room wasn't spinning a minute ago and now it's going as fast as a damn Tilt-A-Whirl.

"Kara."

"I should get home."

He lowers his voice. "I'll drop it."

I keep my back to him. "No. You'll ask about it until I tell you. So get it over with now."

"Anyone ever try?" he asks.

"Yes. My ex... he used his hands once. It's not that I don't like it. It's..." I press my palms flat against the table. It's impossible to breathe.

A sob wells up in my throat. No, not here. I'm not crying over this. Not over how that asshole Jake treated my scars. They're mine and no one is ever going to see them again.

Ever.

Drew presses his chest against my back. He runs his fingertips over my arms, all the way to my hands.

"I have a good reason. I swear." I pull away. I try to wipe the distraught look off my face. I try to shake off the memories that threaten to surface.

It's not working. I close my eyes but the only thing I can feel is the disgust on Jake's face. The way he looked at me like I was damaged. No longer worth his time or attention. No longer worth his desire.

My hand is shaking. I shove it into my jeans pocket but

it's still shaking. Drew is here with me now. Would he still be here if he knew about the scars?

Would he still like me?

I step back. I can't let him see how this hurts. I can't let him know how deep it goes.

But, dammit, the smile isn't coming to my face. It's taking all of my energy to keep up a neutral expression.

Drew squeezes my hand. His voice is soft and even. "I'll take you home."

I nod and I follow him to the car.

———

EVERY MINUTE STRETCHES TO FOREVER. I CHECK THE clock on the dash. Four minutes. I've been in the passenger seat, carefully avoiding making a noise of any kind, for four minutes.

A yellow light turns red. Drew slams on the brake and the car jerks to a stop. If the guy can afford the rent of that obscenely large house, he can afford a car with some actual handling.

Traffic is totally clear. The only things open nearby are the movie theater and the bar across the street from it, but somehow every street parking space is taken. Meters are off after six. People are cheap enough to hike half a mile if it means they'll save the five dollar valet charge.

Drew is looking at me. My gaze is fixed on the empty road, but I can feel it. I can feel the concern. I've done such a good job not meriting concern the last few years. I can't go back to being the girl everyone worries about.

The light is still red.

Five minutes. I have been sitting in this car for five minutes. I'm pretty sure Drew has spent every one of those three hundred seconds staring at me with concern. It's not safe, really. He should have his eyes on the road.

I turn on the radio and flip through the presets. A Motown song fills the car. It's cheerful. Peppy. I try to grab onto the sensation and manufacture some kind of smile, but it doesn't work.

Drew is looking at me. The weight of his concern is so damn heavy.

Green. Thank God. Drew's attention turns to the road. I lean back in the passenger seat, slide my watch up my forearm, and trace the tiny scars on the inside of my left wrist. They're so faded, they're almost impossible to see. Nothing like the scars on my thighs. Those are deep, and red, and jagged.

The next three lights are green. Drew reaches for the radio and turns it off. The silence fills the car again. He's trying to wait me out. He's trying to make me break.

He's trying to win. As always.

We turn onto my street. The car slows to a stop a dozen or so feet from my apartment. I undo my seatbelt and reach for the door, but he stops me.

"Kara."

His fingertips graze my wrist. I pull my hand into my lap so there's no chance he'll feel the scars.

I make eye contact. Oh, those eyes. Those piercing eyes. "I really need to finish my essay."

"You know you can talk to me about anything."

"And in public, no less." I reach for the door again. "I'm really glad all the salespeople at Urban Home know my feelings about oral sex."

"I'm glad I know."

I try to shake off my mood. I try to remember the upbeat Motown song. "Yes, well you're deranged."

He studies my expression with doubt. He doesn't buy the cheer, but he doesn't push it. "Thank you."

I pull the door handle. He's still staring at me, but I'm not about to fall back into that awful role. "It's a twelve-page essay."

"One question first."

"What?"

His mood lightens. "Do you masturbate?"

I step out of the car. "Goodnight, Drew."

"Yes or no?"

I turn and walk up the steps. In my pocket, my phone buzzes. There's no way he... I pull it out. Yep, it's Drew.

Drew: Yes or no?

I turn back to him and wave goodbye.

"You didn't close the car door," he says.

"Sue me."

He smiles, reaches for the door, and slams it shut. I make my way into my apartment like I don't know he's watching.

Inside, I press my back against the wall so I can hear the car pull away. But it doesn't.

My phone buzzes again.

Drew: It's only two letters. Or three. Let's be real It's three.

Kara: Fuck you.

Drew: Not with your silly rules about how I can't rub you until you scream.

Kara: GOOD NIGHT, DREW.

Drew: One word. That's all I ask.

Nadeen is sitting on the couch with a textbook, staring at me like I'm a freak. Good thing I don't care what she thinks.

I slide my phone into my pocket and ignore its buzzing until I'm safely in my room. Alone.

Drew: One word, Kendrick.

Fine. If he wants to know this badly, I'll tell him.
Kara: Yes.
Drew: ...
Drew: Are those all the details I get?
Kara: Yes.
Drew: Trying to play me at my own game, huh?
Kara: Sure, why not? Do you masturbate?
Drew: Of course.
Kara: So why don't you go fuck yourself?
Drew: Maybe I will ;)
Kara: Enjoy it.
Drew: I always do.

I throw my phone on my bed and boot up my computer. It's just after nine. The essay is due at the start of class tomorrow. If I skip my finance lecture and pull an all-nighter, I have a solid fourteen hours. Way more than I need.

My phone buzzes against the bed.
Drew: So by "write an essay," you really mean...
Kara: GOOD NIGHT!
Drew: Feel free to picture my ass if it helps.

Chapter Six

I wake up to a picture message. It's the album cover of *Born in the USA*. Bruce Springsteen's jean-clad ass over red and white stripes.

It's from Drew, of course.

Drew: If The Boss doesn't get you there, no one will.

Friday morning, I wake up early and focus all of my energy on packing. I have about six hours and there's a ton to do. I get lost in the tasks, emptying my closet and bookshelf. Everything fits into two suitcases and four cardboard boxes.

My existence in this apartment fits into the trunk of my car.

I'm so focused, I don't stop until my stomach is growling. It's well into the afternoon and I haven't eaten all day. I finish off a box of Froot Loops and toss them in the recycling bin.

One last look around my room. Nothing under the bed. Nothing in the closet. Nothing left of mine.

I grab the handle of one of the suitcases—it's a huge pink thing, perfect for moving large amounts of shit—and drag it to the door. Getting it through the door is trickier than I'd like, but I manage okay. The stairs are going to be a bit more difficult.

I roll my shoulders back. The only way out is through. I grab the handle and lift it. Shit. It's heavy.

"You need some help with that?"

It's Drew. What the hell? We're supposed to meet at the new place in an hour, and he's standing at the bottom of my staircase.

"I've got it." I drag the suitcase down the first step and set it down with a thud.

"You're going to hurt yourself."

"Good."

He runs up the stairs and grabs the suitcase right out of my hands. Then he lifts it like it's nothing and descends.

Drew sets the suitcase on the concrete. He opens the trunk of his car—somehow he got a free space right outside the building—and shoves it inside.

"I could have done that," I say.

No response. He walks back up the stairs, past me, inside the apartment. Okay, fine. Apparently, we're doing things his way.

I make my way to my room and grab my other suitcase. Drew plucks my hand off it.

"I can do it," I say.

"It's heavy."

"I'm aware." I grab onto the handle. "Aren't you supposed to protect your hands?"

"My hands are more than capable."

I try to push him out of the way, but he doesn't budge.

Drew raises his eyebrow. He stares at me like he's daring me to do something.

"Please move," I say.

He shakes his head.

Fine. I try to push past him. He grabs my shoulders and holds me in place. I try again. This time, he wraps his arms around me and lifts me off my feet.

What. The. Fuck.

Drew slides one hand under my ass and holds my body against his. I press hard against his shoulders. Not enough to hurt him. Or to convince him to never do this again.

"Put me down," I say.

"Are you going to let me carry the bags?"

"No."

"There's your answer."

"What is wrong with you?" I ask. "When did you get so fucking weird?"

He takes a step forward and drops me on the bed. I land on the mattress—Nadeen's mattress—with a thud. Drew climbs on after me. He slings his knee over my thighs, so he's straddling me.

His fingertips skim the edge of my t-shirt. He leans close. Close enough to kiss me. Close enough to fuck me.

"I don't want to tickle you into submission," he says, but from the way he's smiling it's clear he does.

He runs his fingers over my stomach. It's this strange thing between *I want you so bad* and *I'm going to tickle you until you pee your pants.*

I clear my throat. "Fine."

"Thank you." He shifts off me and grabs the suitcase. "You should let other people help you."

"You should respect other people's wishes."

He's already out the door.

The landlord is waiting in front of the house with the keys in one hand and a takeout coffee cup in the other. She is all smiles now that Drew's money has made us worthy of her attention. Even with me in jeans and a v-neck that does little to cover my cleavage.

"Do you need any help?" she asks.

"I've got it all under control." He takes the key with indifference. "Thank you."

"I'll head back to work then. You really are a lovely couple."

Drew waits until we're out of earshot then turns to me. "We're a lovely couple."

I roll my eyes and grab my key. I copy the landlord's tone as I nod to my car. "Do you need any help?"

"Not at all."

"Great." I trudge up the concrete path. It's hard to stay irritated in front of such a nice house. There's something very soothing about the blue paint and the white trim, like a pastel version of the sky.

Still, I won't let Drew off that easily. I wait until I'm inside the house to let out a sigh of appreciation. This main room is huge. All I need is my ballet slippers and I can turn this place into my personal dance studio.

I slide out of my shoes and change from first to second position and back again. Even with a couch, a TV, and a huge dining table, there's enough space for any of my routines.

My shoulders relax. I check to make sure Drew is still outside, and I practice my turns. Quarter. Quarter. Half. Single. Double.

The door creaks open. I lean into my landing instinctively. There's no avoiding it. These steps are drilled into my brain.

Drew raises an eyebrow. "I haven't seen you dance like that since your seventh-grade ballet recital."

My feet go to first position instinctively. I smile like I have fantastic memories of my long-ago ballet recitals. I haven't done much real dancing since I was on the high school dance squad. Mostly, I get my fix at the clubs on Saturday nights, but I miss the structure of ballet, jazz, and modern dance.

"You want me to keep some space clear?" He asks.

How the hell did he know? "That would be great."

"As long as you don't mind sharing. I need somewhere to do bodyweight exercises and I drip sweat during push-ups.."

I do everything in my power to keep a neutral expression.

He lifts the suitcase and heads up the stairs.

Drew dripping sweat in our living room. Drew dripping sweat. Must not picture Drew dripping sweat, on top of me, his body locked with mine.

Okay. Need to keep my mind occupied or it's going straight to the gutter. I head to the car and grab one of the boxes. I pass Drew on my way inside and he's smirking like he knows I'm fighting off lust with everything I've got.

I trudge up the stairs and place the box in the master bedroom. There are clothes and hangers in the suitcase and there's a perfectly good closet. It's enough to shake the lust out of my brain.

In theory.

I unzip the suitcase and start hanging dresses and blouses. Internship clothes in one corner. Stuff for class in the middle. Stuff for the clubs on the other side.

Drew steps inside the room. His eyes go to my unzipped suitcase. It's lying on the ground and—

Shit.

The last thing left in it is lingerie.

I'm not sure why I own any of it. I certainly never wore anything for anyone. There are a few bra and panty sets, bought so I could pretend to be a normal girl and not a damaged freak. At least the lacy thongs have a practical use. They don't show under my bodycon dresses. Anything else means panty lines, even under tights.

Drew smiles a wide, smug smile. "You need any help with that?"

"No, I'm fine."

He offers his hand. "Good. Then we can go."

"Where are we going?"

"Early dinner. Then there's a show. A friend's band." His gaze goes to a pink bra and panty set. "You're free to change if you want."

My cheeks flush.

"Or to skip the underwear entirely."

"Thanks for the permission."

"Anytime."

Chapter Seven

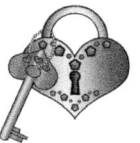

We eat at a cozy restaurant in Hollywood. The host must recognize Drew, because everyone else here is dressed to the nines. We're the only people wearing jeans and sneakers.

I order three courses and savor every bite. I'm starving and the food here is amazing. A caprese salad with sharp basil and thick tomatoes. Pasta packed with fresh shrimp and fresher vegetables. Just sweet enough flourless chocolate cake. We linger at the table with our post-dinner beverages, black tea for me, black coffee for him.

Dinner with my best friend should be effortless and casual. But it's far from that. Every time he looks at me, it's a little harder to breathe. My heartbeat picks up. My head fills with images of me and Drew naked and rolling around his bed, his nails on my skin, his lips on my neck, his cock deep inside me.

Okay. Time to catch my breath. I excuse myself to the bathroom.

My hair and makeup are about average for someone who just moved. If this concert is anything like a Sinful

Serenade show, most people will be in band t-shirts and jeans, their hair and makeup carefully messy. But there will be a few dozen girls in tiny skirts and tall shoes, made up to perfection and waiting in line to flirt with their favorite band member. Or maybe even take him home.

I can fit into the former group. I part my messy hair so it looks on-purpose messy and I apply a little concealer, some thick eyeliner, a brush-on lipstick. My reflection looks less tired and more game for wherever the night takes her.

At the table, Drew is signing the check.

"I wanted to split that," I say.

He shrugs like it's not a big deal. Must be nice to shrug off a hundred dollar dinner like it's a cup of coffee.

"What happened to things being even between us?" I ask.

"They are." He stands and motions to the exit door. "This is because you're going to have to put up with Gavin."

I stare at him. Am I supposed to know who Gavin is?

"Singer of Dangerous Noise."

The band we're going to see. I nod, yeah, of course, like I'm cool enough to know all about Dangerous Noise. They must be decent if Drew likes them. I've never met anyone more specific or demanding than Drew is.

I follow Drew to the street. The setting sun casts an orange glow. It's beautiful and gritty all at once.

We walk a few blocks. There's no line at the club. The band isn't as popular as Sinful Serenade, but then who is?

We do not go to the main entrance. We walk through an alley, straight to the side door. There's a bouncer sitting in front of it, his attention devoted to a game on his phone.

He looks up and nods like he recognizes Drew. "Nice to see you, Mr. Denton."

"Mr. Denton is my dad. It's Drew." He nods to me.

"This is my very good friend Kara. If you see anyone giving her shit, find me immediately, so I can beat him to within an inch of his life."

"You know what musicians are like."

"That's why I asked."

The bouncer shakes his head knowingly. Used to over-protective boyfriends, no doubt. Never mind the little detail that Drew and I are only friends.

The bouncer opens the door for us. We make our way through the backstage area. It's much more low-key than any other show I've ever been to. Twenty-something guys are setting up on stage. Everyone else is milling around a dressing room. No doubt milling around a bottle of alcohol.

Drew motions to the guys on stage. He steps through the curtains. His hand tightens around mine, like I'm supposed to follow him on stage. Sure, the doors aren't open yet, but I'm not going to be on a stage. I haven't been on stage since my high school dance performances.

The bright lights are familiar. Like my high school dance performances. They're the only thing I can see and they're so, so hot. Already, I'm sweating and it's only going to get worse the longer I'm around Drew.

Drew high-five hellos a tall guy with light hair. The guy turns to me.

He offers his hand. "Gavin. You must be Kara."

"I must be." I shake. "You guys opening?"

He nods. "The headliners are taking shots backstage. Sure they'd welcome the best guitarist—"

"Stop with that shit." Drew shakes his head. "As far as you know, I'm just another guy."

"Everyone knows your face. You're pretty much royalty around here." Gavin turns to me. "Don't let it go to his head."

"I couldn't."

Gavin motions for us to leave. "Doors open in fifteen. Get lost before you steal my thunder."

We head backstage. Someone from the headlining band recognizes Drew. He introduces himself and launches into this long speech about how amazing Drew's guitar skills are. It's far too technical for me to follow. I nod, uh huh, taking delight in the awkward look on Drew's face. Call me crazy, but I'm pretty sure he's blushing. The man does not like attention. He especially hates admiration.

Just when I think we're free of idolatry, another musician comes up to Drew and sings his praises. And here I thought rock stars only had to contend with rabid female fans. I scan the backstage area again. As far as I can tell, I'm the only woman here, and everyone is keeping a very wide radius. Either Drew gives off a protective aura or people here know enough about his penchant for threatening people to punches to avoid flirting.

Really, who does he think he's kidding? Like a guitarist is going to punch anyone in the face.

By the time the third fanboy is done praising Drew's musical abilities, the show is about to start. Drew rolls his eyes as his admirer leaves.

"Must be difficult hearing so much positive feedback," I say.

Drew sighs. "That guy didn't have a clue what he was talking about. It's just 'cause Sinful Serenade is famous, not that he actually appreciates our music."

"Still—"

"Do you admire me, Kendrick?" he asks.

"I don't know. We're friends. It's not really like that."

"Exactly. We're on the same level. We can communicate like real people. You don't have me up on this pedestal." His bad mood shifts into a smile. "Which must be hard, given how dead sexy I am."

"Yeah, very hard." Not thinking about Drew hard. Not at all.

The rest of Dangerous Noise makes their way on stage. There's a small chorus of cheers from the audience.

Drew takes my hand and leads me closer to the performance. We're right by the curtains. It's a perfect view of the stage. Well, the back right side of the stage. Too bad I lack interest in checking out any ass besides Drew's, because I have an eyeful of rock stars in tight jeans.

The band launches into their first song. It's not half bad. Catchy. Rhythmic. They have a great energy and they're fun.

It's impossible to see the audience with the bright lights, but their cheers are plenty loud. The next two songs only get everyone more hyped.

The singer turns toward the backstage area, like he's looking right at us. "We have a very special guest here today. One Mr. Drew Denton." He turns back to the audience. "Do you guys like Sinful Serenade?"

The crowd goes wild. Way louder cheers than before.

"What you might not know is that Drew was in Dangerous Noise for a hot second. Back in the day, we shared custody of his very talented hands with Sinful Serenade. But there were a few creative and personal differences, and he left us for fame and fortune."

No doubt about it, Drew is red, though I'm not sure if it's from anger or embarrassment.

"There was this song that we couldn't agree on." Gavin looks back at us. "I hated it. Drew loved it. How about you come out and play it with us, Drew?"

The band's guitarist looks back at us, apparently

unfazed by the stunt. He must know he's not as talented as the man he replaced.

Drew shakes his head. Under his breath, he mutters, "No fucking way."

I nudge him. "Do it."

He leans close enough to whisper. "The differences were more personal than creative."

"What happened?"

"My ex... Vivian. She was with Gavin before she was with me. He didn't take it too well." Drew shakes his head. "Stupid way to leave a band."

"So go make amends." I press my hand into his lower back and push him onto stage.

He looks back at me and shakes his head. "Kendrick, you're going to pay for this."

"Break a leg." I blow him a kiss. For good luck. Only for good luck.

Drew's demeanor changes the second he's on stage. No longer irritated. He's right where he belongs. A roadie runs out with a guitar, slinging it around Drew's shoulders and plugging it in.

Drew looks back to me with that same *you're going to pay for this* expression. Then his attention turns to the crowd.

The song starts with a guitar intro. It's amazing and spotlight-hogging. I close my eyes and soak in the music. There's a great energy and finesse to Drew's playing. The rest of the song falls away, until there's nothing in this entire club except me and Drew's hands and that guitar.

When the song ends, the crowd is screaming. Drew's posture is proud and confident. He really belongs here, on stage, lost in his music.

Gavin steps up to the mic again. "How about those hands, huh?"

The band's actual guitarist pouts.

Drew slides the guitar off his shoulders and takes a bow. The crowd goes wild, screaming and cheering and clapping. Drew waves goodbye as he walks backstage.

His eyes find mine. "Pleased with yourself?"

"It was a good song."

"The guitar part." He takes my hand. "Let's avoid any more of this by going to the front."

"What if I want to find a hot rock star boyfriend?"

"Over my dead body."

———

We spend the rest of the concert in the main area. I don't know the headlining band, but that doesn't stop me from swaying along to the music. Drew sits on a bar stool, watching me and shaking his head.

"You can't dance to rock music," he says.

"Then what the hell am I doing?" I step further into the crowd.

It's only a few seconds before Drew's hands are on my hips. He pulls me toward the bar. "You're not leaving my sight."

"I'm dancing."

"Not out of my sight."

Drew's overprotective attitude is not going to keep me from the one thing that relieves the tension in my body. I make my way toward the stage. He's right. No one is dancing. But that isn't going to stop me either.

I move in time with the songs. It's half-jumping, half-dancing, but I fit right in with the enthusiastic fans. Drew stays close to me, his arm tight around my waist. What the hell is that supposed to mean?

It's dark enough that no one recognizes him. Or maybe it's considered rude to ask a rock star to sign an autograph at another band's show. Either way, we make it all the way to the final song without interruption.

Everyone is cheering. It's so loud I can't hear myself think. Drew's grip tightens. He pulls me closer, his mouth mere inches from my ear. His breath sends goosebumps down my spine.

"I should say goodbye," he whispers.

It's too loud to respond with words, so I nod. We make our way backstage. Security waves us through without batting an eye. It seems Drew is known by everyone, even when he'd rather be invisible.

There must be a few dozen people here. I guess the headliners have quite the posse. Drew cuts through the crowd, his hand tight around mine. He finds Gavin in the main dressing room.

Drew stares daggers.

Gavin stares back.

Drew speaks first. "Consider us even."

No comeback. Gavin nods. And that's it. Conflict big enough to break up a band settled. Men. Who can understand them?

A fan paws at Drew. A woman. She's in a tiny dress and she's teetering like she's drunk. She laughs, a loud obnoxious laugh. Definitely drunk.

"Oh my gawsh, I love Sinful Serenade. Will you sign something for me?" she begs.

Nope. Not watching this. I go to break Drew's grip. He squeezes harder, but I fight it enough to slip away. I cut through the crowd. Time to find a nice bottle of tequila and something to mix it with. That's the only way I'll survive watching this flirting disaster without vomiting.

The booze is in the corner, and there are half a dozen mixers. I fill a red plastic cup with plenty of tequila and plenty of orange juice. It's no Paloma, but it will get the job done.

"Oh, you better hope Drew isn't looking."

Fuck my life. That's Tom.

He's standing there with a blonde woman on his arm. This could be Drew. He could be the one about to take home a pretty girl and never speak to her again.

Tom turns to his conquest. "Meet at my car in five." He taps her ass and sends her on her way.

"That was a beautiful display of affection. Thank you for that." This drink can't fill my throat fast enough. I drink with greedy sips. Not great tequila. It burns.

Tom is unblinking. "You like Drew."

Time for another sip. Heat spreads through my cheeks and throat. "I don't know—"

"Yeah, you do." Tom points to Drew and the flirty fangirl. "You looked like you were gonna deck her right in the jaw."

"I don't hit people."

"Drew does." Tom looks at me. "When he was with Vivian. And then after, when he was fucking his way out of his bad mood."

"What are you talking about?"

"You want those details?" Tom leans closer. "You want to think about him fucking a different girl every night, driving them all insane with that look in his eyes that promises he'll love them?"

"Seems like I don't have a choice. You're doing a great job explaining it. Really evocative language."

"You like him a lot, huh?"

I finish the rest of my drink with one long gulp. "I should go."

"I want to help."

No, Tom doesn't help. Tom is only out for Tom.

I study his expression. It seems genuine.

"Why?" I ask. "You don't help anyone."

"That's not a very nice thing to say."

"You only care about yourself and what you think is best for the band."

He takes my plastic cup and pours me a refill. "This is what's best for the band. Drew's pleasant when you're around. Shows up to practice in a good mood. Doesn't argue that we need guitar solos in our singles."

"Is this supposed to be a compliment?" I take my drink from Tom and take a long sip. It's a lot stronger. At least Tom does something right.

Tom looks me right in the eyes, dead serious. "You're good together. And you're normal. That's what he needs."

"How do you know I'm normal?" I ask.

"If you'd seen him with Vivian, you wouldn't have to ask." Tom's phone buzzes loudly. He picks it up and glances at it. "I have things to do, but I want to help."

"Things?" I raise my eyebrow.

"Okay, I have a woman to fuck. Two, actually. That a problem with you?" He throws his shoulders back, all self-righteous. "You trust me?"

"No."

"Follow my lead. I'll make him figure it out."

"Figure what out?" I ask.

"That he likes you too." Tom steps toward the exit and waves goodbye. "I'd get him home if I were you. Drew hates attention."

"I know."

"You want him or not?"

I bite my lip. I'm not about to trust Tom to help me. But he is right about this. Drew does hate attention, and I hate standing here watching him get flirted with.

Tom shakes his head. He motions to one of his friends

and whispers something in the guy's ear. Then his attention turns to me. "See you soon."

He steps out of the room.

The friend, a short guy with broad shoulders and a dark t-shirt, saunters up to me. He leans close. "Tom asked me to flirt with you. Any clue why?"

Some clue. I turn back to Drew. Sure enough, his eyes are on me. He's staring daggers at this guy, and all the guy is doing is standing near me. Really near me, but still.

"Tom is an idiot," I say.

The guy laughs. It's a big, hearty laugh. He grabs my arm like he needs it to steady himself.

Ten seconds later, Drew is at my side, his arm wrapped around my waist. "Let's get out of here," he says.

I nod goodbye to the guy whose name I don't know.

Once we're outside, Drew softens. His grip moves to my hand but it's still tight and protective.

So Tom is smarter than he looks.

I just might have to trust him.

———

I WAKE UP WITH A THROBBING HEADACHE. SLEEPING ON AN air mattress didn't help in the hangover avoidance front. Downstairs, Drew is sweating on the floor. Doing push-ups, more specifically. The muscles of his back tense and release. So back muscles can make your legs go weak. Who knew?

I make my way downstairs. He pops up with ease. His footsteps are so, so loud. And it's awfully bright in here too.

"I know that look," he says.

"Ugh."

"You shouldn't drink so much."

Yeah, and maybe he shouldn't allow hyena fangirls to

flirt in front of me. I try to offer him a smile, but the pounding in my head won't allow it.

"Thanks for the tip." I sit cross legged on the floor.

He does something in the kitchen. I guess he unpacked a set of pots and pans. It's extra bright over there so I'm not about to look.

"I'm making eggs. You want some?" he ask.

"Yes. Thank you."

He moves closer. His hands graze my shoulders. "You want to come with me?"

Mind going straight to gutter. I clear my throat. "Come to what?"

"To practice. It's in an hour."

Not with this headache. Just the thought of groaning vocals and a screaming drum set...

Tom. He knew what he was doing last night. And maybe today too.

A heavy dose of ibuprofen and a greasy breakfast should be enough to make band practice tolerable.

"Sure," I say. "As long as you drive."

"Wouldn't have it any other way."

Chapter Eight

The guitar's wail fills the room. It's a riff I've never heard before. It's heavy and melodic and totally captivating.

Either the drugs did wonders for my headache or the music is so beautiful it's chasing the pain away.

I dog-ear my page and drop my paperback in my lap. My eyes flutter closed. Nothing to distract me now. Nothing here except the sound of Drew's playing.

The music shifts. Something faster. It's not like the normal Sinful Serenade stuff. It's rawer. It's harder. It's way more aggressive.

Something stirs inside me. Like the song is throwing open a hiding place and letting all the dust free.

The music shifts back to the melody. All that dust swirls around my brain. I shake my head, willing it to settle down, but it does no good.

I don't want to think anything. I don't want to feel anything but Drew's song washing over me.

I play with the pages of my paperback. Something for my Russian Literature class. I'm supposed to be reading it.

My eyes open and my gaze goes straight to Drew. He's completely oblivious to anything except his guitar. There's this look on his face—a mix of concentration and serenity. His fingers glide over the fretboard, fast and exact.

We're early. It's just us. By all accounts, the room is huge. But it feels small. It feels like a closet. Like there's absolutely no room to move or even breathe.

The song ends. I grab my paperback and pretend to read it. Drew is looking at me, checking on me. I can feel it. I bury my eyes in the text and read the same sentence five times. There's a highlighter and a pen in my purse. If I'm going to pretend I'm doing homework, I should sell it better.

I sneak a peek at Drew as I reach for my purse. He's tuning his guitar, a pick between his teeth. He closes his eyes and plays a note. It must be right, because he moves to the next string. He does it again and again.

His eyes blink open. He glances at me. Crap, I'm staring at him. I nod like it's a coincidence. He doesn't seem to notice. He takes the pick from his mouth and rubs it between his fingers.

He plays.

A different song. Another song I've never heard before. This time, I don't fight the feelings whirling around inside me. I close my eyes and let the song wash over me. How can something that sounds so beautiful make me hurt somewhere so deep? It's like there's a hole in my gut out of nowhere.

The music picks up. Faster, harder, but still distinctly melancholy. Still threatening to tear me in pieces and leave me to blow away in the wind.

I open my eyes and watch Drew play. There's a hint of sadness on his face. He's off somewhere else, somewhere that hurts him. But even with his eyes turned down and his gaze drifting off into the distance, there's something comfortable and satisfied about his expression.

He's at home. Exactly where he belongs.

The door swings open and the music stops.

Pete storms inside, his hoodie up around his head, his attention on the floor. He pulls his hands from his pockets and flips off the open door.

Oh. Tom steps inside, all huffy and puffy. He must be the object of the middle finger. God knows he deserves it.

Tom spots me. He winks at me then turns to Drew. "What happened to our no-girls rule?"

Drew only barely looks up from his guitar. "Miles happened."

"You really going to bring one of your floozies to practice?" Pete asks.

"That's my prerogative." Tom pulls his hoodie over his head and tosses it on the ground haphazardly.

Pete rolls his eyes and kicks the hoodie into the corner.

"Don't take your blue balls out on my clothing," Tom says.

"Fuck off, asshole." Pete hides behind his dark hair.

Drew lets out a sigh. "You want to fight or you want to play?"

"You volunteering to fill in for Miles?" Tom asks. "Fuck knows I don't ever need to hear Pete screaming or groaning again."

Drew glares. "We don't need the fucking vocals to practice."

Apparently, Tom agrees. He shakes his head as if to say *whatever* and hightails it to his drum kit.

The instruments are all set up in the same area. It's not quite a stage. It's more like a large section of the room.

Still, I scoot back until I'm pressed up against the wall. There's a good ten, fifteen feet between me and the guys in the band, but it still feels awfully close. It still feels like Drew can see inside me.

Then again, it always does.

Drew looks at Pete as if to say *e tu, brute?* Pete must want to fight. Pete and Tom are always like this. But, then, Drew did mention that they're brothers. Foster brothers, no blood relation, but they grew up together.

They certainly fight like brothers.

"You two want to pull this shit, fine. I'll leave," Drew says.

Pete pulls his phone from his pocket and stares at it. His face flashes with concern. "You want to indulge Tom's bullshit, go ahead. I'm busy." He taps a reply.

"I can't help it if I'm the only one with a fucking mind for business." Tom snaps his fingers at me.

I fight a scowl. I'm playing along here. "Don't snap at me. I'm not a puppy."

Tom pulls his t-shirt over his head and tosses that on the ground. "Let me ask you something, Kara."

"Yes?"

"You go to Club Blue?"

It's one of my favorites, actually. Good music. Decent drink prices. Plenty of room on the dance floor. "I do."

"You like dancing," he says. "And I like dancing."

Oh God.

Tom makes eye contact. He winks. "We could go dancing together."

Pete laughs. "Are you really hitting on his girlfriend in front of him?"

Cue the death glare from Drew. It doesn't scare Pete or Tom, but it's nice to know the idea of dating me is still just that disgusting.

"She's not his girlfriend," Tom says. "And it would not be a date. Just two sweaty people moving their bodies together." He looks back to Drew. "What do you say—do I have your permission?"

"Are you here to play or are you here to talk?" Drew glares.

"The guitar prince is so temperamental." Tom looks at me. "Doesn't sound like a no."

"Leave her alone." Drew huffs.

He's about fifteen seconds from protective caveman mode. Tom looks at me, raising his eyebrows as if to suggest success. I'm not so sure. It's easy to make Drew protective. It doesn't do anything to convince the man I'm anything more than a friend.

Tom grabs his drumsticks and stretches his arms in the air. Done with flirting for now. It's funny. Tom is clearly attractive. He's handsome. He's ripped—more than Drew even. Yes, he's controlling and bossy and slutty as all hell. He's also funny and competent and totally take-charge.

He's the kind of guy who used to make my heart race and my breath hitch.

But, right now I'm staring at his defined, tattooed chest and... nothing. My heart is plodding along at some sixty beats a minute. My breath is slow and even. There isn't a hint of heat in my body. In fact, the thought of dancing with Tom makes me utterly queasy.

My gaze shifts to Drew. His guitar strap is tugging his t-shirt down his shoulders. Mmm. That chest piece is begging for my fingertips. My tongue.

I press my lips together. My heartbeat picks up. That flutter builds below my bellybutton. Drew's shoulders are broad. His chest is strong.

My breath picks up. The guitar strap isn't doing

enough. It should pull his shirt all the way to his belly button.

The door opens and everyone's attention turns to it. Thank God. Miles is here. His hair and clothes are messy like he just got out of bed. More likely, he just got out of Meg.

"About time." Tom huffs. "Where's your girl?"

"Recovering from last night. She needs to catch up on sleep after—"

"You're late." Tom glares.

Miles glances at the clock—ten minutes after noon—and he shoots Tom a sarcastically sweet wave.

Miles nods hello to me. "Nice to see you, Kara. These guys giving you trouble?"

"I'm fine, thanks," I say. "I should really get back to reading. Thanks for inviting me to practice."

Tom motions to Miles. Miles moves close enough for Tom to whisper something. Both the guys laugh.

They look straight at me.

Miles turns to Drew with a smug look in his eyes. "What happened to living alone?"

"Helping out a friend," Drew says. His voice is impossibly even.

I nod to my book like I'm just so done with this conversation.

The guys banter for another ten minutes. Mostly, I stare at my book. The words *housewarming party after practice* are thrown around half a dozen times before Drew finally agrees.

Someone dims the lights. I set my book back in my lap and turn all of my attention to Drew. It's dark enough that he can't make out my expression, the way my gaze travels over his body, the way my tongue slides over my lips, the way my fingers dig into the fabric of my jeans.

The flutter builds to my belly and thighs. I get lost in Drew's playing—the intense expression in his eyes, the delicate curves of his lips, the hard lines of his shoulders, the finesse of his hands.

It's magic.

Chapter Nine

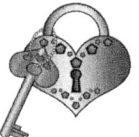

There's furniture in the house. When we left, it was empty. Now it's furnished.

I rub my eyes to make sure I'm not seeing things. It's still furnished. It's not a lot—a couch, a TV, a table and chairs—but it's still shit that appeared magically during a three-hour absence.

"I took care of it." Drew nods to the rooms upstairs. "I figured you'd want a queen bed, a dresser, and a desk."

"How the hell did you make that happen?"

"Trade secret." He drops takeout sushi bags on the table and digs out the plastic silverware. "You better stake a claim on this before Meg gets here and eats all the sashimi."

Pete and Tom walk in the open door. Pete is still hiding in his hoodie, his gaze on the floor.

He plops down on the couch and pulls his phone from his pocket. He stares at it with this strange mix of anger and fascination.

Tom grabs my arm. "Give him space."

Drew glares at Tom like he's going to hit the guy. Tom smirks as he releases his grip.

"Either of you fuck with Pete and you're dead." Tom frowns, empathy in his eyes. "He and Cindy were up all night screaming. He said some bad shit. Kind of shit you can't take back. I couldn't hear quite as much from her side, but it didn't sound good." He shakes his head and returns to a demanding look. "Stay out of it."

"You don't stay out of shit," Drew says.

"Because I know what I'm doing."

Tom tries to shrug it off but there's worry all over his face. He and Pete are foster brothers. It's easy to forget since they look nothing alike, but they fight like brothers and they care about each other in that *I love you enough to tell you I hate you because we're family* way.

Was Drew right? Do the guys talk about each other because they like to gossip? It sure seems like Tom likes to gossip.

But there's something in his eyes, and in Drew's eyes too.

They really do care.

―――

"I haven't seen you in a million years." Meg throws her arms around me and squeezes tight.

"More like five days."

"It sucks we don't have any classes together." She bites a piece of salmon sashimi in half.

"It was bound to happen eventually." I glance at the guys in the band. They're all sitting at the table together— even Pete—and whispering about something.

Meg follows my gaze to the guys. She leans in close and

lowers her voice. "Are you really going to be okay living with Drew?"

"Better than Nadeen."

Apprehension flares in her expression. "What if he brings another girl home?"

I clear my throat. "That crush is ancient history."

"I'll do you a favor and not call you on that today."

My cheeks flush. "Thank you." An immediate change of subject is the best way to avoid any further discussion of my feelings for Drew. "How's everything with Miles?"

A dreamy look spreads over Meg's face. "It's like paradise spending the day with him up in Malibu." The dreamy look fades. "Of course, it means I have to spend all day Sunday studying."

"Small price to pay for paradise."

Someone clears his throat. Sure enough, it's Tom, calling our attention.

Okay, fine. Meg and I join the discussion at the table.

Tom nods to the bottles of liquor. "We're going to play a game: truth, dare, or drink. Except for Miles. He's stuck with truth or dare."

Meg looks at me as if to ask *okay?* I nod. Yeah. Fine. I'm not fourteen. Truth or dare doesn't scare me.

Drew looks at me the way Meg did. Like he's concerned about me. I turn on the bubbly. I am not about to be some kind of pity homing beacon.

Meg slides into Miles's lap. She kisses him on the cheek. "I'm not drinking either."

"I'll start." Tom turns to Pete. "Truth or dare."

Pete mumbles his answer. "Dare."

"Call Cindy and tell her what you really think about—"

Pete grabs the bottle of whiskey, pours a shot, and slams it. "That's the drink part of the game." He turns back to Tom. "Truth or dare, Tom?"

"Truth."

Pete shakes his head. "Pussy choice." He rubs his chin like he's thinking. "Is the reason you've never had a girlfriend that women can't tolerate your personality, or is it that you're so bad in bed no woman dares let you touch her twice?"

Tom raises a brow. "I've fucked plenty of women three or four nights in a row."

"Must be the former then," Pete says. "Your turn."

Tom holds Pete's stare for a moment. He shakes it off and turns to me. "Kara, truth or dare."

"Truth." I hesitate. Dare is a better choice. Dare can't open me up or make me reveal anything personal.

I shake my head. This is a stupid game. It won't open me up. Worst case scenario, I can take a shot.

"Do you regret moving in with Drew yet?" he asks.

My neck relaxes. An easy question. "Not yet. But there's always time." I clear my throat. I have to smile. I'm supposed to be the fun friend. "Meg."

"Truth," she says.

I throw her a bone. "Is Miles as good as he says he is?"

She turns back to Miles and plants a kiss on his lips. "Don't know. Miles has a big mouth."

"Pretty sure you like it." He sucks on her neck. She giggles. "So cocky. So smug. Why do I put up with you anyway?" She leans into his kiss with a slight groan.

He grabs her and holds her against him. Okay. Now they're making out. She turns away with a little giggle and a "Miles" that seems to mean *oh my goodness, not in front of our friends.*

"You're not doing that in my place." Drew glares.

Meg pushes off Miles. She turns back to the table with a shy look on her face. "I'll have to take him to the bedroom to verify. I can't be sure until I test out that mouth—"

"One more word and I'm dragging you to the car, babe." He grabs her thigh.

Tom clears his throat.

They keep making out.

Pete looks up, then his eyes go back to the table. "We can call that a yes."

Meg pushes off of Miles with a desperate sigh. She makes a circle with her finger like she's deciding who to pick. It stops on Pete. "Pete, truth or dare."

He pulls his hoodie up over his head with a sigh. "You pick."

Meg frowns. "Uh, I guess truth. Why do you choose to live with Tom? I don't think I've ever seen you doing anything but fighting." She slaps her hand on the table. "And don't say it's because you're brothers, because I had a sister, and I know how that relationship actually goes."

Pete sits back in his chair. "He's a better friend than he seems."

Tom beams, proud of the compliment. He shifts back into mayhem mode. "The game is only fun if people pick dare."

"The game is only fun if you're fourteen," Drew says.

Tom holds his gaze. "Okay, Drew, I have a dare for you. Kiss Kara."

Is this Tom's idea of helping? If the angry look in Drew's eyes is any indication, it's only making things worse.

I guess subtlety and drumming don't get along too well.

"You can't just dare someone to do something," Drew says. "Those aren't the rules."

"Okay, fine. Truth or dare," Tom says.

"It's not your turn," Drew says.

Pete shrugs. "He can have my turn."

Drew shakes his head. "Truth."

"Pussy." Tom smirks.

"Fuck you," Drew says.

Tom's eyes narrow. "Okay, I have a question. Why didn't you pick dare?"

Drew's gaze fixes on the table. It's almost like he's nervous. He mutters under his breath, pours a shot, and slams it. "You're so fucking immature."

Gee, great. I'm that appealing.

Attention is divided. Half on me. Half on Drew. I maintain my happy face. No way I'm going to allow all the pity in the room to land on me.

Drew presses his palm against the table. "Tom. Truth or dare."

"Truth."

"Why are you such a miserable piece of shit?" Drew asks.

"I was born that way." Tom turns to me. "Kara. Your turn."

No sense fanning the flames here. If I act like this is cool, everyone will calm down. This will all be okay. "Truth."

Tom lowers his voice. "Were you hoping Drew would pick dare?"

My lips feel heavy. No way to pry them apart. I push myself out of my chair. "Drew should do whatever makes him happy."

Drew is staring at me, this strange mix of anger and concern.

"You know, I just remembered. I have a paper due Monday and I haven't even started. I should get to that." I take another step toward the stairs. "It was great to see you guys. Have fun."

Drew's eyes find mine. Something passes between us,

but I haven't got a fucking clue what it is, why we're both dodging these questions.

I turn and rush up the stairs with as much calm as I can muster.

The tension in my neck relaxes once I'm alone in my bedroom. Hurt bubbles up in my chest, the same hurt I felt when I was listening to Drew play. I push it away, lock myself in the bathroom, and run the shower.

———

I TURN THE WATER AS HOT AND HEAVY AS IT WILL GO. It pounds the porcelain with a loud *tap tap tap*. The tiny white room fills with steam. It turns everything into this bright blurry haze

The band is still downstairs. No signs anyone is on their way out. I throw my head back and rinse my hair in the water. I didn't exactly play that cool, but I didn't throw a fit.

I shampoo, condition, and soap. My fingers trail over the scars on my inner thighs. They're still raised well above my skin, thick and red and ugly. But no one can see them.

No one will ever see them again.

"Kara."

It's Drew. Outside my bedroom door. He must be yelling pretty loud to make it all the way to me.

I pretend like I can't hear.

"Kara." The bedroom door opens. He's inside my bedroom now. His footsteps move toward the shower. He knocks lightly. "How is the paper going in there?"

"Great," I yell over the shower.

"You want to come downstairs? I made Tom promise to shut the fuck up."

"No thank you." I turn the water off. "I really do have

to finish my homework."

"Do it after everyone leaves." He taps the door lightly. "Things are falling apart without you. Pete is sulking on the couch. Meg and Miles are necking on the table."

I pull my towel—one of my few belongings—from the rack and pat myself dry. I'm naked and Drew is on the other side of the door.

"Give me a minute," I say.

He taps the door with his fingers. Okay. He's not leaving. I pull the towel around my chest and check my reflection to make sure I'm covered. It's acceptable.

Drew's eyes pass over me as I move to the closet, from my eyes all the way down to my toes and back up again. His gaze lingers at my chest. For a split second, his pupils dilate. His lips part.

He wants me. Some part of him, at least. Even if it's subconscious, it's something.

"Why does it make you so angry?" I ask.

"What?"

"When Tom teases that we're together. Dares you to kiss me. Whatever."

"I asked Tom a million times to leave it alone." He runs his hand through his hair. "He knows I swore off relationships after Vivian."

"Oh."

He shifts. "Are you okay?"

"Great."

His eyes fix on mine. "Were you?"

I pull the towel a little tighter. "What?"

"Hoping I'd pick dare?"

My heart races. So not going there. So, so not going there. "I'm not a teenager. If I want a guy to kiss me, I make it happen."

He stares at me, studying my expression. His fingers

brush my shoulders. His lips part, but he doesn't say anything. He just stares.

I press my knees together. "Why didn't you?"

He shakes his head. "I'm not a teenager. If I want to kiss a girl, I'm not going to do it because of a dare."

He sits on the bed, his back to me. He can't think I'm changing with him here.

I grab a dress and underwear and change in the bathroom. My makeup is smudged from the shower. I wipe it clean with a sheet of toilet paper.

In my room, Drew is lying on my bed, arms stretched over his head. A thin sliver of his stomach is exposed.

It's enough to make me pant. God, he's cut. He looks damn yummy.

I dare you to kiss Kara.

My head is swimming. The suggestion made him angry. And every time anyone hints there's something between us...

But he flirts with me and he runs his fingertips over my shoulders and he looks at me like he wants me.

Drew turns toward me. This time, he's obvious about his double take. Of course, I'm wearing a tight dress and no bra. Not that I wore it so his gaze would be drawn to my chest or anything.

He pushes himself off the bed and leads me to the hallway.

Downstairs, someone is clapping. Tom, of course.

He yells in our general direction. "That was fast, Drew. Kind of embarrassing."

Drew glances at me for a second. No telling what's going on in that head of his. He brushes a wet strand of hair behind my ears and leans in close.

Then he pulls back and he makes his way down the stairs like nothing has changed.

Chapter Ten

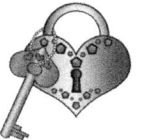

My dance workout relieves the tension wrecking my body. So Drew dodged a dare to kiss me, then stared at me like he wanted to consume me, so what?

I focus on hitting every step in my routine. It's been a long time since I've done any real performances, but the steps are drilled into my brain.

By the time I'm finished practicing, I'm dripping with sweat. My heart pounds against my chest. No lust, just good old-fashioned exercise.

I pull off my tank top and use it to pat dry. No sense in wearing more than a sports bra and leggings. Not for modern dance.

One more time. The track is on repeat. I get into position and wait for the song to finish. The instrumental intro kicks in. Five, six, seven, eight. I launch into my routine, throwing myself into every movement.

I hit the ending pose, catching my breath as the music fades into the outro.

Something is different.

I turn around. Drew is standing at the front door in a t-shirt, running shorts, and sneakers. I must not have heard him come in.

"You're amazing," he says.

"Thank you." I go to put my music on pause.

I can still feel his gaze on me. My sports bra and leggings are tight as hell. That must be it. He's just checking me out. Whatever that means.

I nod to the exercise mat sitting in the corner of the room. "I was going to do some floor work."

"I'm afraid I can't allow that, Kendrick."

"That right?"

"I have push-ups and crunches to do."

Well then. The mat is just big enough to fit the two of us, side by side, even if half of my exercises involve opening my legs as wide as they'll go.

I bite my lip. I can handle this. Maybe. "You can do push-ups on the floor."

He shakes his head. "How do I tolerate such a selfish best friend?"

I roll out the exercise mat and lie on my back. I pretend like I don't care Drew is watching me and do my first set of leg lifts.

He drops on the floor next to me and puts himself in push-up position. He lowers and raises his body with a grunt. There's sweat dripping off his chest and shoulders. He's practically glistening.

Not going to stare at Drew. Just doing leg lifts here. Not lusting after my friend. Not at all.

He moves to the table for inverse rows. I use the time to do bridges, but he's back by my last set, watching as I lift my ass and torso toward the ceiling.

Okay. Enough of that. I switch to forearm planks. I'm

already spent. My arms and legs are shaking. I shift, lifting my ass higher than I should.

Without a word, Drew grabs my hips and adjusts my form.

My body buzzes. That flutter between my legs goes into overdrive.

Fuck it. I drop to the floor. Drew lies on his back. He lifts his leg in the air.

"Stretch my hamstrings," he says.

"Ever hear of the word please?"

"Never."

I stare at him, waiting.

He shakes his head like he finds me ridiculous. "Please, stretch my hamstrings. I'll do you after."

"Tell me when." I wrap one hand around his thigh—his hard, muscular thigh—and the other around his calf, and I push his leg toward his chest until he groans.

"Ugh. When! When!" He makes eye contact.

I silently count to twenty. We switch and I stretch his other leg. He lets out the same delicious groan.

So. Not. Going. There.

I go to push myself up. Drew grabs my upper arms and wrestles me onto my back. Once I'm flat, he kneels next to me, slides his hands around my upper thigh, and pushes my leg to my chest.

He moves slowly, waiting for my when. "Jesus, Kara. Can you get this thing behind your head?"

"Sometimes."

His voice gets lower. "That must come in handy."

I swallow hard. He shifts so he's putting his weight into the stretch, so he's right on top of me. His crotch hovers a few inches from mine.

The stretch gets deeper. It's about as much as I can

take, but I can't bear to say anything that will move Drew's body away from mine.

My eyes flutter closed. I focus on the pull of my muscle. Slow inhale. Slow exhale. So my every bit of breath goes to my hamstring.

He shifts off me slowly and brings my leg back to the ground. His fingertips trail down my thighs. He's going in the opposite direction, but he's still too close to the scars.

He moves to my other leg. Grabs it right at the upper thigh and lifts it. "Truth or truth?"

"Wow, those are a lot of options." My muscle strains. I bite my lip to keep from groaning. "Truth."

He leans his weight into my leg, his hands still firmly around my thigh. "How close are guys' hands allowed to get to your cunt?"

"I thought we agreed to drop this."

"I'm curious."

"Bring me a shot, because I'm not answering."

"Say we were about to have sex." He slides his fingertips an inch up my thigh. "Would this be okay?"

He's about three inches from the scars. "Drop it."

I motion for him to release the stretch. He does. Slowly.

He stares into my eyes. His voice gets soft. "You don't have to tell me why."

I rise to my feet. "I wasn't going to."

He jumps to his feet and grabs my wrist. The left one. I pull it to my chest. No watch today. No arm bands. Nothing to cover that particular set of scars.

"Why do you do that?" he asks.

"No reason."

"Bullshit."

"Bring me the shot, because I'm not telling you that either."

After breakfast, I bury myself in homework. Senior year is no joke. I have an essay and two tests every week. The one thing I don't have is mental energy.

Two hours of finance and I'm ready to drop. It's not so much that I don't understand business classes. They're just so dull and closed to interpretation. I love my literature classes, even when I have to read long, meandering Russian novels that are so bleak they make me cry.

I flop on my bed and reach for my phone. Time to see if I missed anything important. There's a text from Nadeen.

Nadeen: Hey. This letter came for you. It's like really big. From UCLA. Do you need it?

My throat goes dry. A letter. It must be my acceptance or rejection from the UCLA teaching program. It's really big. Big is good. Big is acceptance packet with financial aid information.

I grab my phone and reply.

Kara: Are you home? I'll come by and get it.

Nadeen: Yeah. Until seven. I can open it now and tell you what it says? It looks like a grad school thing.

Kara: I'll come get it now.

Nadeen: Aren't you going to work at your mom's company?

Kara: Please don't touch it. I'll see you soon.

Nadeen: Okay. You don't have to get snippy about it.

I toss my phone into my purse and slide it onto my shoulder. I need that letter now. I need to know what it says.

I rush down the stairs. Keys. My keys are on the table somewhere.

Drew is sitting on the couch. He's been there for hours, bingeing on some comic book TV show.

There. I grab my keys and make for the door.

Drew turns to me. "Where are you rushing off to?"

"I have to pick something up at Nadeen's."

"You hungry?"

"Starving actually."

He turns the TV off and jumps to his feet. "I'll come with you."

"Why?"

"Because you want me to *come* with you." He takes three steps toward me. "And we can get groceries after."

I can't think about a little thing like groceries at a time like this. But, yes, that makes sense. We do need to eat eventually and there isn't a lick of food in this house.

"I'm driving," I say.

"I like a woman in charge." He practically races to the door. "What's at Nadeen's?"

"You'll see."

And he's already out the door.

Chapter Eleven

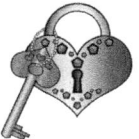

I race up the steps to my old apartment and pound on the door. There's some sound inside—Nadeen's voice and a man's voice too. I smooth my skirt and blouse and fix my hair. No way I'm letting her know I care about this.

There are footsteps and the door opens. It's Alex, Nadeen's boyfriend. We've met once or twice before. He was nice enough then, but the guy did kick me out of my apartment without a second thought.

He shows no signs of embarrassment or regret. "Oh, you're the old roommate right?"

"Right."

Inside, Nadeen gets up off the couch. She grabs something off the table and makes her way to the door.

There it is, in between her selfish hands—my letter. It's a thick manila envelope with a fancy stamped return address. Something that size has to be good news.

I snatch it from her hands. "Nice to see you again." I turn and march down the stairs without waiting for a response. No way I'm letting these two assholes share in my moment.

My car is parked down the street. I hug the letter to my chest. No one else is getting at this. It's mine.

Drew is leaning against my car with a wide-eyed expression. He raises a brow. "And what is that?"

"It's nothing."

"You raced over here to get nothing?" He shakes his head. "You're such a bad liar."

I run my fingertips over the edges of the envelope. A breath escapes my lungs. "You'll see in a minute."

I find the edge of the letter. Okay, here goes nothing. I tear it open at the top. There's a thick stack of papers. Some kind of pamphlet. That must be a good sign.

I let the manila envelope slide to the ground. Drew stoops to pick it up. He stares at the return address for a minute then his eyes dart back to me.

Dear Ms. Kendrick,

We are pleased to offer you a spot in the UCLA Master of Education Program. Please find registration information and deadlines enclosed.

My jaw drops. Drops. I got in.

The ground is spinning. I reach for something to steady myself. Drew. My arm falls on his shoulders. I ignore my balance and squeeze him. He brings his hand to my lower back and holds me against him.

Only to keep me upright.

That's all it means.

I read the letter again.

Dear Ms. Kendrick,

We are pleased to offer you a spot in the UCLA Master of Education Program.

An easiness spreads through my body. My chest and throat and stomach are light and free and airy.

Drew's fingertips dig into my shirt. It pulls back my attention. I take a calm breath but everything is spinning.

He turns my wrist, the right, so he can read the letter. His face lights up with excitement.

"You're going to school for a teaching credential?" he asks.

My lips refuse to open. My mouth is sticky. I pull myself upright. It helps a little.

I shake my head. "Not necessarily."

"When did you apply for this?"

"October."

"You never told me."

"It was a lark." I shrug like it slipped my mind. That's not even close to the truth. I made sure no one knew about this. Not Meg. Not Drew. Certainly not my mother.

Drew shakes his head. "Bullshit." He drags his hand up my back and rests it between my shoulder blades.

I clear my throat. "It's not a big deal."

"You're holding on to me like you're about to jump off a cliff." He pulls my hand off his shoulder and squeezes it. "You're beaming."

"I am not."

"Yeah-huh."

I meet his gaze. "What kind of argument is that?"

"I don't need to argue something this obvious." He brushes a stray hair behind my ear. His eyes bore into mine. "Honestly, Kara. I haven't seen you this happy since... since ever."

I shake my head. "It's really not a big deal. It was a lark. There's no way I can actually become a teacher. My mom has a job lined up for me at her company after I graduate."

"Is that what you want?"

"She's expecting me to take it."

Drew slides his hand to my hips. He stares at me with a penetrating gaze. "Fuck her."

"Drew!"

"Seriously. Unless you want to work at her company."

"I might. Once I get the hang of finance." My voice wavers. It's so soft I can barely hear it. There's no way Drew is buying this. I'm not even buying it. "It's possible."

His fingertips graze my chin. "Look me in the eyes."

I do.

"No bullshit." He holds my gaze. "Do you want to work in finance or do you want to be a teacher?"

"I don't know."

"I said no bullshit. I'll have to punish you if you bullshit me again."

My mind flashes with a truly, truly beautiful image. Drew, naked, sinking his teeth into my neck until I beg for mercy.

I shake my head in an attempt to get my concentration back, but it's not working. Drew naked. Drew naked. Drew naked.

"Kendrick, get your mind out of the gutter and look at me."

My cheeks flush. "You started it."

He brings his hand to my chin and adjusts me so I'm staring into his eyes. "Truth or dare."

My nostrils flare. Fine. I'll entertain this. "Dare."

"I dare you to call your mom and tell her what she can do with her job."

I step back, breaking from his touch. His hands go back to his sides. Suddenly, I'm cold. It's seventy degrees and sunny and I'm cold.

"That's not the spirit of the game," I say.

Drew drops into his serious voice. "Do you want to

move back to San Francisco to work at your mom's company?"

"It's a great opportunity."

"Yes or no."

"You can't say 'yes or no' in that voice, like that gives you some right to my feelings. I have to take that job. She needs me. She doesn't have anyone else and work is the only place she isn't miserable."

"So what?"

"She's my mom."

His voice is soft. "Kara."

"I know my name." I take another step back, my gaze on the sidewalk. There's a jagged crack going straight through the middle of it. "It will make her happy and I'll make twice as much money."

"Since when do you care about money?"

I shrug. "Everyone needs money."

Drew steps toward me. He brings his hand to my cheek with a delicate touch. "Will it make you happy?"

I look into his eyes for a second. It's too much. I have to look away.

"You applied to grad school for a reason," he says.

"It was no big deal."

"Bullshit." He drops his hand to his sides

Everything is spinning again. It's so much harder to stay upright without him touching me. I lean against the car to keep my balance.

"You take any tests?" He asks.

"The CBEST is easy."

"You write an essay?"

"Three."

"Did you have an interview?"

"Yes."

"Did you volunteer at a school to get a feel for teaching?"

"That was for my tutoring job."

He grabs my forearm, his voice stern. "Look me in the eyes, Kara."

I do. His eyes are this gorgeous clear brown. Bright and dark all at once. This is my best friend. His gaze shouldn't feel so intense. It shouldn't feel like he's picking me apart. But it does.

"Truth or dare," he says.

"We were over this."

"And you bullshitted me." He leans closer. "I'm giving you another chance."

"Then give me a drink because I'm not answering."

He rubs my forearm with his thumb. "Do you want to work at your mom's company?"

That heaviness floods my body. It's all wrong. My shoulders tense. A crick develops in my neck.

"Do you want to work at her company?"

"No." I let out a deep exhale. "I don't."

And, suddenly, all that heaviness and tension is gone. I don't want to work with my mom. I don't want to do business. I've never admitted it before, not out loud, not even to myself.

I want to go to grad school.

I want to teach English.

My breath is steady. No tension in my chest. Nothing too heavy or too light. I'm okay. I admitted I don't want to work with my mom and it didn't destroy me.

I'm okay.

But that doesn't make it possible.

I bring my gaze back to Drew. His expression is softer. Sweet even. He plays with my ponytail.

"I'm proud of you." he says.

"I can't do this," I say. "She pays for my school. My rent. She puts money in my account every month. It's all contingent on me following her plan."

"You know what I think?" he asks.

"You think that you know better than I do."

He shakes his head. "You deny yourself the things you want."

"When have I ever done that?"

He cocks a brow. It's like he's daring me to think about it. I'm not stupid. I see this is still about sex, but Drew doesn't have a clue what he's talking about.

That's not how it is.

"I did the same thing," he says. "Went to Stanford to please my parents, even though the only thing I ever wanted was my hands on a guitar. Didn't do any good. When I dropped out to focus on the band, they cut contact. My dad got over it eventually. Mom didn't."

"You want to talk about it?"

"No. Fuck them if they won't support what I want." He runs his fingertips along my neck. "Fuck anyone who denies you what you want."

I lean back against the car. My shirt must be filthy by now, but it doesn't concern me.

Drew's fingertips brush against my left wrist. Just above my silver watch. I pull my hand to my chest and hold it there. He looks at me funny, but he doesn't call me on it.

"This is an amazing accomplishment," he says. "Whatever you decide to do."

"Thank you."

"We're going to celebrate."

I turn to face him. "How?"

He smiles. "I'm making you dinner."

"You cook?"

He shakes his head, *tsk tsk*. "I'm an excellent cook."

"Right."

"You're going to eat those words, Kendrick." He slides his hand into the pocket of my denim skirt and pulls out my keys. "Of course you'll be so full from my delicious cooking that you'll have no room for the words."

I nod, uh-huh, but truth be told, I'm still stuck on the feeling of Drew's hand in my pocket.

Chapter Twelve

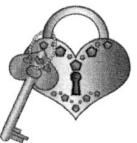

We are in and out of the grocery store in a breeze. Drew knows exactly what he wants and exactly where to get it. When he tries to pay, I shove $40 in the pocket of his jeans. He doesn't object. Maybe he likes my hands in his pants.

A girl can dream.

At home, Drew chops and dices, lost in his cooking the same way he gets lost in the guitar.

I measure flour, sugar, and cocoa powder. A few minutes and this cake will be ready for the oven. "Could you set the preheat to three-fifty?"

He murmurs some kind of affirmative, but he doesn't turn toward me. I focus on stirring, my fingers wrapped around the wooden spoon. The batter is thick and rich and it smells like some wonderful mix of vanilla and chocolate. I dip a finger and bring a taste to my mouth.

"Mmmm." I groan much louder than I mean to.

Drew turns almost instantly. "Shit. I was worried Meg and Miles were hiding upstairs."

My cheeks flush. "Only me."

"That good?"

I offer him the spoon of batter. Instead of grabbing the spoon, he licks it.

His tongue slides over his lips. He grabs the spoon and licks it again.

"Hey!"

I try to grab it back, but he holds it over my head. Damn, Drew is so much taller than I am. There's no way I'll manage to grab it by jumping.

I push myself up, ass on the counter. I hold onto the cabinet to steady myself and slide to my knees. I reach for the spoon but Drew takes a step back. It's still out of reach. He smirks and shakes his head like he knows he's defeating me.

Oh, that's how he's going to play it? I slide off the counter and plant my feet on the ground. I scoop a glob and take two steps toward him.

I fling the batter on his nose.

His eyes close as he winces. "You're asking for it now." He charges, slides his hand in the batter, and flings it on my face.

Oh, fuck, that's cold and sticky all at once.

Drew looks at me as if to call a truce. But the words truce do not flow from his lips. Nice try.

I flick a scoop in his direction. He ducks but it lands on his neck and his otherwise perfectly clean white t-shirt.

He shakes his head. His eyes narrow. He reaches around me and dips his hand in the bowl.

He moves closer. Until his crotch is pressed against mine. He shifts, pinning me to the counter. My lungs empty. My interest in our food fight evaporates. He feels damn good against me.

Drew smiles as he hovers his batter-covered fingers over

my nose. He draws a line down my face, chin, neck, chest. It stops at the neckline of my t-shirt.

That flutter builds between my legs. His fingers are inches from my breasts.

I take a deep breath, willing my body to calm down. It doesn't work.

"Truce," I offer.

He draws another line down my face. His lips curl into a smile. "Truce."

"Asshole."

He laughs. "Here." He wets a towel in the sink and tosses it to me.

I wipe my face, chest, and neck and toss the towel to Drew. He doesn't quite manage to get clean.

"Come here," I say.

He slides one hand around my hip and presses me into the counter.

Somehow, I stay focused on my task. I rub my thumb over his cheek to wipe off the batter.

His eyes find mine. They're not playful anymore. They're wide with desire.

He takes my wrist and brings my thumb to his mouth.

His tongue presses against the fleshy pad. It's strange how sensitive my skin is. How good his mouth feels.

Desire shoots through me, but I maintain a hint of sense. We're not in too deep. Not yet.

Drew releases me. I run my thumb over his lower lip. It's soft. Kissable.

His stare is intense. I pull my hand back to my side and stare back. We're about to cross some line that can't be uncrossed.

It's a terrible idea but I can't talk myself out of it.

Drew drags his fingertips across my chest. He picks up a smidge of batter and brings it to my mouth. I part my lips to make way for his finger. His skin is hard and calloused.

I take it deeper. Suck harder. My head fills with all sorts of ideas.

It's not enough. I need more. I need all of him.

He traces the outline of my lips and slides his hand into my hair. His eyelids flutter together as he brings his lips to mine.

Eyes closed, I lean into his kiss. It sends me straight into a frenzy. I have to grab onto his shoulders to stay upright.

Drew's lips are against mine. Drew is kissing me. It's not for show. It's not a dare. It's because he wants me.

He sucks on my lower lip. He digs his hands into my hair, holding my mouth against his. All I can do is react. Press my fingers into his skin. Part my lips to make way for his tongue. Shift my hips against his.

I don't breathe until he releases the kiss.

His eyes find mine. He runs his thumb against my cheek. "Kara."

I swallow hard. Talking just might ruin this. So I close my eyes and I slide my hands into Drew's hair and I kiss him.

His lips are soft and they taste like chocolate and sugar. He doesn't hesitate. He kisses back, hands on my hips, tongue in my mouth.

Every part of my body is awake and alive and every part of it wants Drew. I arch my back to press my chest into his.

No waiting. He grabs my t-shirt and pulls it over my head. He drags his fingertips down my arm and shoulders and traces the outline of my bra.

That flutter spreads through my stomach and chest and thighs until every part of me is buzzing with electricity.

Drew is touching me.

Drew is kissing me.

Drew is mine. For the next few minutes at least.

He unhooks my bra. I moan into his mouth. Drew is going to take off my bra. Drew is going to see me topless.

It's like I'm a desperate high school student again. The only thing I want is Drew feeling me up. Every second he's not touching me is horrible agony.

He breaks our kiss. His fingers hook around my bra straps. He drags the left strap down until my breast spills out. My sex clenches. I swallow hard.

Then the right.

His eyes go wide. Pupils dilate. "Fuck." He lets out a breathy sigh. "You have no idea how badly I've wanted to see you like this."

He cups my breast and I'm warm all over. Hell, I'm on fire.

My eyes flutter closed. I arch my back to push my chest into his hands. "How badly?"

Drew rubs his thumb over my nipple. "I go out of my fucking mind thinking about you." His voice gets low and heavy. He rubs me harder. "But you're so much better than I imagined."

Heat spreads through me. "You haven't..."

One hand goes to my hips and holds them in place. He presses his crotch against mine, so I can feel his erection straining against his jeans. Drew is hard because of me. I swear I must be dreaming.

I pinch my forearm and pull my eyes open. He's staring at me with this look on his face that says he's desperate to touch me.

Not dreaming.

So much better than dreaming.

"I have. Since forever," he growls. "You dress like you're trying to kill me."

I bring my lips back to his and speak in between kisses. "You flirt like you're trying to kill me."

"I am." He rubs me harder.

I hook my arm around his neck. "How long have you wanted me?"

"Since I can remember." He kisses a trail down my neck and chest.

"Why didn't you try anything?"

"Didn't want to fuck this up."

His mouth closes over my nipple and he sucks hard, the way he sucked on my thumb. Heat spreads through me. Pleasure builds between my legs. I can barely think anything except *Drew*. He's wanted me since he can remember.

He wants me.

He's hard because of me.

My untouchable rock star best friend is hard because of me.

He moves to my other nipple. One of his hands goes to the inside of my knee and traces a line up, up, up.

I press my legs together and shift away from him. God, I want Drew's hands on me, but it's not worth the risk of ruining this completely.

His hands go to my hips and he kisses his way back up my chest and neck. His lips meet mine and his tongue plunges into my mouth.

I let out a low moan and grab the counter to stay upright. I reach for his shirt and pull it over his head. He lifts his arms to help me. And then his hands are on my hips. They trail down the outside of my thighs. He plays with the hem of my skirt, getting closer and closer to my inner thighs.

It feels so good. I'm warm everywhere and I'm so desperate for his touch, but I can't let him see those scars.

"Drew." I shift back and press my legs together.

His eyes find mine. "Oh, shit. I forgot."

I smooth my skirt over my thighs. "It's nothing personal."

He takes a step back. His demeanor changes, so it's tense and awkward. "So, what... we can keep going as long as I don't touch you?"

I swallow hard. "Please."

He takes another step back. His eyes turn down, like he's confused by his own reaction. "I can't, Kara. I have to touch you. I've been going out of my fucking mind thinking about touching you."

The oven *beeps*. The preheat is done. What perfect timing. Drew's eyes are on the floor. It's like he's suddenly lost all interest in me.

I take a deep breath and push myself off the counter. "I understand." I reach for my top, but it's too mortifying standing here half-naked and mid rejection. I turn and make my way for the stairs.

"Kara."

"I'll see you later."

"At least tell me why."

I run up the stairs like I didn't hear him.

Chapter Thirteen

I try devoting my energy to peer editing an essay. Most days, I can spend hours fixing grammar and offering constructive comments. Today, everything about my classmate's writing stands out as wrong. I tear apart her argument with angry red comments. It's all filler. It's all pointless. It's all a distraction from her total lack of a thesis.

When I finish, my head is aching and my neck is sore. I power down my computer and resolve to bullshit my way through the rest of my homework in the morning. The bed is this wonderful supportive foam—it must have cost Drew a fortune. It beckons me, so I flip the lights off and belly flop onto my comforter.

The solitude is soothing. No way anyone can pick apart my expression. Or stare at me with this confused look in his eyes asking for an explanation with his inhale, and rejecting the whole thing outright with his exhale.

It's not his fault.

He was always clear. He was joking, but he was clear. I find my phone and pore over my text messages in search of evidence. The muscles in my chest, neck, and back tense.

He's so demanding and playful and arrogant and sweet at the same time. I want to scream and cry and laugh at the same time.

There. Only a week ago, but that feels like an eternity.

Kara: Fuck you.

Drew: Not with your silly rules about how I can't rub you until you scream.

I play with the hem of my skirt the way Drew did. I drag my fingers over my thighs the way Drew did. Over my quads and up my inner thighs. Up, up, up, until they trail over my first set of scars.

If he'd felt them...

These stupid things change everything. I managed to keep them from my ex-boyfriend by insisting on fucking in the dark and keeping my skirt on. I had to take the lead, to take care of the condom, to move things forward before he even tried to touch me.

To tell him I came even if I didn't.

We were together a year and I managed to deter all his advances. Then, one night, we were drinking. I was relaxed and fucking him wasn't getting me there. I thought it might be okay. He was so excited until he saw them. Until he touched them. His eyes went dark and his dick went soft. He stared at me like I was this awful damaged freak.

One minute I was irresistible. The next I was broken.

The asshole dumped me the morning after. That usual *it's not you, it's me* bullshit.

Then it was like I didn't exist. Like he'd never said he loved me. Like he'd never even met me.

That can't happen with Drew.

I can't be the damaged, unlovable girl. Not to him.

There's a soft knock on my door. I throw the comforter over my head and will the sound to go away. I can't explain this and I can't bear to take another second of the awful look in Drew's eyes.

There are footsteps in the hallway. He's leaving. Another door, must be the one to his bedroom, opens and closes.

It's like he's playing some weird grown up version of ding dong ditch.

I climb out of bed and check the hallway. It's empty except for a plate on the ground—the pasta he was making for dinner. It's still steaming and it smells like garlic and lemon.

It smells like heaven.

There's a napkin-wrapped fork lying next to it. I bring both into my room and set them on my desk. My chest pangs. This was supposed to be a celebration dinner. This was supposed to be ours.

My bad mood can't overpower my appetite. I unwrap the fork. It tumbles onto my desk with a clang.

There's something written on the napkin in a black marker. Drew keeps the damn thing in his pants in case he's asked to sign something.

His handwriting is neat and emotionless. *The cake is cooling on the counter.* That's it.

It's not like I expected a love letter, and it's good that he managed to take the cake out of the oven in time, but I don't need this message. I certainly don't need the taste of sugar and chocolate in my mouth.

I stab a piece of penne with my fork and take a bite. The pasta is amazing—fresh vegetables and shrimp in some white wine sauce way beyond my cooking skills—and I'm positively starving. I try to take my time to savor every bite, but I finish quickly.

Music turns on in Drew's room. He's occupied. Good.

I creep downstairs and wash my plate in the sink. The cake is sitting on the counter, already cool. I cut a tiny sliver to check if it's done. It's perfect; not too soft or too hard or too dry. And it tastes like chocolate and sugar.

Like Drew's lips tasted.

All those muscles in my neck tense again. It was barely an hour ago. We were on the counter. If I hadn't stopped him, if I didn't have these stupid scars...

I fix a cup of tea, English breakfast to keep me awake while I tackle my reading. Caffeine is supposed to help with concentration. It should help me focus on work and not on how good Drew's lips tasted.

They were so soft.

And he was so hard.

The kettle's whistle snaps me out of my daydream. I fill my cup with hot water, cut a slice of cake, and trudge upstairs.

Drew's door is open a tiny sliver. There are no sounds coming out of it except angry heavy metal.

My stomach twists. He's hurting all alone and I'm hurting all alone. I need to explain it's not his fault, that I still want him badly enough to scream, that he's still my best friend, whatever happens.

But I can't bring myself to knock.

I step into my room, slam the door shut, and drown myself in Rage Against the Machine and cake.

───────

MY MORNING DRAGS. INSTEAD OF GOING HOME BETWEEN school and work, I change in my car, arrive half an hour early, and eat lunch at my desk.

I have an email from my mom. A question about

spring break. She'd missed me over the holidays, when I stayed in LA for winter quarter. It was the only way to make my double major work, and it meant I wasn't there to make Christmas dinner or put up the tree or call Grandma. It meant there was nothing in the house but crushing silence.

I shake my head. It's not that I doubt my mother loves me. She does, in her way, but she doesn't see me. Not really. She doesn't have a clue how much I hate finance, how little I want to work at her company, how hard it was being the one who kept everything together after Dad died.

I do my best to concentrate on today's work. It's very basic finance stuff, 201 at most. A slightly more advanced version of this will be my life if I take a job at my mom's company.

By six, the office is empty and the sun is setting. And no doubt Drew is at home, eating dinner on the couch with that same disappointed look in his eyes.

I check the Sinful Serenade Twitter for a clue. There's a new picture of Drew posing with a fan. They're outside in the sun. She's wearing a sports bra and tiny little shorts. Her thighs are scar free, and they're tan and toned to boot.

He has his arm around her shoulder. No flirting. Just a friendly guy fulfilling his duties as a celebrity.

There are no other hints on Twitter. In all likelihood, Drew is at home.

After another hour of work, I change in the bathroom, drive to the gym, and run until my legs are aching.

———

IT'S THE SAME THING FOR TWO WEEKS. I LEAVE FOR SCHOOL early, kill time at my internship, and take the latest cardio dance class the gym offers. If that isn't late enough, I run until I'm too tired to think. I arrive home no earlier than ten.

There is no contact between us except for the Post-it notes Drew leaves on the counter. It's always something about what he made for dinner and then there is a Post-it note marked "Kara" on some neat piece of Tupperware.

I eat the food he cooked for me in my room and I try to avoid wondering what it means that he's still making me dinner.

———

On screen, guns blaze. Except for the loud movie, it's been a mercifully quiet morning. Nothing but screen and cereal.

Meg finishes her can of green tea and gets up to toss it in the trash. Her gaze darts to the curling staircase. "We missed two brunches in a row."

"I know."

She plops back on the couch. "I shouldn't have let you get away with that after that party."

"But I'm glad you did."

She reaches into the paper bag sitting on the table, pulls out a bottle of black tea, and hands it to me. "Are you though?" She looks me in the eye. "You dragged me out of bed every Sunday after Rosie died."

"You were despondent." I twist the cap. "Your sister overdosed. You needed emotional support. This is nothing... I was busy with homework."

She pops open a can of green tea. "Right."

I take a swig of my drink. Perfect excuse not to respond. Meg isn't as perceptive as Drew is, and she hasn't known me as long as he has, but she does see through me.

She follows suit. Her attention returns to the action on screen.

"I'm out of my element here," she says. "I'm so used to you being the one dragging shit out of me. How do you do that? It's annoying at first, but I always appreciate it." She sits up straight and looks me in the eyes. "You're going to tell me what's going on with Drew."

"Very convincing."

"Thank you." She puts her hand on her hip and turns her head like she's posing. "More importantly, you're going to swear to me that you're okay. You don't have to talk to me if you don't want to, but if you're not okay, I'm going to drag you to the damn clubs and fill you with drinks until you feel okay."

I shift back into the couch. "It's eleven a.m."

She laughs. "Valid point."

I look Meg in the eyes. "I'm okay enough."

She accepts my answer and turns back to the action movie. It's some cheesy thing from the eighties. There's a built guy running around in a ripped shirt and tight pants. He has a mullet and a giant gun. Somehow, he always manages to hold it so it's jutting from his hip.

Meg finishes her can of tea, tosses it back in the bag, and pops another top. "Drew has been in a funk all week."

"Yeah?"

"Oh, yeah. I've got all the gossip. I was at practice Friday."

Fantastic. Drew is gossip. Drew and I are gossip.

"It's no big deal. You know those guys. They're like brothers the way they talk."

I nod.

"What happened after the party?" she asks.

"You don't have that gossip?"

"Only what Miles said the next time I saw him."

"Before or after he made sweet, sweet love to you?"

She smiles. "Before. We do need to eat."

The girl is beaming. Still out-of-this-world, over-the-moon in love.

Meg turns to me. She rests her head on her hand and lowers her voice to a whisper. "It's kind of gross."

"Not as gross as hearing the two of you come."

Her cheeks go red. She drops her voice an octave as if imitating Miles. "If the guy is so good with his hands, why doesn't he use one and spare us from his blue balls?"

My drink slips from my hands, landing on the hardwood with a thud. My cheeks burn. "Was that in front of everyone?"

"Just me."

Thank God. I pick up my drink. The cap is on. Not a horrible spill. "Will you hate me if I slap your boyfriend?"

"Go ahead." She looks at me. "Did he end up taking the dare?"

"Kind of."

Her eyes light up. "Drew kissed you?"

"We kissed, yes."

"What the hell do you mean 'we kissed, yes?' You've been crushing on Drew for ages."

"Yes, okay. Drew kissed me and it was the best kiss of my entire life. I thought I was going to stop breathing. But we stopped before—" I clear my throat. "At second base."

Her voice softens. "What happened?"

What happened? There's no way to explain it without telling her the whole story. And that's off the table. I come up with an acceptable half-truth. "He stopped things."

"Did he say why?"

Yes. He was crystal clear. I rack my brain for another half-truth. Screw it. I'll lie. "Said it was a mistake."

"Are you okay with that?"

I don't have a choice. "I'll get over it eventually."

"You shouldn't live with him. You can stay with me while you're looking for a place. Stay at my place even. I can stay with Miles for a week or two."

"He's still my friend. We just have to get past the sexual tension."

She shakes her head. "You can lie to me if you want, but don't lie to yourself. It's more than sexual tension."

"*I will* get over it."

She studies my expression. I must look miserable because she pulls me off the couch and into the kitchen. We scan the pantry for proper discussing-how-shit-goes-wrong-with-guys snacks. There's nothing except chocolate.

Even the smell of it makes me dizzy.

Back at the couch, I keep my eyes on the movie. She doesn't pry. Thank goodness the girl respects my privacy. Unlike some people.

Upstairs, a door opens.

Speak of the fucking devil.

It's Drew. He moves down the stairs slowly. He's in jeans, Converse, and a tight, v-neck band shirt. My gaze goes right to that chest piece peeking out of his neckline. Such a perfect chest. Such a horrible thing to cover.

He nods to us. "Nice to see you again Meg." He makes eye contact for a split second. "I'll see you later."

I'm cold all over. He's got such an icy look in his eyes, like I've hurt him so much he can't stand it. It's like I've been punched in the gut. I can barely breathe. All the muscles in my stomach clench.

He turns his back to me, walks out the door, and slams it shut.

I'm trying so hard not to hurt him and I'm failing miserably.

Chapter Fourteen

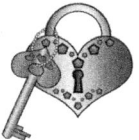

Meg stays through the movie. She asks if I'm okay a dozen times, then goes home to study.

I soak in my time in the living room—lounging with a cup of tea in the kitchen, lying on the couch with my Kindle, spreading my shit out on the table to write an essay. Every hour feels like a gift. Soon, Drew will come home and I'll have to rush back to my room or brave that awful look in his eyes.

Afternoon turns to night. My stomach rumbles and it won't tolerate any more dry cereal or black tea. There's another little Tupperware container in the fridge marked "Kara." Delicious, I'm sure, but it makes my stomach twist in an awful way. My silence is hurting Drew. He's making me dinner and I'm hurting him.

I make a sandwich. Grilled cheese and tomato. Nothing special—my cooking skills haven't evolved much since high school.

The smell is comforting but the sandwich holds no appeal.

This isn't me. I've never been one to lose my appetite.

No matter how awful I feel, I still get hungry.

I push my plate aside and turn my attention to my computer. I dive in to lecture notes and study them like my life depends on it. An hour passes. I eat three bites of my sandwich, pour myself a glass of water, and drift back to work.

The front door swings open. Drew steps inside. There's something off about him. It's like someone sucked every bit of happiness from his body.

I did this to him.

I hurt him.

He glances at me but doesn't look me in the eyes. "There's stir fry in the fridge."

"I know."

He steps onto the staircase. "Living room is yours. I'm going for a run."

He turns his back to me and jogs up the stairs.

It's the same as this morning. The room goes cold. I pull my hoodie over my head, but I'm still freezing. I sip my tea, but it's lukewarm.

Drew jogs down the stairs, headphones around his ears, gaze averted. He throws his hand up as if to wave goodbye and then he's out the door.

Again.

―――

I GO STRAIGHT TO MY ROOM AND PUT MY MUSIC ON MAX, so I won't hear Drew slamming every door in his path.

My back and shoulders are tense. There's this crick in my neck and stretching does nothing to chase it away. My bed is hard and cold. Even my finance homework is better than this awful feeling in my gut.

I need my best friend back.

My stomach grumbles. Most of that sandwich is sitting on the kitchen table, mocking me with its blandness. It's almost ten. I need to eat something if I want to make it to midnight, and there's no way I'm going to finish reading *Crime and Punishment* before midnight.

There's light streaming from the hallway bathroom. Water running too. It sounds like the shower. So Drew is back from his run. Either my music was loud enough to drown him out or he's worked out enough tension he doesn't need to go slamming doors.

The sandwich is still sitting on the table. I finish it in four bites and wash it down with the remnants of my now-cold tea.

My stomach settles. That's got to be good enough. I trudge up the stairs with my eyes on the stark, white ceiling.

The water stops running. The bathroom door opens and Drew steps into the hallway.

In a towel.

In only a towel.

His hair sticks to his head. His lashes and lips are wet. Water drips off his chest, down his cut abs, all the way to that perfect V above his hips.

"You want me to drop the towel so you can get a good look?"

More than anything.

I clear my throat. "Excuse me."

My face and chest flush. It's not every day I get to see Drew like this. My body wants his. It's not like I control how the damn thing reacts to him. It's not like I want to be tied up in knots every second I'm home.

It's not like I want this kind of tension building between my legs, begging me to ignore my better senses completely, begging me to throw myself on his bed.

He's staring at me like he's daring me to say something.

I force myself to look him in the eyes, but that's worse. He has that same hurt, confused expression.

"I should read," I say.

"You should get a better line."

The crick in my neck spreads all the way to the back of my skull. Tension headache, here I come.

I press my eyes closed to will it away. I can't keep doing this. I miss Drew. I miss his laugh, his music, his arms around me.

"How about we pretend it never happened so things go back to normal?" I offer.

He stares through me. "No."

"Please." I play with the waistband of my jeans. "If we forget about the kiss."

His eyes narrow. "I'm never going to forget about that kiss."

I hold his gaze.

"I'm still going out of my head over the taste of your lips and the feeling of your groans in my mouth. I'm still going out of my head dreaming of running my tongue up your thigh and licking you until you come. I can't concentrate for shit. Anytime my hands aren't on my guitar, I'm dreaming about getting them on you."

My eyes go wide. I can barely breathe. I can barely think. I open my mouth to reply, but I can't form a single word.

He takes a step toward his room, his eyes still on mine. "So, no, Kara, I can't forget kissing you. Not ever."

Want spreads to my thighs, stomach, chest. It works its way down my limbs until every inch of me is buzzing. My lips part. My fingertips press together. I will an explanation to form in my mouth. Anything to keep Drew here, to explain this to him. "I had a reason."

He pulls open his bedroom door. "And maybe, one day, you'll trust me enough to explain it."

He steps into his room and slams the door shut.

———

Two a.m. passes and my book is still unread. My body is still heavy. My breath is still strained.

About time I give up on finishing this tonight. I turn off my music, change into my pajamas, and brush my teeth.

Yellow streams through my bedroom door. Hallway light must be on. I go to turn it off.

There's Drew's door, across the hallway, utterly closed to me. There's familiar music in his room. A guitar. It's so soft I can barely hear it, but I recognize it immediately.

It's the song he was playing at practice before everyone showed up. The one that threatened to tear my heart into a million little pieces.

Heaviness builds in my chest. I need to hear that song, to be near him, even if we're not going to talk.

Even if he hates me.

His bedroom door is open. I knock lightly and step inside. Drew turns to me. He's sitting on his bed, acoustic guitar in his lap.

He's wearing nothing but boxers.

That flutter builds below my belly. His back is so strong. It's like he's cut out of marble. I want to touch him and have him touch me.

Maybe I can tell him.

Maybe he won't run away.

"Can I listen?" I ask.

He pats a spot on the bed next to him. "It's pretty rough."

"I like it rough." My face flushes. "I mean... I don't mind."

"I'm afraid I don't have it in me to tease you as mercilessly as you deserve." He turns back to his guitar.

I sit on the edge of the bed opposite him. The three feet between us might as well be a million miles.

An acoustic version of Drew's song fills the room. I lie back and hug a blanket to my chest. The music is beautiful and sad. It presses on the walls of my heart, threatening to collapse them completely.

I can tell him.

I have to.

Drew lets out a heavy sigh. I keep my back to him, my attention on the clean, white wall in front of me.

The song bleeds into an outro until our breath is the only sound in the room. There's something so intimate about it, but that only makes the horrible space between us hurt more.

I play with the blanket. "Is that a Sinful Serenade song?"

"No." He plays a chord. "It's mine."

"Are there lyrics?"

"Yeah, but you're not going to get me to sing. I don't sing."

"What about..." I shake my head, but it's too late. The memory is already there. The sound is already drilled into my brain.

"That was a special circumstance." He leaves it at that.

Music fills the room again. "Fire and Rain," the James Taylor song. The only song he's ever sung.

It was the night of my father's funeral. After everyone left. I was in my room, alone, finally out of sight of everyone who was concerned about how I was handling it.

Finally about to give in to how much it hurt and cry myself to sleep.

He had cancer. It was a slow, agonizing death. I was half-glad he wasn't in pain anymore, half-miserable I'd never see him smile again. But there was no time for any of that. That last year, he was too weak to help. My mom was either at work or shuffling him to treatments. Everything else fell to me.

I cooked dinner, did the shopping, paid the bills. I didn't mind the work. It kept me busy.

Staying strong was the hard part. I was their happy little girl. I had to smile for them, to convince them it would be okay, to convince them it was fine.

It was the same thing at the funeral. Everyone was proud of me for being strong, for being there for my mother, for taking care of things. I wanted so badly to cry, but I couldn't, not until I was alone in my room.

Drew and I weren't close anymore. We had drifted apart my first year of high school. But he was there that night and he refused to leave, refused to believe me when I told him everything was okay.

He sat there in my bed and he played and he sang to me. And then I cried and he held me until I was too numb to cry anymore.

That was the last time anyone saw me as anything besides their rock.

A tear forms in my eye. He's playing loud enough he won't hear, so I do nothing to hold it back. It rolls down my cheek and off my chin.

My eyes sting. I choke back a sob. I pull the blanket over my head to cover the sound. I pinch the skin on the inside of my forearm. I'm not supposed to do anything like that—it's two steps away from cutting—but I need some filter for my feelings before they consume me.

The music stops.

"Kara." Drew's voice is soft and sweet. He pulls the blanket off and runs his fingertips over my shoulder. "I know you usually start with 'I'm fine,' but this time you've got no chance of selling that."

A laugh breaks up the tension in my chest. "I'm sorry. I was just thinking about that night."

"We never talk about it." He lies behind me.

"I know." I relax into Drew's body. "You're the only person who's ever seen me cry."

"You're the only person who's ever heard me sing."

"That can't be true," I say.

"It is. And I can't hit the notes James Taylor can. Not anymore." He holds me closer. "You must have cried in front of someone else."

"Not that I can remember." I wipe a tear from my eyes. "My parents, even before my dad was diagnosed, they were so happy when I was happy. And after he was gone, my mom fell apart. There were months when she spent the entire night on the couch with a bowl of melting ice cream in her lap. And she'd look at me with these dead eyes and tell me how lucky she was to have such a strong daughter."

"Kara."

"It was like she wasn't there anymore. I tried to get her to eat, but she refused. I tried to get her to leave the house, but she wouldn't even get dressed. It was sweet, almost, how empty she was without my dad. But it left me without a mom, more or less."

Another tear rolls down my cheek. That was when my cutting got really bad.

I know it doesn't make sense. But it was like the weight of the world was on my shoulders, and I was desperate for any kind of release I could find. The pain in my body was like an outlet for the ache in my heart. It made me feel alive. It made me feel in control. It made me feel okay, like I could survive going back to being the girl who kept everyone happy.

It was the only way I could deal with my feelings. Mom needed me to take care of her and there was no one to pick up the slack.

The only time she was happy was when I did well.

When I came home with straight A's.

When I made it onto the varsity dance squad.

When I got into UCLA.

My experiments started with my wrists, but those marks were too visible. So I cut my thighs instead. I couldn't wear shorts or go swimming, and I had to be careful to make sure my skirts fell below mid-thigh, but, otherwise, no one asked questions.

No one stared at me with that concern in their eyes the way they did after Dad died.

Drew wipes a tear from my eyes. "Hey."

"Hey."

"I should have been there," he says.

"We'd already grown apart."

"Still." He slides his arm around my waist. "You deserved better than going through that alone."

My eyelids drift together and I soak in the feeling of Drew's body wrapped around mine. It's perfect—calming and exciting all at once.

I take a deep breath. "I'm sorry about what happened. It wasn't your fault. It was me."

He doesn't say anything, but he squeezes me tighter.

"You know, I always hoped I'd find you on my bed, playing guitar. That was the last time in so long that I really felt okay."

Drew holds me tighter. I close my eyes and block out everything except the feeling of his body next to mine.

Chapter Fifteen

I wake up in Drew's arms. I lie there for half an hour, soaking in the comfort of his body, trying to sort through what the hell last night meant.

He stirs, kisses me on the forehead, and shifts out of bed. "It's almost nine. You're gonna be late to class."

Dammit. I hightail it to my room, shower, dress, and pack my backpack.

Drew is at his door, doing pull-ups from a bar hanging off the frame. No shirt. Running shorts. Sweat dripping off the hard lines of his back and shoulders.

A buzz of want builds between my legs. By the time I walk down the stairs, it's everywhere. Even my fingertips want Drew. Especially my fingertips. They're desperate to touch every inch of him.

He drops to his feet with a heavy sigh, then makes his way to the kitchen. His eyes flash with a hint of something mischievous. His gaze meets mine and his lips curl into a smile.

Like he knows I'm staring.

Like he knows I'm desperate.

Like he knows I'm powerless to do anything but melt.

———

My internship runs late. The second I'm home, I change into jeans and a t-shirt and collapse on my bed. I barely have time to catch my breath when there's a knock on my door.

"Come in," I say.

Drew opens the door. He's wearing pajama pants. No shirt, just pajama bottoms.

"You want to mock *Batman and Robin* together?" he asks.

I should finish my homework, but this sounds like a lot more fun. "Sure."

He helps me off the bed and walks me to the couch.

Drew turns the lights off one by one. Downstairs gets dark in stages until the only light is coming from the pool outside.

He pulls the blinds so that's gone too.

Drew sits next to me. Not on the middle cushion, but on mine. Our knees touch. He leans into the backrest, shifting his hips up ever so slightly.

I must be imagining things.

There's no way Drew is this evil.

He turns on the TV and loads the DVD. I try to keep my eyes on the screen and not on the light flickering over Drew's shoulders and chest. It's quite the challenge.

He shifts to the middle seat in one smooth movement. There's no relief from the ache building inside me.

Whatever this is, it's not back to normal.

Maybe he was right. Maybe normal is impossible after that kiss. It's still burned into my brain, my lips, my skin.

His attention is on the movie. I try to follow suit. We watched this all the time when we were younger. Every time, we mocked it mercilessly. Today, nothing. We're silent.

Drew turns to me. He pats his shoulder like he's offering me a pillow. I swallow hard. Not a good idea if I want to keep things anywhere in the vicinity of platonic.

I want him to push me on the couch and rip off my jeans and t-shirt and fuck me until I'm screaming his name so loudly the neighbors call the police.

But it's not worth losing him forever.

———

I GET UP FOR A GLASS OF WATER, BUT IT DOES NOTHING TO cool me off.

I try patting my neck and chest with the water, but that only fills my head with that same beautiful image of Drew coming out of the pool naked and dripping wet.

There are footsteps behind me. Drew slides his arm around my waist. He rests his head in the crook of my neck.

"You up to finish?" His breath is warm against my skin.

"Sure." I set my glass on the counter and turn so I'm facing Drew.

His crotch is pressed against mine. He has me pinned against the counter, more or less. Just like the night when everything went to shit.

Of course, my body shares none of my cautious sentiment. It's practically buzzing with electricity, with the most desperate need to feel his hands again.

It's not the worst idea in the world.

Bottom five maybe, but not the worst.

He steps back and stretches his arms over his head. My eyes go straight to the muscles of his torso as they constrict and relax. There's that little line of hair under his belly button. They shouldn't call it a happy trail. More like a *this is driving me out of my fucking mind trail*.

Drew drags his fingertips over my palm. He nods to the TV like everything is normal and he isn't trying to torture me.

I follow him back to the couch. He plops in the corner and pats his shoulder the way he did earlier.

This time, I take his offer. I slide onto the middle cushion and rest my head on Drew's shoulder.

He runs his fingers over the elastic band in my hair and pulls out my ponytail. My hair falls over my face and shoulders. Drew brushes it behind my ear.

The TV flickers. There's absolutely nothing about it that can draw my attention. I lean into Drew's touch as he runs his fingers through my hair.

There's nothing demanding about his touch. It's soft. Sweet. Patient.

He traces a line down my neck and over my chest and back again. His touch moves lower and lower, until he's tracing the neckline of my t-shirt.

Heat builds between my legs. This might ruin everything, it might make him run away, it might torpedo our friendship forever.

But none of that can compete with the desire spreading through my body. Whatever the consequences, I need Drew and I need him now.

I let out a low moan. I shift my chest into his hands. He doesn't need it explained. He slides his hand under my shirt and over my bra. He traces its outline from one side of my chest to the other and back again.

And again.

And again.

He slides his fingers into my bra and draws slow circles around my nipple.

My sex clenches. Drew is touching me and it feels so damn good.

He plays with my other nipple the same way. His free hand goes to my hair and he tilts my neck so we're face to face.

He's three inches away.

His eyes close and he kisses me. Soft to start, then harder and harder.

He cups my breast inside my bra and rubs me with his thumb. His tongue slides into my mouth, exploring it. I kiss him back as hard as I can.

Drew is kissing me. Drew is touching me. It's still so novel and amazing. My best friend, the guy I've wanted for as long as I can remember, is touching me.

He releases my hair. His hand goes to the space between my shoulder blades. The other goes to my side. He pushes me onto the couch, pinning me with his hips.

I run my hand over his chest and shoulders, exploring every inch of them.

I sigh into his mouth. He releases our kiss and brings his lips to my ears, neck, collarbones. He pulls off my t-shirt, breaking my grip on his shoulders to get it over my head.

I arch my back into him. I let out a loud moan. No holding back. I want Drew to know how much I want him, and I want him more than I've ever wanted anything.

My body is buzzing. Every part desperate to be touched. Even... maybe...

I'm doing this, whatever it means.

He sucks on my earlobe and all that apprehension drips away. His mouth feels damn good. My nipples tighten. That flutter spreads to my stomach and thighs.

Drew grabs my hips and adjusts my position so my crotch is right below his. I can feel him through my jeans.

He's hard and he's pressed up against me. I shift my hips to grind against him.

It's just the right amount of friction. Pleasure rushes through me.

Drew lets out a low groan. He unhooks my bra and pulls it off in a huff.

His lips close around my nipple. He runs his tongue over it with just the right amount of pressure.

He rocks against me. The weight of his body feels so damn good. He's warm and he's hard and he's mine.

His hand slides up the inside of my leg. My breath hitches. My chest tightens.

"Drew." I try to relax as I exhale but it's not working.

He brings his lips back to my ear. "I want to touch you, Kara."

And God does that feel good. Every place his fingertips touch buzzes with need. All these clothes in the way. Usually they protect me from questions, but now they're keeping me from Drew.

"I'm going to go insane if I don't touch you." He drags his teeth over my neck. He grabs my hand and slides it over his. "Show me."

Okay. I can do that. I relax into the couch. The tension in my chest eases.

I guide his hand up my thighs and between my legs.

There.

He rubs me over my jeans. Just hard enough. Just heavy enough.

Pleasure shoots through me. I arch my back and surrender to it.

The pressure builds, tighter and tighter, until I'm almost there. I groan. I dig my nails into the skin of his back and hold his body against mine.

Drew kisses his way back to my lips. I moan into his mouth. I sink my nails into his skin.

Pleasure builds. More. More. More. Until I'm almost on the edge. I buck my hips. I kiss him back as hard as I can.

The smooth fabric of my underwear presses against me. Almost. I break free of our kiss and pant.

"Drew," I groan.

His teeth scrape against my neck. He rubs me with that same perfect pressure. That pressure inside me builds until I'm on the edge. I let out a low moan and rake my nails over his back.

There.

An orgasm builds inside me, more and more and more. And then I'm there, and everything inside me releases. Pleasure washes over every inch of my body. It's in my hips, my chest, my fingers and toes.

Drew shifts to his side. He undoes the button of my jeans. His lips hover over my ear. "I want to hear you say my name like that again." He sucks on my earlobe. "And I want to feel you come on my hand."

Oh God.

My body is begging me to say yes. Drew wants to feel me come on his hand. It would be criminal to resist.

He unzips my jeans and goes to pull them down my hips. I stop him. I'm not ready for that. Not yet.

But I can manage this if it's on my terms.

I grab his hand and place it on my stomach. I guide it down, below my belly button, under my panties.

There.

His fingers slide over my clit.

Yes. God, yes.

Drew's eyes find mine. It's that same penetrating look

he always has, the one that makes me feel exposed. But this time it's dripping with desire.

He kisses me so hard I get dizzy. I grab onto his hand and hold his mouth against mine as he rubs me. Harder and harder until it's perfect.

My body fills with ecstasy. It doesn't seem possible that anything could feel this good.

His strokes get shorter, faster, harder, until his finger is rubbing exactly the right spot.

"Drew," I groan.

I melt into the feeling in my body. I say his name again and again.

An orgasm rises up inside me, higher and higher, and it crashes over me in a rush of pleasure.

He keeps his hand pressed against me as I come. His kiss gets harder. His free hand digs into the skin of my shoulders.

I relax into the couch, panting in a desperate attempt to catch my breath.

Drew brings his mouth to my ear. "So much better than I imagined."

He holds me until I fall asleep.

Chapter Sixteen

I wake up in my bed with only the faintest recollection of Drew taking me into his arms and carrying me upstairs. The room is bright and warm.

The air smells better.

Even my toothpaste tastes better.

I throw on jeans and a sweater and rush down the stairs. No signs of Drew but there's a cup of tea on the counter.

That tastes better too.

———

CLASS FLIES BY. MY INTERNSHIP IS A BREEZE. EVERYTHING is perfect until I collapse on the couch and pull out my cell phone.

Three Missed Calls from MOM.

One new message.

Fantastic. I roll my shoulders back. A preventative measure for the crick threatening to form in my neck.

There's the faint sound of music coming from upstairs.

A recording of some kind. Not Sinful Serenade. Drew must be relaxing. There's no sense in disrupting him over nothing.

I listen to the voicemail.

Hey, Kara, sweetie. I miss you. Mr. Reeves tells me you're doing really well at Giffin. I'm so excited for you to start at Sugar and Spice in June. I've got a great visit planned for you during spring break. You'll be shadowing Stacey for two days—you remember Stacey? She adores you.

Call me soon.

Her voice is void of energy. She's not doing well.

There's no way I can tell her when she's this off-kilter.

What if she's not eating or sleeping again?

What if she's self-medicating again?

The crick in my neck spreads to the back of my skull. It will be a throbbing tension headache in five minutes flat.

Fantastic.

A glass of water and an ibuprofen might destroy this thing before it overtakes me. I push myself to my feet. My phone slides off my chest and onto the floor with a thud.

It's face-down.

I go to pick it up. Sure enough, there's a crack running down the middle.

It fell two feet onto hardwood and there's a crack.

It's so ridiculous it's funny.

A tiny laugh escapes my lips. It breaks up a tiny hint of tension in my chest, but it's not enough.

My throat is dry and ragged. The pounding in the back of my head starts. I move to the kitchen in a daze. Water. There's ibuprofen in my purse, but where the hell is my purse?

A door opens upstairs. Drew. God knows what he'll think of me in this sorry state. I plant my ass on the couch and dig through my purse. Those painkillers must be somewhere.

Footsteps rush down the stairs. And then I can feel it, even through the haze of my increasingly obnoxious headache. Drew is staring at me the way he always does. He's looking through me and picking me apart.

My fingers hit plastic. That must be it. I pull the bottle from my purse, align the child safety symbols, and pop off the top.

Drew sits next to me. "Let's skip the part where you lie and say you're okay."

I pop two Advil and down half my glass of water. "I have a headache."

"Where?"

I point to the back of my neck.

"Turn around."

I do.

Drew drags his fingertips up my back. He tugs at the collar of my shirt and traces its outline all the way to my chest.

He leans closer, so his breath is on my neck. Somehow, that dulls the awful throbbing.

He undoes the top button of my shirt. Then the next. The next. His fingertips skim the fabric of my bra and all the nerves in my body turn on at once.

"What are you doing?" I ask.

"Besides feeling you up?"

I swallow hard. "Yeah."

His fingertips trace their way up my blouse until they meet at the back of my collar. He rolls the shirt down so it's at my waist. He pulls my bra straps off my shoulders.

All that need for an explanation vanishes. I don't give a flying fuck what he's doing as long as he keeps doing it.

His hands settle at the edge of my neck and he rubs my

shoulders.

I let out a low moan. That awful crick in my neck melts away. The throbbing in the back of my head dulls until it's barely a whimper. And then he rubs my neck and any remnants of pain are gone.

All I know is how good his hands feel.

How much I want them on my body.

On every part of my body.

"Should we take it from the top?" He presses his thumb against the place where my neck and shoulders meet. "You tell me what's wrong. I get my hands under your bra."

"I like the second part of that."

"Unfortunately, I can't do anything to change the order."

"Don't you find it inappropriate to feel up a girl after she pours her heart out?"

His voice drops an octave. "You don't want me touching you?"

"Don't say stupid things."

He mumbles some kind of affirmation and rubs me a little harder. No wonder all those flirty fans giggle over jokes about his skilled hands. These things are magic.

I close my eyes and relax into Drew's massage. He's quiet for a long time. There's nothing in the room except the sound of our breath.

And then he stops. He drags his fingertips down my shoulders and sides. "If you don't talk to me, I'm not going to touch you."

Quite the card he's holding there.

My eyes flicker open. "My phone broke."

He leans down and scoops it off the ground. "It's only a scratch."

"It's more than a scratch."

He presses his lips into my neck. "But it's fixable." He

plays with the screen. 'It's still usable like this.'

He kisses me again, a little harder. I moan into his mouth. This is much better than conversation.

He pulls back. "I'll still replace your screen tomorrow." He tugs at my ponytail, pulling the elastic band from my hair. His lips hover over my ear. His breath is soft. "You don't really expect me to believe you're this upset over a phone."

"I'm not—"

He brushes my hair behind my ear. "You remember how I touch *after* you talk to me?"

My cheeks flush. "Yes."

"Well, I'd hate if we didn't get to the touching part."

"But... I... we..." I want so badly to know what this means—if he likes me or loves me or simply wants to fuck me, no feelings required—but I'm not sure I'm prepared to hear the answer.

Drew has my shirt halfway off and he's whispering flirtatious dares in my ears. He clearly wants me. And there's no doubt he's my best friend.

But that could be it. It's entirely possible his feelings for me are only lust and friendship.

I pull my shirt back over my shoulders and rebutton it.

Drew lets out a low sigh. "I wish you wouldn't do that."

I turn to face him. "It's no big deal."

His stare is penetrating. His expression shifts. Not fun or flirty but serious

He traces the hem of my pencil skirt. "Why do you play this game? You always tell me eventually."

I shrug like I'm not affected by him. "I had a message from my mom and she didn't sound happy."

His eyes narrow. He stares at me like he's daring me to tell him the truth.

"Okay. It was worse than not well. She sounds

depressed again, the way she was after my dad died." I play with my skirt, my hands a few inches from Drew's. "My mom has plans for me to shadow at Sugar and Spice over spring break. She's super excited for me to work with her and fulfill all her dreams and I'll crush her if I turn down the opportunity."

"How do you know that?"

"She's my mom. I know." My gaze drifts toward the soft blue leather of the couch. "She's been either depressed or halfway to depression since my dad died. And she's almost there again."

Drew's voice gets soft. "Hey." He plays with my hair. "It's sweet you want to help her."

"I have to be there. No one else will."

He brings his hand to my chin and tilts it so he's staring straight into my eyes. "And how will you feel working at her company?"

"I'll live."

He shakes his head. "You're so full of shit. Why do I put up with you?"

"Because I have a great rack."

His eyes flare with desire. "True."

I fight a blush. "Okay, fine. I'll be miserable working at her company." I meet Drew's gaze. "Happy?"

"Very." He leans closer. "And what do you want?"

"You're obnoxious."

"And handsome." His voice gets serious. "Make me a promise."

"Why?"

"Because it's your only hope of staying on my good side." His fingertips brush my cheek. "Promise you'll get your teaching credential."

"You don't have the right to make me promise anything."

"So do it because it's what you want."

He says it like it's so easy. Must be easy for him—he's a talented musician with tens of thousands of fans. His future is set.

He can do whatever the hell he wants—drink or fuck or trash hotel rooms—and it's all excused under the guise of rock stardom.

"I'm not going to promise. Even if it means you never touch me again." I bite my lip, willing all my determination to rise. "Besides, I think you're bluffing."

He runs his hand through my hair. "That right?"

"Yeah." I close my eyes and relax into Drew's body. Whatever is happening between us, I need to be around him. I need him to hold me, touch me, whisper sweet things to me.

He tilts my chin so we're eye to eye. "Come on. I'm taking you out."

"I don't want to go out."

"You'll feel better."

I hold his gaze, but he's not backing down.

"Besides, I want to see you in one of those tight dresses you wear." He nibbles on my ear. "And out of it."

"Those are for dancing." I fight a groan. "And you hate dancing."

"No." He drags his fingertips over my neck. "I hate not being able to touch you."

I swallow hard. "Okay."

He smirks like he knows how dizzy he's making me.

I slide off the couch, change in my room, and add a little dramatic flair to my makeup.

Drew's door is half-open. He changes into a clean band t-shirt and grabs something from his dresser and slides it into his pocket.

A condom.

Chapter Seventeen

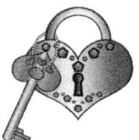

We have dinner in Hollywood. The place is too loud and dark for much conversation. Truth be told, there's not much room in my head for conversation. My thoughts are in the gutter. Every last one of them.

My favorite club is three blocks away. We walk like a couple: arms around each other's waists, barely any space between us.

Even in my fuck-me heels, I'm several inches shorter than Drew. I force myself to take long steps to keep up.

It's a tiny little place. Fits a hundred people, maybe, and it's used for rock shows as often as it's used for all-out raves. Tonight is a rave, thank goodness. I want to get lost in the dark and the music and the feeling of Drew's hands on my hips.

Drew nods to the bouncer like he knows the guy. We cut in line and walk into the club.

Even in the entrance hallway, the music is pounding. It sinks all the way to my bones. My hips sway as I walk. It's pure reflex. Utterly out of my control.

We step into the main room. The lights are blue and white and the dance floor is packed to the brim with people lost in the rhythm.

I squeeze Drew's hand and pull him onto the dance floor. He slides his hands around my hips and brings my body into his.

Either the guy dances more often than he lets on or he's a natural.

I hook my arms behind his neck and look deep into his eyes. There's something there—something so much more than friendship or attraction or his obnoxious-yet-sweet need to protect me.

His hands go to my ass and he holds me tighter. No coyness. No games. Nothing but the purest, sweetest want.

Everything except the beat drifts away until I'm only aware of the sensations in my body. The strain of my thighs. The stretch of my chest. The warmth of Drew's body against mine. His hands digging into the fabric of my dress. The ache between my legs building until I want to scream.

He drags his hands down my hips and thighs. His fingertips skim the edge of my skirt. I pant. I grab onto his shoulders as tightly as I can. Half of me wants to strip right here on the dance floor... anything that gets his hands on my body. The other half wants to run screaming. Drew discovering my scars in a loud, sweaty club has catastrophe written all over it.

I take a step back, breaking his grip. I'm cold all over and the ache inside me is so much more desperate.

His expression flashes with concern. Then it's back to that awful confused look, the same one he had in the kitchen when everything almost went to shit.

I offer my best *I'm not at all freaked out about you seeing my scars* smile. "Let's get drinks."

He presses his palm flat against my back as he leads me to the bar. His hand slides around my hips and over my ass.

I bite my lip to keep from panting. It's loud and crowded here. The light is strange. After two drinks, it's possible Drew won't notice the scars.

It's possible I'll be able to avoid this for another month. A week. Hell, even a day as someone other than the poor damaged girl would be fantastic.

I search Drew's expression for any signs to how he'll react, but all I see is desire.

He leans over the bar and signals the bartender. He turns to me. "Paloma?"

I nod.

He orders for us. Paloma and a tequila on the rocks.

Drew turns back to me, his eyes are wide with excitement.

I bite my lip. I can't tell him now. Not here. Not yet. Maybe after a drink or two or three. Maybe after I'm sure he won't run away.

He makes eye contact. "You're going to drive me out of my fucking mind if you keep looking at me like that."

My tongue slides over my lips. "Like what?"

"Like you have to tell me something awful."

Drew slaps two twenties on the bar. "Keep the change." He hands me my drink and presses his palm into the small of my back. His eyes get serious. "Tell me it's not something awful."

I clear my throat and offer my perfect calm smile. "I thought you could read my mind."

"Usually."

"You're so obnoxious sometimes, you know." I take a step toward the dance floor. "Ever consider that I have something on my mind that I don't want to talk about?"

"No."

"Or that I'd rather not talk at all?"

"No." He slides his hand around my hip. "I have to know everything about you. I have to know every part about you."

"What about the ugly parts?"

He runs his fingertips over my cheek. "There are no ugly parts."

I bury myself in my drink. Sugar and citrus and loads of tequila. But this isn't coming out easier. "You've really hurt your bargaining position by admitting how badly you want to fuck me."

He grabs my ass and holds my body against his. "I see that hint of desperation in your eyes. You want it even worse than I do."

I shake my head.

His lips close over mine and he kisses me so I almost topple over.

Fuck. That's amazing.

The kiss breaks. I go back to my drink like I'm not even fazed, but I'm not selling that story. I'm flushed and panting. My legs are shaking. My arms are riddled with goosebumps.

I don't know who wants it worse, but I want it so badly I could kill someone.

Drew, I have to warn you about something. It's not a big deal, but I have some scars on my thighs. Who am I kidding? It's a huge deal and I wouldn't even consider letting anyone else touch them.

I will the words to form in my throat, but they don't. Drew's expression gets serious. If I don't act fast, the next thing out of his mouth will be something about not fucking me until I tell him what's wrong.

I take a deep breath. "I should probably tell you something."

"Is it important?"

"It might be."

He raises a brow. "Kendrick, you know if it's important."

"It is." I take a long sip. "But I'm terrified it's going to change the way you feel about me."

"There's nothing you can say that will talk me out of fucking you." Drew finishes his drink and sets it on a side table in one smooth motion. He moves back toward me. His hands skim the hem of my dress. "But first, I want to have you here."

My breath catches. Here as in on the dance floor here? That's so... I can't even...

I can't even believe I'm considering this.

Drew grabs my wrist, the left. I go to pull my hand to my chest but stop myself. He looks at me funny for a second but he shakes it off.

We move to the middle of the dance floor. No pretenses. No waiting. No conversation. His lips slide over mine. His hands go to my hips and he grinds against me.

My body is buzzing already. I hold his head against mine so I can suck on his lips. He tastes so good. Like Drew. The word dances around my brain. It's better than the music. Better than anything I've ever felt.

I rock my hips against his in time with the bass line. He's hard and he groans with every brush of my body against his. I turn and press my back against him, my ass against his crotch. He sinks his teeth into my neck. He drags his hands to the neckline of my dress.

I arch my back to press my crotch against his. Drew lets out a low groan. He sucks on my ear so hard I almost scream. His hand trails over the jut of my hip bone, until his fingers are right over my clit. The dress is in the way, sure, but there's no mistaking the pleasure flooding my body.

My cheeks flush. I'm suddenly aware that we're in a crowded club, surrounded by other people. I straighten my back and turn around so I'm facing Drew.

He sucks on my neck. Then my ear. I dig my hands into his hair. I let out a low moan.

We're barely dancing now. I'm too caught up in the sensations in my body to tune in to the music. I only shift my hips to press my body against his, so I can feel his cock straining against his jeans.

Every shift of his hips sends a wave of pleasure through my body. I relax into his touch, utterly powerless to feel anything else.

He traces the neckline of my dress then slides his hand under it. His fingertips brush against my nipples. A shock of pleasure rushes straight from my sex to my toes. I'm going to go mad if he doesn't fuck me properly.

He plays with my nipple until I'm panting. His lips sink into mine. His tongue plunges into my mouth. I hold onto his arms for dear life.

Drew breaks our kiss. He brings his mouth to my ear and adjusts my dress so I'm fully covered everywhere. "Follow me."

His hand slides to my hip. He leads me off the dance floor and toward the back of the club. There's a small hallway and a door marked *Crew Only*.

Drew opens the door carefully. The room is black, almost dead black, and it's stuffed with equipment for shows—costumes, amps, vanity. It's a tiny room, but it's empty.

He pulls me inside, pushes the door closed, and presses me against it in one smooth motion.

I open my mouth to speak, to really warn him, but before a word can form, Drew is kissing me.

He pulls the straps of my dress off my shoulders and pushes it to my waist. I'm not wearing a bra, thank God. To torture him and maybe myself.

He kisses his way to my breast and flicks his tongue against my nipple. My hands go to his hair. I press my back against the door. God, he feels so good.

"Drew," I gasp. "Now."

He brings his lips back to mine and kisses me hard. I lift my dress enough to kick off my underwear and then I pull it back in place.

Drew pulls the condom from his pocket. I unzip his jeans and push them off his hips. Then the boxers.

Holy shit.

He's huge.

I wrap my hand around his cock and rub him until he shudders. He bites my neck hard, groaning into my skin.

I unwrap the condom and slide it over him.

He grabs onto my hips and lifts me. I take a deep breath and hook my legs around his waist.

There's that sharp tug of rubber as he slides inside me.

He thrusts into me. It's deep enough to hurt. I gasp, digging my nails into his shoulders until the pain turns to pleasure.

This is exactly where I should be.

He holds me against the door and thrusts into me. "Fuck. You feel good."

I attempt to verbalize some kind of agreement but it comes out as a loud moan.

Drew brings one hand to my mouth and slides two fingers between my lips. There's something magical about those hands. They do something to me.

I suck on his fingers, pressing my tongue against their

soft pads. He holds me against the door, thrusting into me harder and harder and harder.

Every muscle in my body is awake and alive. Hell, every nerve is tuned to the same frequency and they're headed straight to an orgasm.

I suck on Drew's fingers so I won't groan. It's not enough to contain the pressure building inside me. His hand digs into the delicate skin on my hip. A few inches from my scars, but right now I don't care.

The only thing that matters is him inside me.

I pull my mouth off his fingers and kiss him as hard as I can. He plays with my nipples. It's just soft enough to send pang after pang of desire shooting through me.

My body buzzes. I hold him tighter. Kiss him harder. Buck my hips to drive him deeper.

He groans into my neck. His nails sink into my skin. He's close. I'm fucking Drew and he's close.

I must have died and gone to heaven.

He rubs his thumb over my nipple. There. I break our kiss to let out a low groan.

He does nothing to keep me quiet. He rubs me the same way. He thrusts into me until I let out a scream. And then he keeps doing it. Just. Like. That.

The pressure tenses and tenses, until it's almost too much to take. I hold him tighter. Groan louder. Rock my hips to push him even deeper.

There.

An orgasm rises up inside me. Tighter and tenser and harder.

He thrusts into me again and I teeter over the edge. I come in spasms, all that delicious tension releasing into pure ecstasy.

"Drew," I groan.

His name is still the best thing I've ever heard.

Drew kisses me deeply. He shudders. Almost there. Almost all mine.

I lose myself in the feeling of him inside me. Drew is about to come. I pinch myself to check if I'm dreaming.

Wide awake.

He groans into my mouth. There's this desperate need pouring from him to me and back again. I've wanted this for so long. And he has too.

And it's perfect.

He releases the kiss and groans my name into my ear. "Kara." His nails dig into my skin as he thrusts one last time.

And he comes. I can feel his cock pulsing, even with the condom. I can feel it in his breath and his hands and the muscles in his chest.

"Fuck." Drew releases me.

I unhook my legs, plant them on the ground, and pull my dress back on.

He shifts back into his jeans and discards the condom in a trash can on the other side of the room.

And then he's back to me.

He's mine.

He squeezes my hand. "You're amazing."

"Drew." I wrap my arms around him. "Take me home so we can do that again."

"I thought you'd never ask."

Chapter Eighteen

On the ride home, I play with the hem of my dress to keep my mind from spinning out of control.

Drew and I had sex.

And now we're going to do it again.

It's enough to make me dizzy.

He stops at a red light. His attention turns to me. His lips curl into a smile. He drags his fingertips over the inside of my knee and up my thigh.

And there it is: the only snag in such a perfect plan. I can't put it off anymore.

I have to tell him and pray he won't run away.

He's staring at me with that same penetrating look he always has. His eyes are wide, filled with this strange mix of enthusiasm and concern. Usually, that kind of concern makes me feel empty and exposed. On Drew, it's not so bad. It's almost sweet.

The light turns green and Drew hits the gas. My attention goes back to the road. His hand stays on my thigh.

Close enough to my knee that I can delay this conversation until we're home.

———

Drew throws open the sliding door. Cold air rushes inside. It doesn't faze him at all.

He looks at me with wide-eyed enthusiasm. His voice is light. Teasing. "We still haven't gone skinny dipping."

"It's still freezing."

He pulls his t-shirt over his head and tosses it on the concrete. He raises a brow. "Don't you want to see me naked?"

My cheeks flush. I try to think of some excuse that isn't *I'm not ready to tell you about this yet* but nothing comes.

He takes a backward step, planting his foot on the concrete outside. His hands go to his jeans. Button, undone. Zipper, unzipped. The things fall to the floor.

Nothing but boxers.

Heat builds in my body, until the air doesn't feel cold anymore. Even my cocktail dress is far too much clothing. If I don't get in that pool, I'm going to catch fire.

It's glowing with an aqua sheen. The light dancing off Drew's torso is utterly gorgeous but it also means there's nowhere to hide.

Deep breath. Here goes nothing.

"Drew, I have to tell you something," I say.

He drops his playful expression. "Important?"

I nod. "I'm terrified you're going to run away."

"How could you think that?" Hurt flashes in his eyes. "You're my best friend."

"But that doesn't mean..." I bite my lip. "Can I get that promise in writing?"

His eyes pass over me. That same penetrating look. That same concern.

This might be the last time he ever looks at me as anything besides the pathetic, damaged girl.

My chest gets heavy. A deep breath does nothing to break it up. He's staring at me all curious and confused and there's nowhere to go.

I try to hold Drew's gaze but it's too intense. I look at the concrete instead. "I used to cut."

My stomach drops. It's like I'm on one of those free-fall roller coasters, only there's no bar for me to hold. There's no harness keeping me safe.

"I have scars all over my thighs," I say. "Deep, ugly, red scars."

I finally meet his gaze. His eyes are filled with the most awful hurt.

"When?" His voice is heavy.

"In high school."

"When in high school?"

This isn't how he's supposed to sound. He's supposed to hold me and stroke my hair and tell me it's okay. He's not supposed to stare at me with all this awful accusation.

Like I'm letting him down.

Like I'm failing him.

Like I'm not good enough.

I keep my eyes on the concrete. "It started when my dad was sick and everyone was expecting so much from me." I run my fingers over my shiny silver wrist watch. "My wrist at first, but that was too hard to cover. So I switched to my thighs."

Drew's stare guts me—rips me into little pieces and pastes me back together again.

"We were friends," he says. "Why didn't you tell me?"

"I didn't tell anyone."

"I would have helped you."

"When?" I ask. "Because the way I remember it, you ditched me the second you got popular."

His voice softens. "It wasn't like that."

"Then what was it like?"

He runs his hand through his hair. There's this look of agony on his face, like there's more to the story.

But he doesn't say anything. He never does.

It's always questions directed at me. He's always desperate to know all of my feelings. But the second I bring up something that hurts him, he shuts down or changes the subject.

My temper flares. "You have to do more than show up at my house with a guitar and a promise that we can be friends again." I play with the hem of my dress. "I didn't want a pity friendship and I still don't."

His expression hardens. "And what about the last six months?"

"No one knows about this. No one but my asshole ex-boyfriend who dumped me for it."

He reaches for my wrist, the right, and holds it tightly. "You think I'd dump you over this?"

"We're not anything that can be dumped." I take a step backward. "Where do you get off getting upset about this? What secret have you ever told me?"

His grip slips. He grabs onto my hand. "You're the only person I tell anything."

"What about Vivian? There must be a reason why I never hear a word about her."

"Because it's not important."

"Bullshit."

I back into the house. He's still staring at me with the same look he had in the kitchen that day: sad and angry and utterly confused by his own reaction.

"You're my best friend, Kara."

"But that doesn't give you the right to my feelings." It's dark, but I can just make out the stairs. I stumble over something. Stupid heels. I brush myself off and climb the first step. "They're mine. I don't care how much you want to hear them or how much you want to know every part of me. You don't get to unless I say so."

"Kara."

I rush up the stairs and into my room. I press my back into the closed door, sink to my ass, and hug my knees.

That awful heavy feeling spreads from my chest to my stomach and shoulders and hips. And then it overtakes me completely.

Chapter Nineteen

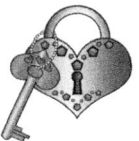

I was never one of those kids who was afraid of the dark. I never worried there was something lurking under the bed or in the closet.

I loved the dark.

The older I got, the more people expected from me, the more I loved it. It's this beautiful blanket of invisibility. No one can see the expression on my face. There's no reason why I need to smile or nod or even hold together some semblance of calm.

In the dark, in my bed, under the comfort of my so aptly named comforter, I can frown or cry or weep until my throat is ragged and sore.

No one sees me.

No one expects anything from me.

No one looks at me like I'm a poor, unfortunate soul.

But, right now, I hate the dark.

I hate my room.

I hate my bed.

And it's all because Drew is somewhere outside my door.

We're in the same house but we're eight million miles apart.

And for some strange reason I want him looking at me, expecting something from me, listening to me.

I want him to understand.

I want him to love me, even with the ugly scars.

Chapter Twenty

An hour passes. A door across the hallway opens and shuts. There are footsteps heading down the stairs and out the front door.

Drew's car turns on and pulls onto the road. God knows where he's going at this time of night.

If he's ever coming back.

If he's ever speaking to me again.

I brush my teeth and change into my pajamas. Then it's back into the not-at-all comforting embrace of my bed.

It's so cold in here.

It's so empty.

I toss and turn, not really attempting to sleep or think or do anything but breathe.

Even that is difficult.

Another hour passes.

Another.

The street goes dead quiet. It's closer to morning than it is to night. God knows I should be asleep. God knows how I'm going to make it through my homework tomorrow.

A car pulls onto the street. Then into our driveway. It stops. Turns off. A moment later, the front door opens and slams shut.

Drew.

His footsteps move up the stairs. They're steady. Not rushing. Not hesitating. Just coming.

There's a soft knock on my door.

I hug my comforter a little tighter. For a split second, I consider throwing it over my head and pretending I'm asleep.

But this awful pang in my stomach won't allow it.

"Come in," I say.

The door opens with a quiet creak. There's a footstep and then the door is pressed shut again.

I keep my back to Drew and my eyes on the window. There isn't much to see besides the sky. It's nearly black. No stars. There's too much light pollution.

He sits on the bed behind me. His fingertips brush over the side of my cheek. "Hey."

"Where did you go?"

"To think."

"You need to hop in your car to think?" I ask.

He shifts closer. "When it's about you." He lies on the bed behind me. "And even that only helps so much."

I hug the blanket to my chest.

"I didn't ditch you in high school because you weren't cool." He moves closer. "I got caught up in the attention. Stopped trying to hang out. When I saw you around, you never seemed like you wanted to talk to me. I should have thought about how much you were going through, but I was a stupid kid, and I was distracted by my parents getting divorced."

"That was around when my dad got sick, wasn't it?"

"Hard to remember exactly. They fought constantly. It

was a long time coming. But after... shit happened with Willow." He tenses, like he can't stand the memory of what happened with his sister. "I won't betray her trust but it snapped me out of my bullshit. By then, you had new friends. You seemed better off without me."

"How could I be better off without you? Drew I... don't you realize how much you mean to me?"

He runs his fingertips over my shoulder. "I didn't. Not then. I didn't appreciate how lucky I was. You were the only person I ever trusted besides my sister. You still are."

"What about Vivian?" I say her name like it's some disgusting food.

"That was different. Messed up." He's quiet for a moment. "It's not an interesting story."

"It's interesting to me." I shift so my back is pressed against his chest. The second our bodies come into contact, I feel warm and safe. It's the same sense of freedom I get from the dark.

I can stomach Drew seeing me, really seeing me.

And I want to see him too.

"You can admit she broke your heart," I say.

"I'm not good with relationships, Kara. I can't even fuck a girl without fucking her up." He drags his fingertips over my neck. "I don't want to do that to you too."

"You're a little late for that."

"I don't want to hurt you." His voice gets low. "But I can't stop touching you. I can't stop talking to you. I can't stop being around you."

This warmth builds in my body, but there's something off about it. This is no confession of love. It's not even some high school request to make things official, so we're really boyfriend/girlfriend.

It's nothing.

"What is that supposed to mean?" I ask.

He exhales so slowly. He drags his fingertips down my arms and hips. No answer, I guess. Or maybe this is the answer.

Drew wants me enough to throw out all those concerns of hurting me. I don't know whether to be flattered or offended.

"Is that really it?" I ask. "Or do you not want to get hurt?"

"I drove for two hours straight and the only thing I could think about was how badly I want you." He hooks his thumbs into my pajama bottoms. "All of you."

I open my mouth to ask for an explanation, but I can't force the words out. They'll only confuse me more. The truth is, I feel the same.

I can't think straight.

I can't think anything but *I want Drew.* All of him. Whatever that means.

He runs his thumbs over the waist of my pajamas. His lips press into my neck.

I want Drew.

All of him.

Whatever that means.

He tugs at my pajama pants and pulls them off my ass. All the way to my knees.

My head is swimming, but common sense has no chance next to the desire rushing through my body.

I kick off my pajamas and rub my body against Drew's. He's strong and warm.

He runs his fingertips over my outer thigh, starting at my knee and working his way up. His fingers graze one of my scars. His touch is soft and gentle. There's no sign he's repulsed.

He presses his body into mine. "When was the first time?"

"It was the day my parents told me about the diagnosis." I trace the light scar in my right wrist. "They were both so scared and so sad. They looked at me like they were worried I'd be scared and sad too, like it would kill them if I wasn't sweet and bubbly anymore."

I take Drew's hand and bring it to my wrist. He runs his fingertips over the line of one scar after another. Until he's felt all of them.

My body fills with the strangest warmth. It's something more than lust or friendship. Something pure and deep and impossible to ignore.

I try anyway.

I close my eyes. I arch my back to press my ass against his crotch. I turn my head to press my neck against his cheek.

But that feeling won't go away.

"And?" he asks.

"And I stayed their rock. I nodded and told them it would be okay, that I could cook dinner, and clean the house, and walk to school instead of getting a ride. I sat there with a smile on my face for the rest of dinner while they explained everything that might go wrong, that my dad might not have that much time left. They kept looking at me like they were waiting for me to break. Like it would kill them if I did."

He runs his fingers over the scars on my wrist.

"And I did. But I waited until I was in my room. I was scared and angry, but I couldn't manage to cry or scream." I push through my discomfort. "I locked myself in the bathroom and broke my compact mirror on the ground. When I was cleaning up the mess, I nicked my arm. It hurt like hell, but there was something so relieving about that. It took me out of that awful sense that my dad was going to die. I tried it again, on purpose. The pain made me feel like I was in control."

Drew slides his arm around my waist and holds me tight. "How does it feel?"

"You have plenty of tattoos. It's like that. It hurts but there's something exhilarating about it. It's like all the awful feelings inside me pour out with the blood." I play with the fabric of the sheets. "I know it sounds grotesque, but—"

"I get it." He runs his fingertips over my hips. "I've had plenty of nights like that."

"Tell me about them."

"Another time." He drags his fingertip over one of the scars on my thighs. His voice is strained. "When was the last time?"

"Before I moved to LA."

"If you ever want to do it again, you call me first."

"I won't." I hug my arms against my chest. "I'm damaged enough already."

He traces another scar. A deeper one. "Everyone is damaged."

"Not like this. Not this ugly."

Drew presses his lips into my neck. "There are no ugly parts of you." He slides his hand over my inner thighs. "Every part of you is beautiful."

His fingertips pass over dozens of scars. Even in the dark, they stand out. They're raised and rough and harsh.

He moves his hand to my other leg and traces a line from the inside of my knee all the way to the edge of my panties. He touches every scar with tender care, like he's committing them to memory. His fingers are rough, calloused, but his touch doesn't hurt. It's sweet. Gentle.

His breath catches. His hips shift, so his crotch is pressed against my ass.

He's hard.

I let out a sharp gasp.

Drew laughs. "You didn't believe me."

My cheeks burn. The heat spreads to my neck and chest. All the way to my stomach and thighs. And then it collects right between my legs.

He's not turned off.

He's not running away scared.

He's hard.

He pulls the strap of my tank top off my shoulders. I'm not wearing a bra. I never sleep in a bra.

Drew cups my breast. He brings his lips to my ear and sucks gently. "More than beautiful." He swirls his finger against my nipple. His breath strains. "Sexy as fuck."

"That's poetic."

"Thank you." He nips at my ear. "I go out of my fucking mind thinking about touching you."

He rubs my nipple harder. A pang of pleasure shoots through me. I let out a low groan.

"You've never been eaten out, have you?" he asks it without a hint of shyness.

I bite my lip to keep from blushing. "Never."

Drew presses his lips into my neck. "So that makes me your first."

He kisses his way to my chest and sucks on my nipples. Harder and harder until I'm ready to scream. I buck my hips.

He pushes my tank top to my waist.

He kisses the skin between my breasts.

Then just under it.

My eyes close. I move my hands to the sheets and brace myself. Touching my scars is one thing, but he's going to be face to face with them.

My body is screaming at me to ignore the apprehension growing in my chest. Somehow, Drew's lips are even better than his hands. It shouldn't be possible for one person to be blessed with such talents, but he is.

He pushes the tank top down to my hips, all the way to my knees. It meets my pajama pants and he pulls both off my feet.

"Drew, I..." I take a deep breath. That heavy feeling is still right there on top of my chest.

"I'm going to go out of my fucking mind if you ask me to stop."

"Don't stop." I like the way those words feel on my tongue, but my heart is still pounding against my chest. "The scars are... they're ugly."

He grabs my knees and pins them to the bed. "Take that back."

"They are."

His voice gets low, deep, desperate. "Everything about you is sexy." He lowers himself so he's right between my thighs. He presses his lips into the skin just above my knee. "Even your scars."

I swallow hard.

"I'm still waiting to hear you agree."

"Not happening."

Drew kisses me again, a little higher, a little closer. "You're lucky I've been dreaming about you coming on my face."

"Is that right?"

"Or else I would never let you get away with this bullshit." He plants a soft kiss on the inside of my thigh. "You're going to admit it."

"Fat chance."

He kisses his way up my thighs until his lips are two inches away from my sex. I lose any interest in making or hearing comebacks. I lose any concern over what he thinks of my scars.

There's only one thing on my mind.

I need Drew.

Now.

Drew wraps his hands around my inner thighs and pins me to the bed. He flicks his tongue against the space where my crotch and my leg meet.

So, so close to where he needs to be.

His fingers trail over my inner thighs. Over my scars, sure, but it doesn't bother me. All that apprehension is gone.

As long as Drew is touching me, I'm sexy. Every part of me.

His tongue slides over my sex.

I let out a slow exhale. It's so strange and wonderful all at once. His mouth is wet and warm. It's soft but the pressure is intense.

All that need whirs around me. I close my eyes and dig my hands into Drew's hair. Not to guide him or hold him. Just to make sure he knows how fucking good I feel.

He licks me from top to bottom and back again. He sucks on my lips. Soft at first, then harder. Harder. I let out a low groan and tug at his hair.

There.

He does it again. Again. He lavishes my other side with the same attention. He draws zig zags over me with his tongue.

I've come before. Some with the ex-boyfriend. Some by my hand. Okay. More than some.

But this is a whole other level of bliss.

Every one of my nerves is on fire. Every part of me feels alive.

Drew's tongue slides over my clit.

Oh, hell yes.

I tug at his hair. Every flick of his tongue sends another wave straight to my core. I buck my hips and he buries his face between my legs.

Licking.

Sucking.

Biting softly.

I'm lost in the feelings he's stirring inside me. It's so intense I can barely stand it.

He flicks his tongue against my clit. It's hard and fast. And then it's exactly where it needs to be.

I surrender to the warm, wet sensation of his mouth. It's better with every flick of his tongue. Better, better, better, until I'm there. I'm at the edge, about to come. The pressure inside me builds to a crescendo.

I groan. "Drew."

My sex clenches. Almost. Every flick of his tongue pushes it higher and higher.

I scream his name. "Drew, Drew, Drew."

And then I'm there. I come in waves. Pleasure spreads through my body, bouncing off every single one of my nerves.

I use his words. "You're amazing."

He groans an "I know" into the skin just above my hipbone and kisses his way up my body, stopping at my chest to flick his tongue against my nipples.

Oh, hell yes.

That want spreads through me again. I need to feel him. I need him tugging at my hair and screaming my name as he comes.

Drew plants his lips against my collarbones. My neck. My chin.

And then he kisses me. He tastes like me. It's strange,

but it only makes me want him more. It only makes me more desperate to feel him inside me again.

He pushes himself up and locks eyes with me. "Are you on birth control?"

I nod. "Still on the pill."

"I'm clean."

"Me too."

He drags his fingertips over my stomach. "If you want to be careful, I can get something."

"No." I pull off his t-shirt. "I want to feel every inch of you."

"Fuck yes." He plants his hand right above my shoulder. His eyes find mine. "Say my name like that again."

My cheeks flush. I shake my head. "You'll have to make me."

His eyes flash with desire. He kisses me hard and drags his fingertips over my breasts. "You're asking for it now, Kendrick."

I explore the muscles of his chest with my fingertips. "And what am I asking for?"

"Coming until you scream."

"I better ask for it again."

"Until you can't take it anymore." He sucks on my lower lip. "You taste so fucking good."

He bites my neck.

I groan.

"And you sound so fucking good."

I reach for his jeans. There's the button. And now it's unbuttoned. Zipper, unzipped. "*You* sound so fucking good."

He slides out of his jeans. Then the boxers. It's dark but there's just enough moonlight to cast a gorgeous shadow over the hard lines of Drew's body.

He grabs onto my thighs. My chest tightens for a split second. And then it relaxes.

Drew pries my legs apart. He moves closer. The tip of his cock brushes against my sex. A desperation builds between my legs. I need him inside me. It's the only thing I know. The only thing in the entire world that makes a lick of sense.

He thrusts, entering me. I can't help but gasp. He feels so damn good. I drag my hands over his chest, taking in every contour of his muscles.

He shifts, going deeper. Then he shifts back, until his cock is at my tip again. He rocks into me, filling me again.

Again.

Again.

I shudder. This is exactly where I need to be.

I look into Drew's eyes. His expression is heavy with desire. It tightens the knot building inside me.

He adjusts my leg, pinning it to my chest the way he did when we were stretching. "I want those behind your head."

I nod.

"I want you pinned to the bed so you're totally at my mercy."

He slings my other leg over his shoulder. My back curls. My ass shifts into the air.

And there I am, pinned and totally at his mercy.

He plants his hands outside my legs and thrusts into me. It's hard and deep. It hurts for a minute and then that drifts away.

Drew holds my gaze as he fucks me. His breath gets heavy. He moves faster. Harder. I let out a groan when it's just right.

"Drew," I breathe.

He keeps the same rhythm. Every thrust brings me closer. I scrape my nails against his chest.

"Drew," I groan his name again.

God help me, I love the sound of it on my tongue. I love the flash of need in his eyes when I say it. The way he goes harder. Deeper.

I can't bear to keep my eyes open. It feels too good.

"Drew," I groan.

He sinks into me, pushing my legs all the way behind my head, pushing my ass further into the air.

He thrusts into me again. Even harder.

Even deeper.

All I can feel is that perfect tension. It aches in the best possible way. I lose control of my breath. I claw at his shoulders and back.

"Drew, Drew, Drew."

The pressure hits its peak. More and more. So much it hurts.

An orgasm overtakes me. I come in spasms. Pleasure spreads out from my core.

He sinks into me. Harder. Deeper.

His breath strains.

He's almost there.

Drew is almost there and there's nothing in between us.

I pull my eyes open to watch the ecstasy build on his face. His teeth sink into his lip. His eyelids press together. He squeezes the sheets between his fingers.

He groans.

There.

I can feel him come inside me. It's amazing. His cock pulses. My sex clenches instinctively.

Drew lets out a dreamy sigh. He kisses me, sucking hard on my lip. I dig my hands into his hair, holding his mouth against mine.

He's mine.

Whatever we are, he's mine.

And I'm his.

And I'm not about to ask any questions that will ruin how good this feels.

He shifts, unpinning my legs and collapsing next to me in one fluid motion. His fingertips trail over the space between my breasts. "You want to come again?"

I shake my head. "I'm spent."

"Too bad." He wraps his arms around me and pulls me closer. "I'll have to get you tomorrow."

I pinch myself.

Still awake.

Chapter Twenty-One

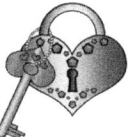

Drew is on the couch in his boxers, hands wrapped around a PlayStation controller, messy hair falling in every direction.

"You want eggs for breakfast?" he asks without looking up from the TV.

"Cereal is fine." I descend the stairs and take a better look at his game. It's colorful and bright. Not one of those gritty shooters where you take out wave after wave of zombies.

I stare at him for a minute, trying to figure out what I want to say about last night, what I even think about last night.

The words never stream together, but it sure is nice looking at Drew. The muscles in his shoulders tense and soften. His biceps too. The forearms. He's pressing his fingers into that controller with so much attention and care.

Dammit, I need to get ahold of myself. I pour a bowl of cereal, fix a cup of tea, and take a seat at the table.

Drew pauses his game. He pats the spot on the couch

next to him. "What do you think you're doing so far away, Kendrick?"

I scoop cereal into my mouth. "Eating breakfast." No way any words are going to stream together if my body is pressed against Drew's. I'll be lucky if I can manage anything more complicated than *don't stop.*

"You eating dry cereal again?"

"I like it this way."

"Eat it over here." He turns back and makes eye contact. "I won't bite." His eyes light up. "Unless you're into that."

Yes. Please. All. Freaking. Day.

I chew my cereal and swallow hard. I need control of my senses.

I like him too much.

Drew rises from the couch. The light streaming from the window falls over him just so.

It's wrong how sculpted his body is. The way his tattoos curve over his muscles like they're highlighting every delicious line. Right now, he's not my best friend. He's pure rock star perfection. A wet dream come to life.

And he wants me next to him.

"I fixed your phone screen. Took a few pictures to test it." Drew motions to my cell phone on the kitchen table.

I play it cool. "I should check for myself."

"Do."

Sure enough, the screen is replaced. It's easy to forget that Drew is a computer geek at heart. I look up at him. "Do you keep replacement screens in your room?"

"About a dozen. A lot of broken iPhones on tour. It comes in handy."

"So they're going with you in April?"

"This really what you want to talk about?"

I shake my head as I navigate to my photos. Sure

enough, there are half a dozen pictures of Drew. None are naked, tragically, but they come close. From his lips all the way to the driving-me-out-of-my-damn-mind trail. Okay. That really doesn't have a good ring to it.

He's fucking yummy. And he's right here. In front of me. Dammit, I'm only human. I can only tell that flutter between my legs to shut up so many times before it takes over.

I join him on the couch. He pulls me onto his lap, spreading my legs so they're hanging outside his. Then he grabs his controller and turns his game back on.

The hell?

"I'm not sure what arrangement you had with your last roommate, but I'm not big on watching people play video games."

He slides the controller into my hands. "Try it."

"I'll be terrible."

"It's easy." He drags his fingertips over my shoulder, stopping at the straps of my tank top. "And I need my hands back."

It's warm in here. It didn't feel this warm two minutes ago, but all of a sudden it's way too hot to be wearing clothing.

"It's a fun game," he says. "And the villain looks just like Aidan, our manager. He has a suit and a ponytail and this pompous fake accent. Actually, the villain is lot more pleasant than Aidan."

"That's very special."

He pulls the strap of my tank top down my shoulder. "You're a Lombax with a robot best friend." His hand goes to the controller and he presses a few buttons. "Triangle to switch guns. O to shoot. X to jump. Kill the bad guys. You know they're bad because they're big and ugly."

His hand goes back to my waist. He plays with the

bottom of my tank top, pushing it up my stomach. His lips flutter against my neck.

"Drew," I breathe. "I'm not going to have any concentration available to play this game."

He slides his hand under my tank top. "Why is that?"

"Gee, I wonder why." Concentration is a distant memory. My body is kicking my brain out of the driver's seat, and it's going to be one hell of a ride.

Drew laughs. He presses his lips against my neck. It's a soft kiss and it sends a shock wave straight to my core.

"You'll appreciate it later." He slides my tank top up my stomach and over my chest and head.

It falls in a heap on the floor.

Drew drags his fingertips over my arms. He pulls my hands from the controller and tosses it onto the floor. It skids until it hits my tank top. Quite the combination—video games and Drew. But, then, anything and Drew is an excellent combination.

I close my eyes and exhale deeply. My body relaxes into his. He lifts my ass and pulls my pajama pants to my knees. They fall to my feet. Another heap on the floor.

His fingertips trace the edge of my panties.

"I like these new rules." His voice is thick with desire.

I rub my ass against him. "What rules?"

He drags his fingertip over my sex, pressing the fabric of my panties against me. "Touching you whenever I want." His thumb is pressed against my clit. "Wherever I want." He drags his other hand up my waist and over my chest. "However I want."

Uh-huh. I have the faintest sense that this is important, but it's awfully hard to think with his hands on my body.

I force myself to concentrate on his words. "Is that right?" I ask.

"Yes, it is." He tugs at my panties.

"And what if we're at the bank? Are you going to start fingering me in line?"

He pulls my panties to my knees. His teeth scrape against my neck. "Why would we be at the bank?"

"The store, the beach, whatever."

His fingertips slide over my inner thighs. There's not a hint of self-consciousness left in my body. I want these rules. I want Drew touching me anywhere, everywhere, any way he wants.

"If that's what I want." His thumb rubs against my clit. "Then, yeah. In line at the bank, at the beach, in a club, in my car. Anywhere."

Pleasure builds inside me. He's making a convincing argument. I've spent a long time not being touched and now Drew wants to touch me anywhere, everywhere, all the time.

It would be criminal not to agree.

I nod. "Okay."

"Just okay?" He nips at my ear. "You can do better than okay."

He slides his fingers over my clit, rubbing me a little harder, a little faster.

And then he hits just the right spot.

I gasp. "Yes. There."

"Here?" He does it again.

Yes, there. Absolutely there. Pleasure shoots through me. It's so much, so fast I can barely take it. My breath hitches. I pant.

"Yes." I arch my back. I pant. "I agree. Whatever you said, I agree. Just don't fucking stop."

"Never."

He grabs my thighs and spreads them a little further. With one arm, he holds onto my chest, keeping me pressed against him, toying with my nipples. Every flick of his fingers sends a shockwave of pleasure straight to my core. Yes, yes, yes.

His other hand goes between my legs. He teases my sex with a light brush of his fingertips. Just enough to leave me panting and desperate for more.

His touch gets harder. He draws a line from my core to my clit. He does it again. Again. Harder. Faster.

And then he's there, right back at that perfect spot.

"Drew," I gasp.

He palms my breast. His breath gets heavy and he sucks on my earlobe. "Say it again."

His hands are magic. So much better than mine. So much better than anything I ever felt with my ex-boyfriend.

He has just the right pressure, just the right speed.

The bliss inside me builds. "Drew," I groan. More. I need to tell him more, so he knows how fucking perfect this is. "You feel so good."

He sucks on my earlobe.

"Come for me, Kara," he breathes.

His teeth sink into my neck.

And there it is.

I go higher and higher, until I'm absolutely at the peak. And it feels so good, so tight I can't take it anymore.

"Drew," I groan.

One more touch of his hand and I'm there. An orgasm spills through me, sending pleasure to every inch of my body.

I dig my hands into the couch to contain the sensation.

Drew presses his lips into my neck. He slides his hands around my waist and pulls me to the couch next to him.

His eyes pass over me. "I told you I'd get you tomorrow."

My cheeks flush. "But who knew you'd start so early?"

He reaches for the controller and slides it back into my hands. "Now that you can concentrate, I'll explain again."

He's wrong about the concentration, but I try my best to listen anyway.

———

We spend an hour playing the game. It's called *Ratchet and Clank*, apparently, and it's certainly the most fun I've ever had with a video game.

An alarm on Drew's phone rings. He groans and pushes off the couch. "I better get dressed for practice. Miles is picking me up in ten." His eyes pass over me. "You should come."

"I have homework."

"Do it later."

"Tempting, but..."

"You disappoint me, Kendrick. If you weren't naked I'd be very angry with you."

"But I am."

"Yeah, you are." His eyes go wide with desire. He shakes his head like he's sorry he has to leave, grabs his phone, and takes a step toward the stairs. "We'll be in Hollywood all day. Come when you're done with your homework."

"I don't know."

"If you don't come, how will I get to make you come again?"

The man really does make a convincing argument.

"I'll see what I can do," I say.

He shakes his head with mock disappointment. "It's more fun when you're there."

This wonderful lightness passes through my body.

Music is the only thing Drew cares about and it's more fun when I'm there.

Sure, it's band practice. Even someone as disciplined as Drew must get tired of practice.

But it's more fun when I'm there.

I watch him climb the stairs. "It will be at least three hours," I say.

"I'll save the good stuff for last." He winks.

It's not possible to fly, but I'm pretty sure I could come close if I tried.

―――

HOMEWORK IS A SLOG. IT TAKES UNTIL WELL INTO THE afternoon, but I finish. I shower, change into skinny jeans and a t-shirt, and hustle to my car.

I went with Drew to practice last week, but where the hell was it? I turn my phone on to an avalanche of text messages.

The first text is the address of the studio. Then:

Drew: You ever gonna show up, Kendrick?

Drew: My hands are getting lonely without you.

Drew: And Tom is even more unbearable without you around.

Drew: Don't make me tempt you with pictures. I can't afford a nude photo scandal.

Drew: And now Tom is shooting me a dirty look.

Drew: You have any idea what you do to me? I can barely concentrate on playing. My hands don't want to do anything but touch you.

Does he have any idea what he does to *me*?

I tap a reply.

Kara: On my way.

I put the address into my maps application and follow it mindlessly. Ten minutes pass, and my phone buzzes with another flurry of text messages. I keep my eyes and attention on the road, my hands on the wheel or the gear shift.

The texts sure are damn tempting.

There's a smattering of traffic on the 10. The 110 and 101 are a crawl. It's far enough into the afternoon that I'm brushing up against rush hour. But, then again, rush hour is a constant state in Los Angeles.

I pull off the freeway. My phone buzzes. Another flurry. Almost there. I park outside the studio. It's a rundown little street in Hollywood. The concrete is dirty. The buildings are dark and covered with posters for concerts.

It's very rock and roll.

I'm more out of place than I'd like to be. I'm usually good at blending in, but I just don't wear my jeans and t-shirt in a very rock and roll way.

My phone rings again. Drew's never this impatient. Is it really possible he wants me around this badly?

I answer. "Hey."

"Kara, sweetie."

Crap. That's not Drew. It's my mom.

"Hey Mom," I say. "How are you doing?"

Her voice sinks. "Did you get my message?"

"Yeah, absolutely. It sounds like we have a really busy break." I bite my tongue. I have to find a way to tell her without crushing her.

"I'm taking Friday off. We can go to Napa for the weekend."

"That would be nice." I take a deep breath, willing it to fill me with confidence. It doesn't.

"I was thinking you could take your old room. Rents in the bay are getting so expensive." Her voice brightens. "It would be great having you at home."

Yeah, and it will be awful having me away.

It will be awful if I tell her no.

"Maybe," I say. "I haven't thought about it."

"There's always a place for you here, sweetie."

If I do it fast... like a Band-Aid. I take a deep breath. "I..." And I stall. "What if I didn't start immediately? I'm, um, I'm really liking Los Angeles and I think it would be nice to spend the summer here."

"Oh." The happiness drains from her voice.

It's like I just punched her in the gut.

Like I told her I go around beating puppies.

"If that's what you want," she says. "But Sugar and Spice would love to have you right away. You're going to be so great for the team."

Of course. It's not just Mom who needs me. It's the whole damn team.

I hold the phone to my chest and take three deep breaths. Each is less calming than the one before it.

I bring the phone back to my ear. "Maybe it would be better if I didn't work at your company. I don't want anyone to resent me for being the boss's daughter."

"Kara, sweetie. Everyone loves you. Everyone wants you there."

I fight my desire to backpedal, to apologize and promise I'll do whatever it takes for her to feel better.

"You'll be great," she says. "We can talk more over break. I have a meeting in a few minutes." Her voice stays dead. "I love you, sweetie. I'm so proud of you for finishing your degree."

"Thanks." I back into the concrete wall of the studio. "I'll talk to you later."

I hang up the phone without waiting for her reply.

She sounds miserable.

How can I add to that?

I shove my phone back into my purse. Two weeks until spring break. I'll figure something out. Somehow.

The entrance to the practice space is around back. I make my way through the alley. The music gets louder. It's unmistakable. That's Sinful Serenade and that's Drew playing.

The door is open a few inches. No sounds except the music. But, then, this song is the last in their second set and it's almost over. Not that I have their setlist memorized.

I wait until the song's outro and I step inside.

Eyes turn my way. Pete looks worried. Miles frowns. Tom shakes his head as if to say *great, someone is throwing gasoline on the fire.*

And there's no describing the look on Drew's face. Happy and smug and impatient all at once.

Meg is sitting in the corner with a giant textbook in her lap. She waves at me. It seems she's the only person here who isn't expecting something explosive.

Drew and his ex must have been more of a train wreck than he's let on.

Or maybe the expression on my face is more tortured than I think it is.

"Hey, Kara," Miles says. "How was the drive?"

"Fine, thanks."

Tom glances at his watch. "You want to take five, loverboys?"

Death glare from Drew. Of course. I guess the idea of us together, really together, is still awful to him.

So that answers the whole *does he actually like me or just like fucking me* question.

Drew pulls his guitar over his head. "Give it a rest, all right?"

Tom shrugs as if to say *who me?* "Not everything is about you. I was speaking to Miles and Pete."

Pete rolls his eyes. "Make it ten. I'm going to get a drink." He motions to me and Meg. "You two want anything?"

"Iced tea." Meg looks at me as if to ask, you too?

I nod.

"Green for me and black for Kara."

"You buying my girl drinks?" Miles asks.

"I am," Pete says.

"Better watch out," I say. "Meg is only loyal to whoever provides her with the most caffeine."

Miles makes his way to Meg. He takes her hands and pulls her to her feet. And then his arms are around her and his lips are on hers.

And they are making out.

Tom shakes his head. "What happened to the 'no girls' rule? It was such a great rule." He hurls his drumsticks in the general direction of the floor and makes his way to the door.

And then it's just Drew, standing next to his guitar and looking at me with all these expectations.

What the hell am I supposed to do with that?

"Let's leave them to it." He nods to Meg and Miles.

"Let's," I say.

He takes my hand and leads me back outside. It's not much here—a black concrete alley surrounded by warehouse buildings. There's music coming from down the street. It's vaguely familiar, certainly something I've heard on KROQ, but I can't place it.

No sign of Tom or Pete. No doubt they're both sulking in their own unique way.

"Hey." He rubs my shoulder, sweet. "You want to tell me why you look so miserable?"

"Not really, no." I hug my purse. "I'm here to listen to the music."

"I can rephrase it so it's not a question."

"I don't want to talk about it." The sun is beating down on the black concrete. I move toward the little alley on the side of the building. There should be shade there.

Drew follows me. He's close. A foot behind me maybe. I can hear his breath. I can feel the warmth of his body. My heartbeat always speeds up when he's around. My lungs always struggle to keep up.

I lean against the concrete wall. "I'm exhausted. Can we leave it at that?"

"I don't like seeing you upset."

"It's just stuff with my mom. I'll figure it out. I promise."

He runs his fingertips over the back of my neck. "I can help you figure it out."

"You can't." I look into his eyes. "It's something I have to do."

"Kara."

"Come on," I say. "It's not like I beg you to talk about whatever it is that made all your bandmates so cagey around the subject of you and relationships."

"That's just Tom being an idiot."

I shoot him a *yeah, right* look. "Why do you stop flirting with me the second someone else is around?"

"It's private."

"Am I not good enough for your friends?" I press my fingertips into the concrete wall.

"How could you not be good enough?"

"I don't know. You tell me. What quality do I need to have to be worthy of girlfriend status?"

"Kara."

"Which is it? Because I'd like to know now if this is just sex. Do you want to be with me or not?"

His gaze goes to the ground. "I told you before. I'm not good with relationships."

"Yeah, but, it's me. We've been friends since forever."

He makes eye contact. "I don't know. I can't think straight when it comes to you."

"But why?" My heartbeat speeds. "If you don't want a girlfriend then what is there to think about?"

"I didn't say that." Drew's eyes find mine. "I fuck women up. That doesn't mean I don't want to be with you."

"But do you?" I ask.

He presses his hips against mine, pinning me to the wall. "What do you think?"

I bite my lip. He knows I was asking about more than sex. He's not going to answer me.

Drew's hands slide over my cheek. "Why don't you talk to me about your mom?"

"Why don't you talk to me about why you're not 'good with relationships' or why it is you can't think straight when it comes to me? Or maybe why you're dodging questions about what this means by trying to fuck me?"

There are footsteps coming toward us. Tom or Pete, probably. Which means Drew is done having this conversation. God forbid someone think we're together.

Drew steps back. Big surprise. The affection-repelling footsteps belong to Tom, apparently. Never mind that Tom knows exactly what's going on. Anyone could put the pieces together at this point.

He nods to me. "I think Pete has your drink inside."

"Thank you. It's hot out here. I'm going to go find that."

"Kara." Drew says it with this pained voice like it's just killing him I'm not willing to entertain this bullshit.

Like it's just killing him that I want more than *I'm not good at relationships.*

I round the corner.

Tom says something that sounds a lot like, "What the fuck do you think you're doing?"

I brush it off.

Inside, Meg is sucking down her iced green tea instead of sucking on Miles's face. She takes one look at me and shakes her head.

"Let's get out of here, huh?" she offers.

"Good thinking." I grab my drink and take a very long sip.

She waves to Miles. "I'll see you later."

"Babe—"

"I can't study here anyway." She makes goo-goo eyes at him. "You'll get me all day tomorrow. I promise."

"I warned you about the caffeine allegiance," I say.

He nods. "Babe. I give you something much better than caffeine."

"Yeah. We've all heard it." Pete waves goodbye to us and turns back to Miles. "You want to put out the fire or you want to give 'em ten minutes to cool off?"

"Make it twenty," Miles says. "Drew has been extra pissy since that *Guitar Hero* business."

"Can't blame him. *Guitar Hero* is played."

Miles shrugs. "He'd be in a better mood if he—" Miles turns to me with an apologetic shrug. "Nevermind."

Meg pushes the door open and motions for me to follow. "Come on. You can't wait for them to stop acting stupid. It will never happen."

Chapter Twenty-Two

It's only five blocks to the Hollywood and Highland center, the mall slash tourist trap center of the neighborhood. It's right along the Walk of Fame and adjacent to just about every club on the boulevard.

Meg eyes me cautiously. "I'm guessing you don't want to talk about it, but I'm going to channel you. And I think that means I need to make you talk about it.'

"That sounds like what I would do." I slurp my drink until it's nothing but ice. "Of course, I'd bribe you with caffeine."

"Oh, my dear, your wish is my command." She nods to the coffee shop across the walkway. "Unless you want something alcoholic."

"Are you drinking now?"

"Every so often." She sits on a concrete bench and pats the spot next to her. "It still makes me think about Rosie. And, it's not like I'm going to drink when Miles is around." She looks me in the eyes. "I still remember meeting Drew. He seemed so normal. Last guy in the world I ever thought would leave you in knots."

"That's a good way to describe it."

"What happened?"

"He's 'not good at relationships.'"

Her eyes narrow. "I can find some way to have him killed, you know. More than happy to."

"Don't. I... I care about him. A lot. So much it hurts."

"I know the feeling."

I press my heel into the concrete. "This how you felt with Miles last semester?"

"You can't sleep or think and you feel like your body, heart, and head are waging this terrible three-front war?"

I nod.

"Yep." She slurps the last drop of her tea. "It wasn't pretty, but it was worth it. He's just so..." She sighs. "Sorry, I don't want to brag at a time like this."

"It's sweet."

"I know Drew cares about you," she says. "Loves you even. You should have seen the way he was acting today. He was desperate to see you. And any time Tom even said your name, he got all angry and protective."

"Yeah, it's not hard to make him angry and protective. But what do I do with that?"

"You don't like it?" she asks.

"It has a certain appeal. And the sex is amazing." I press my back against the railing behind us. "But then I have this guy who has been my friend for ten years telling me he's not good at relationships."

"Maybe he's not."

"Obviously not," I say.

"You could teach him. Help him." She tosses her drink in a trash can. "I really do think he loves you. So if you love him..."

"Maybe," I say. "I kind of miss breathing and sleeping and being able to concentrate."

"It's so unfair that you have to choose." She pushes herself off the bench. "Come on. I'm buying you another tea."

"Okay."

"Now, let me ask you something—do you want to talk about it or do you want to force Drew to listen to you?"

"I want to think about something else."

"Well then, the Arclight is a quick walk down the street. I'm sure they're playing something with subtitles."

———

WE ARRIVE AT THE ARCLIGHT JUST IN TIME FOR A FRENCH film. Something about a woman on the verge of a sexual awakening. The plot is simple. A married woman has an affair with a much younger man. Somehow, despite all the scenes of said much younger man naked and rolling around in bed with the married woman, the movie is long and slow. Mostly them screwing or talking about the meaning of life and youth and philosophy. Everything that gives foreign films a bad name. Besides the sexy naked people.

It's not all bad. We have chocolate and iced tea. The theater is mostly empty. No one comments when we laugh at dramatic parts or slurp the last drops from our drinks.

After the movie, we head back to my car.

"You know," Meg says. "I don't work Fridays anymore."

"Yeah?"

She looks at her phone. "And I just got word from my bae—"

"You did not just say bae."

She winks. "Let's just say I know where you can find all four of the members of Sinful Serenade."

"That so?"

She taps her screen a few times. "Of course, everyone who follows Tom on Twitter knows where you can find them. But let's not let that ruin our fun." Her eyes narrow. Determined. "That is, if you want to deal with your hot, sweaty guitar boy."

I nod. "I'm game."

She smiles and takes my hand. "Then follow me, sweet pea. Let's get that boy so desperate to get under you that he doesn't have a lick of blood left in his brain."

"That doesn't sound medically possible."

"Hey, you gonna trust your own medical ideas or you gonna trust the future doctor?"

She laughs with glee that would make any super villain jealous.

I STEP OUT OF A FITTING ROOM IN A TANK TOP AND A TIGHT skirt. The top is cut down halfway to my bellybutton. It's black and lacy, little more than a bra, really. The skirt is pleated and plaid. I look like I belong in a music video or on a stripper pole. Or maybe in a music video on a stripper pole.

It looks good. Sexy. Not that I've ever had a problem looking sexy. No bragging. It's just not all that difficult to appeal to the base male mind. Tight pants, lots of cleavage, red lips in a pout—done.

"Holy shit, I always forget how giant your cans are." Meg laughs. She looks in the mirror and adjusts her outfit, a crop top and skinny jeans. "I think that's going to do it."

"I have plenty of slutty outfits at home," I say. "I don't think my issue with Drew involves lack of boob-revealing clothing."

"Yeah, but you don't have it now. And right now, guitar

boy needs your loving." She unlocks her phone and holds it up to me.

There's a text from Miles:

Miles: The guitar prince has blue balls again. I like your friend, but she's making my life difficult.

"He can be an idiot," she says. "But, what can I do? I love the pervert."

"You're cute together. I'm glad you're happy. Still going to medical school next year?"

"Best school I can get into, even if it's all the way across the country."

"The guy can afford to visit every weekend."

"Yeah." Her eyes get dreamy. "But I'm thinking about staying close. To my family. And to Miles. I don't want to run away from everything."

"It will be good to have you around," I say.

"Aren't you working at your mom's company in San Francisco?" she asks.

"Maybe." Deep breath. This doesn't need to be a secret. "I got into a teaching program at UCLA. For English."

"You have to do that." Meg turns to me. She grabs my shoulders and stares right in my eyes. "Screw the boy bullshit. You'll make a perfect English teacher. And you hate finance."

"I do." I check my reflection again. Add a little eyeliner and dark lipstick and I look like the perfect groupie.

We'll be at a show. There will be musicians there. They will flirt.

And if Drew really is around, well, I'm sure he'll get jealous.

Meg's plan is simple but effective.

"You want to talk about it?" she asks.

"No," I say. "I want to make this happen."

She checks her reflection. "I think a skirt. Better to convince my pervert to drag me to the car to have his way with me."

"Does he need convincing?"

"No." She blushes. "But it will be easier in a skirt." She takes a look at me. "There's no way Drew is going to think anything but *need girl now*."

I laugh. "That's a very flattering impression."

She steps into the dressing room then emerges in a short denim skirt. "I've been working on it."

THE CLUB IS THROBBING WITH THE HEAVY BEAT OF A ROCK song. There's a band on stage—four guys with dark hair and dark clothes. They're no Sinful Serenade, but they're not half-bad.

Meg hooks her arm with mine. It's alarming how much we've swapped roles. I am supposed to be the one giving makeovers and pep talks. I am supposed to be the one who drags her out to have fun, who meddles in her love life to fix it.

I suppose there's not much meddling left to do now that she's found the one. A silly concept I know, but I can't get it out of my head.

We push through the crowd, until we're in the most well-lit part of the mosh pit slash dance floor. There's a VIP area upstairs. No sign of any of the Sinful boys. Likely they're up there, shrouded in the dark.

The song picks up. I sway my hips and throw my arms over my head. I'm desperate to burn off some energy, to distract myself from that nagging feeling in my gut telling me how fucked things are with Drew.

So much for falling in love with my best friend and

living happily ever after. The guy is a rock star. It's way too good to be true.

The singer has a throaty, breathy voice. If my body wanted anything besides Drew, I'd find it sexy. But my poor, stupid body is desperate for Drew. Nothing else will do.

Maybe it will subside in time.

Meg dances with enthusiasm. She jumps up and down. She whispers in my ear and motions to the corner of the room. "I think I see the Guitar Prince himself."

"Did I miss this nickname?"

"It's a band thing. I think it's behind Drew's back." She waves to the guy standing next to me. "Hey, have you met my friend, Kara? She loves dancing."

I shake my head. Girl couldn't be more obvious, but she's trying.

I turn back to the guy. I barely register him. It's like my body is flashing with a sign that says *not Drew*. That's all that matters. He's not Drew so who the hell cares?

Still, I throw my arms over my head and I dance. The guy is polite enough to keep his distance. More or less.

Meg cuts through us with a quiet, "Excuse me."

And then she's out of sight and out of earshot, no doubt encouraging Drew's rabid jealousy.

The guy leans a little closer. "Kara, huh?"

"Yeah, that's right. Like the girl in *Battlestar Galactica*."

"Oh, yeah. The butch blonde girl." The guy's hands go to my hips. "She was kind of manly. You're a lot cuter."

Wow, he managed to compliment me and insult an actress all at the same time. This guy is multi-talented.

"You here alone?" he asks.

"That's a tough question." I shake my hips in an attempt to shake off his hands. My body isn't liking his hands. It's flashing *Not Drew's Hands*.

"You going home with anyone?" he asks.

Well, he doesn't waste any time.

He does not step back or release his hands. He moves closer, presses his palm against my lower back. It wouldn't be so bad if I was wearing something resembling an actual shirt, but that's my bare skin he's touching.

It's normal dancing.

No big deal.

But my body is flashing with that same sign.

Not Drew. Not Drew. Not Drew.

The guy looks me up and down. "What was her nickname? Uh, Starbuck, right?"

"Right."

The guy moves closer. So his body is pressed against mine.

Not Drew. Not Drew. Not Drew.

The song launches into a guitar solo. It's decent, but certainly not Drew.

The guy's hands tread way too low. Nuh-uh, no way. Not normal dancing anymore.

I press against his chest, a firm *get the hell off me.*

The hands release my ass.

"Hey, what's the issue, honey?" he asks. "You look like you're ready to party."

He pouts. Poor horny guy is going home alone. I feel awful, really. It's tragic.

"Well, appearances are deceiving." I adjust my skirt and top. Forget this. I'm better off going home and drowning my thoughts with sugar and caffeine.

"Excuse me," I say. "I'm leaving."

"I can give you a ride."

"No thank you. I'm swearing off men. They're nothing but trouble."

I scan the room. Where the hell did Meg go, again?

Doesn't matter. My car is close enough. I can get there on my own.

The guy is still there, still pressed against me. "You looking for someone better?"

"She has someone better."

Drew.

He grabs onto the guy's arms and throws me a look. *Really, this again?* Yeah, sorry Drew, even with your oodles of fame you don't risk some stranger copping a feel every time you go dancing

Not like I'm about to let grabby strangers scare me away from something I love.

"Hey, watch it," the guy says.

"You have two seconds to get lost before I make you wish you did," Drew says.

The guy looks at me. "Your boyfriend has some anger issues."

"He's not my boyfriend." I frown. "He made that very clear."

Drew stares at me. "What the fuck do you think you're doing?"

"I don't know. This is how messed up you've got me." I turn to make my way to the bathroom. Some place where my body might calm down.

Drew growls at the guy. "Touch her again and I'll fucking kill you." He grabs the guy and shoves him halfway across the room.

The guy knocks over three people in his way. He falls on his ass with a scowl. "Girl doesn't care about your opinion."

"You grabbed her ass, dickwad. You think she wanted that?"

"None of your business."

"I make it my business." Drew stares the guy down.

"Now, I like this club, so either back off or meet me outside and we'll settle this like men."

The guy shakes his head and shrugs *whatever*. I guess that releases me from my obligation not to cause a fight. I return to my mission to get the hell out of here.

I need to breathe again.

Chapter Twenty-Three

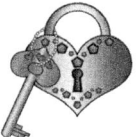

I shove my way out a side door. It's dark outside. Late enough into the night that I won't cause a scene.

The music streams through the walls. Still loud as hell, even as the door swings shut.

I press my back against the concrete wall. Deep breath. I'll survive this, somehow.

But there's no time to rest. The door pushes open. Drew.

His eyes are on fire. He wraps his hands around my wrists and pins me to the wall. "What the fuck are you doing, Kara?"

"We covered this."

"You trying to make me jealous?"

"It doesn't take a lot. You ever think you'd be better off talking to me than starting some dumb caveman fight?"

"You want that guy to touch you?"

"No."

"Then it's lucky for him we're already out here." Drew presses his hips against mine. "You're going to get hurt."

"I am hurt."

He stares at me like he's challenging me to explain. Fat chance of that. I do my best to hold his stare, but it's too demanding. My gaze drifts to the ground. This is not the way to prove I won't put up with bullshit.

All it's proving is how mixed up he's got me.

He digs his hands into my hair and tilts me so we're eye to eye. "You want my attention, just ask."

"Because that usually works so well." My throats gets ragged. I don't have a clue what I'm doing anymore, but I'm desperate to retain any hint of his attention at all.

"Talk to me."

"I don't want to talk about me. I want to talk about you and why it is you're afraid of the word 'relationship' but not afraid of threatening a guy's life for touching me."

"He was hurting you."

"He wasn't."

"You let strangers grope you to make a point?" He squeezes me. "You trying to prove something to me?"

"No. I was trying to dance." I turn my neck, so I'm looking at the street some thirty feet away. It's dark. There are footsteps but no one is looking over here.

He pulls me back to him. Our eyes connect. It's so intense it takes my breath away.

Drew leans in and kisses me. He shifts, pinning me to the wall a little more, rubbing against me so I can feel his erection.

My body responds with a rush of electricity.

Need Drew, need Drew, need Drew.

His tongue slides into my mouth. His hands slide between my legs. Not gentle this time. It's aggressive and rough.

"Is this the reaction you were hoping for?" he asks. "Make me jealous enough I drag you away and fuck you?"

Yes. God yes. Stop talking and do it now.

I hold strong. "That's your go-to move when I ask you about what we're doing here. *Hey, Kara, I don't know, but how about we fuck?*"

"I *don't* know. I swore off relationships after Vivian. I didn't think we... I didn't think." His hands go to my hips. They skim the waistband of my panties. "And now I can't think. I want you too fucking badly to think."

His breath gets heavy. His teeth sink into my neck.

Drew.

My body fills with pleasure. It's unconcerned with little matters like Drew's inability to articulate any feelings of a romantic nature.

It only knows how much it hates the layers of clothes between us.

I try to suppress a moan but it escapes my lips. I want him. There's no denying it.

Hell, it goes beyond want.

I need him.

I crave him.

I'm desperate for him.

"Tell me not to stop." He kisses me, hard.

It's still aggressive. Desperate. But there's something protective about it too.

His lips pull away from mine and he looks me straight in the eyes. It's like he'll go out of his mind if I don't answer him immediately.

"Kara." He presses his body against mine. "I'm not going to be like that asshole in the club. Tell me what you want. Now."

I scramble to regain my breath. There are a million things running through my head. But that big flashing sign is knocking all of them aside.

Drew, Drew, Drew.

I shift my hips so I can feel his cock straining against his jeans. "I want you inside me."

He groans. "Fuck yes."

His pupils dilate. He pushes my panties to my knees and drags his hands back to my hips. I kick the underwear off my feet so there's nothing under my skirt.

Drew's hands sink into the flesh of my ass. He kisses me as he pulls my top down. My breasts spill out. His hands cover me immediately, palming me, teasing me, playing with me.

"You're trying to drive me crazy, aren't you?" He groans.

"You've been driving me crazy for ages."

He scrapes his teeth against my lower lip. It's like he's desperate to taste and touch and feel all of me.

His hand goes to his jeans. Unzipped. He slides them to his feet then grabs my hips and turns me around, so I'm facing the wall.

No wasting time. He pulls me closer. His cock is an inch away from my sex. Almost there. He's almost mine.

I press my hands against the wall. I arch my back to rub against him. Yes. His cock brushes my outer lips. My clit. Every touch is a ripple of pleasure.

His lips hover over my ear. "I'm addicted to you."

My legs go weak. If he wasn't pinning me to the wall, I'd sink straight to the dirty ground.

I shift my hips to rub against him again. It feels damn good but it's not enough. I'm addicted to him too, and I need him inside me, completing me.

I need to be his.

We're thirty feet from the sidewalk.

Two feet from the door.

But I don't fucking care.

Drew enters me. I let out a heavy sigh. All the tense

muscles in my body relax at once. He's inside me. Right now, nothing else matters—not the fights or the lack of communication or the jealousy.

This feels too good to be bad.

Drew groans. He pinches my nipple. It's not hard enough to hurt. Just enough I know he feels as good as I do, wants me as much as I want him.

He rocks into me. It's hard and fast and desperate.

I throw my head back so my neck is pressed against his cheek. He sucks on my skin. He plays with my nipple. He slides his hand down my stomach, below my bellybutton, over my clit.

It's a shockwave. He already feels so good inside me, and now he's touching me.

I moan.

He keeps his rhythm. His chest is pressed against my back. His hands are on my skin, stroking me and filling me with the most delicious ecstasy.

I turn my head and lean into the wall, arching my back to give him better leverage. I'm outside a club in Hollywood pressed against a dirty wall, getting fucked by my rock star best friend.

And my life used to be so ordinary.

His breath gets heavier. "Touch yourself. I want to hear you come."

He thrusts into me. So hard and deep it hurts. But it's a good hurt. It's such a good hurt.

I pull my hand from the wall and slide it between my legs. My balance is gone. I'm at Drew's mercy.

No time for teasing today. I'm all out of patience. I stroke myself with slow circles. A little harder, a little faster, until it's just right.

My sex clenches.

He groans. "Kara."

I arch my back to drive him deeper. He feels so good inside me. He feels perfect.

My hand is quick. I'm already close.

I lose control of my breath. All my focus goes to the feeling between my legs. The pressure intensifies with every brush of my hand, with every thrust of Drew's cock.

It builds. Tighter. Deeper. Harder.

And then I'm there. Right at the edge.

An orgasm rocks through me. I scream so loudly it cuts through the music coming from the club. Yes. Hell yes. All the yeses a million times in a row.

Drew groans. "Fuck, you feel so good." His nails dig into my skin again.

He thrusts harder.

He's almost there.

He's almost mine.

Drew kisses me. All this need pours from him to me. Maybe he can't explain his feelings, but they're there. Right in his kiss.

He pulls out, readjusting me so we're face to face again. He lifts my leg, hooking it around his waist.

His eyes find mine. "I want to watch you come again." He kisses me hard. "It's the best thing I've ever seen."

He grabs my other leg, hooks it around his waist, lifts me and presses me against the wall.

His eyes stay on mine as he thrusts into me. He moves with a steady rhythm. Not quite as fast or hard or deep, but just as desperate.

His pelvis rubs against my clit. It's enough to send me to the edge.

I try to keep my eyes open, on his, so I can watch the pleasure building on his face. But I can't manage it. I have to close my eyes to hold on to the sensation.

I gasp. Almost there. I get closer and closer. That knot tightens with every thrust. And then I'm there.

"Open your eyes," Drew groans.

I do. I look right into his gorgeous eyes. They're fixed on me. They're filled with pleasure.

It pushes me right over the edge.

I dig my hands into his back. I moan. Hell, I scream.

It's an intense orgasm. I feel it in my fingers and toes. Every part of my body feels good. Every part of it is at peace.

Every part is Drew's.

And even though I'm spent, I need to feel him come too.

He keeps his eyes on mine. One hand goes to my ass and he holds me closer so he can move deeper.

A few thrusts and he starts to shake. He was waiting for me. The man has some serious control over his body.

His lips part. He lets out a low groan and everything in his expression changes. Softer and harder all at once.

He thrusts through his orgasm, sinking his nails into my skin, sinking his teeth into his lip. His breath goes wild. His eyes go wilder. He lets out another low, heavy groan.

He's there. Pulsing inside me. Coming inside me.

Mine.

He keeps me pinned to the wall until he's completely drained.

And then he kisses me, hard and aggressive and still desperate to possess me.

Still mine.

———

We drive for what feels like forever. I nestle into the passenger seat, my head resting against the window, my gaze drifting from Drew to the night sky and back again.

It's late. No one on the freeway. No one in our way. Nothing but big, wide open space.

He has one hand on the wheel. The other is intertwined with mine. The crooks of his fingers are pressed against mine. His calloused fingertips are pressed against the back of my hand. He's so soft and hard all at once.

We pass Thousand Oaks and Ventura. The 101 curves so it's nestled up against the beach. The ocean goes on forever—a gorgeous dark blue reflecting a sky full of stars.

Drew gets off the freeway just south of Santa Barbara. He drives like he knows the area well. We take side streets to a wide-open field in the middle of nowhere. It's up on some gorgeous hill across from million-dollar homes. The view is all ocean and sky.

It's perfect.

Chapter Twenty-Four

"I've never actually tried stargazing before." Drew sits on the grass in one smooth motion. He pats his lap.

I sit next to him in a much less smooth motion. The cold night air rushes around my skin. But there's no way I'm getting back in the car now.

He widens his stance and slides me right between his legs.

"I think the point is to cuddle up under a blanket," I say.

"Damn. Should have brought a blanket."

"You need to be prepared. Never know when you'll be taken with the desire to fuck a girl in a field or on the beach."

He laughs. "I can make it work without the blanket."

This tightness forms in my chest. Not thinking about Drew making it work with other girls. It's no secret he's experienced.

He runs his fingers through my hair. "I scared you, didn't I?"

"I know you were a slut."

"At the show. I don't want to hurt you."

"You've said that a few times." I lean into his touch. "But I'm not sure that you really understand what it means."

"Is that a challenge, Kendrick?"

"Yeah, it is." The muscles in my back tense. "You don't get to string me along then make it better by saying things like *I don't want to hurt you*. If you really want to avoid hurting me, then tell me what the hell you want from this. No excuses about how much you fuck girls up." My voice drops. "Not that I doubt you. You're driving me crazy."

"I want all of you. Whatever that means."

"So you want to be my boyfriend?"

He drags his fingertips across my neck. "Do I have to call it that?"

"How old are you?"

"Old enough to know better." He slides his arm around my waist.

"I need more than 'I want all of you.' Do you want a romantic relationship and all that boyfriend/girlfriend shit or not?"

He presses his lips against my neck. "You make it sound awfully tempting like that."

"I'm not going to beg you to love me." Shit. There's no sense in using the l-word. That's only going to terrify him. I clear my throat. "I mean to be with me."

"Will you beg me to do other things to you?" he asks.

Hell yeah. I shrug my shoulders like I'm unfazed. "What other things?"

His fingertips graze the top of my skirt. "I'd demonstrate, but then you'd accuse me of trying to distract you with my unbelievably skilled hands." His breath is on my ear. "Or mouth."

Nope. Not going to get distracted. Not going to lose

sight of my point here. Though, really, is it better to make a point or to get Drew's hands on my—

I clear my throat. "If you earn it."

He laughs. "Why do you have to go reminding me why I like you so much?" He holds me closer. "Makes it hard to negotiate."

"I can remind you of my bad traits."

"What bad traits?"

"I let my best friend drive me crazy instead of demanding he put up or shut up."

"That so?"

"Oh, it's so." I slide my fingertips over his forearms. "I have a weakness for guitarists with tattoos."

"And great bodies?"

"Well, obviously." I take a deep breath. "I hide my feelings from everyone and I never let anyone help me."

"I noticed." His voice is soft, giving. "I didn't get back in touch with you so I could fuck you."

"I hope not. You'd have some really terrible game to take this long."

He laughs. "I was desperate to talk to someone who would treat me like a person."

"As opposed to?"

"Some kind of rock idol." He leans closer. "Vivian and I broke up and then I went through some bad shit. When I bounced back, I tried hard to remember the last time I really cared about someone. And that was you."

"So I'm your rebound best friend?"

"Yeah. But you're more than that." He kisses my ear. "You're everything."

He makes this so fucking difficult.

I take a deep breath. "Why don't you tell me about that?"

He moves closer. " It doesn't paint me in a good light.'

"I want to know the ugly parts of you too."

Drew's voice gets heavy. "My relationship with Vivian was a train wreck. It was the first time I had a girlfriend beyond that high school 'date for a month, make out at lunch because you have nothing in common but popularity' shit."

I cringe, trying not to remember seeing Drew with other girls in high school.

"It was casual until the first Sinful tour. She made this big deal about keeping in touch. It was nice, at first, having someone back home to talk to. Went bad so fast. She manipulated me to get my attention. I was an asshole. When we broke up, I swore I'd never be that jealous again."

I scoff. "This is you trying not to be jealous?"

"I'm trying to give you a meaningful speech here. Don't sass me."

"Then don't say stupid things."

He bites my neck. "You keep using that mouth and I'm going to get distracted."

Sharp inhale. Slow exhale. Not getting distracted. Not at all. "What was so train wreck about it?"

"We'd fight one day. She'd say whatever she could to hurt me as much as she could. Then, the next day we'd make up and she'd cry and say whatever she could to win me over. I don't blame her. I was just as awful. I told her I loved her, but I didn't feel it. I thought it would be better telling her what she wanted to hear, but deep down, she saw through it. It made everything worse."

"You knew you didn't love her?"

He nods. "Deep down, I knew that love felt different. Stronger. But I wanted to make her happier." His voice softens. "The words felt like a lie. They were hollow. Something to recite at the end of a phone call. Ruined any chance we had. I couldn't take it back. I couldn't look at her the same way. She became the girl I was supposed to love but didn't."

"You never fell in love with her?"

"Never. By that point, I didn't even like her. Ask me now, and I can't tell you a single thing I ever liked about her. But I had to win. I had to prove I was right, that I wouldn't be the one to give up on our relationship."

That certainly sounds like Drew.

"I didn't want to see her after the tour. We'd sit there, watching a movie, not talking, not fucking because we didn't care about each other enough to bother. Certainly didn't trust each other enough to go bareback.'

"You are aware of condoms."

"Yes, Kendrick, I am aware of condoms. But asking your girl if you should wear one out of nowhere is accusing her of cheating."

"Was she cheating?"

"Hardly matters at this point. I wasn't invested anymore. Our second tour, shit got really bad. We'd fight, ignore each other, make apologies we didn't mean. One night, I was too fucking tired to do it anymore. She was crying and threatening to end things if I didn't skip the show to talk to her. Aidan was screaming at me to get on stage. So I dared her to end things and that was it."

"You must have learned something."

"Yeah," he says. "I learned I drive girls crazy. I swore off relationships. But touring is hard. You're away from home, you're stuck with loud, opinionated guys for sixteen hours straight. By the end of the night, I needed something that would make me feel alive. Something besides my guitar. I thought it would be okay if I was clear it was just sex, but it never worked out that way."

My head flashes with images of Drew fucking away his pain.

"I don't want that to happen to you," he says. "You mean more to me than anyone ever has."

"Even your ex?"

"That was an immature infatuation."

My heart thuds against my chest. "So what is this?"

"More than that." He takes my hand. "I'm not gonna say it, Kara—not until I'm sure—but my feelings for you are a whole lot more than like."

So I'm mad for a guy who can't say the word love. There are worse things in life.

In theory.

I take a deep breath. "What does that mean?"

"I need you to help me figure out this relationship thing. Tell me what you need and I'll tell you what I need."

"I like that idea."

"Good." He runs his fingers through my hair. "So tell me why you were upset this afternoon."

"What if I don't want to talk about it?"

He rubs his cheek against mine. "I want to hear about it."

I lean in to his touch.

"I need to hear about it." He lowers his voice. "I need to know every thought inside your brain."

"Those don't sound like very healthy boundaries."

"How about we compromise at ninety-nine percent of your thoughts?"

"Your definition of the word compromise is different than mine."

"Yeah, I figured," he says. "So, a flat ninety percent sounds good?"

"Drew."

He runs his fingertips over my outer ear. "I want to help you with this."

The stars are bright and brilliant. It's quiet. Calm. Like there's nothing in the world except for me and Drew.

He plays with my hair. "You don't have to do this alone, you know. Whenever you need me, I'm there."

"It was my mom. Arranging spring break. She's so excited for me to shadow her, and I have to tell her that I'm not coming home. That she's going to be all alone again."

"I'll come with you. We can drive up together. Explore the city while your mom's at work."

"I don't know if that's a good idea."

"Give me one reason why it's not."

Besides my inability to think anything but *need Drew now* when I'm around him? I turn around so we're eye to eye. Drew's hands go to my hips. In one smooth motion, he lies back on the grass and pulls me onto his lap.

I plant my hands on his chest. "You're distracting."

His hands slide up my sides, all the way to my shoulders. He pulls my body into his, so we're only six inches apart. "I'll keep you focused."

"I would be more inclined to believe you if we weren't in the perfect position to fuck."

Drew shakes his head with mock outrage. "Your mind is always in the gutter."

He pulls me into a slow, sweet kiss. There's so much affection in it. Just like in the alley, everything inside him is pouring into me. I can feel him in my bones. I can feel how much he cares about me. Even if it's only care.

The kiss breaks. I stare into his eyes. Those brown eyes are deep and they're filled with tenderness.

The words form in my throat, but I swallow to push them back down. I'm not ready to say it either.

He brushes a stray hair behind my ear. "Hey."

I shift closer. "Hey."

"I want to be there to hold your hand."

A warmth spreads through my belly. It's not lust. Same ballpark, just as demanding, but softer and sweeter.

"Okay," I say. "But just to hold my hand. I'm the one in charge."

His lips spread into a smile. His hands go to my back. He shifts, wrestling me to the ground so he's the one of top of me, straddling me.

The weight of his body sinks into mine. I'm overwhelmed with the feeling of safety. It's like nothing in the world can hurt me.

My body is betraying me again. There's never been anything more dangerous than falling in love with Drew.

My head has no say here. It's been beaten and brutalized by my body and my heart. No sense in resisting how much I want to feel that affection again.

I close my eyes and press my lips into his. He tastes so good. My tongue slides into his mouth, exploring it like this is the first time I've ever kissed him properly.

It's like he can read my mind. His hand rakes over my legs, settling on my inner thighs. He traces the outline of my scars like they're fascinating.

He kisses his way to my ear. "You want to do this here or in the car?"

It is freezing out here, even with all the warmth of his body. "The car."

In one smooth motion, Drew rises to his feet. He takes my hand and pulls me up. His fingers intertwine with mine.

The car is just down the street. Drew unlocks it, slides into the passenger seat, and pats his lap as if to say *come here*.

That looks difficult. I slide into the seat next to him,

pressing him against the center console. He laughs, grabs my hips, and pulls me into his lap.

Drew reaches over and pulls the door shut.

The rest of the world fades away. It's just the two of us in this little car, in this tiny seat.

I shift so I'm straddling him. He looks up at me, all that affection in his eyes, and brushes my hair behind my shoulders. Something passes between us. Neither one of us is ready to say those words, but, right now, I can feel them.

His eyes close. He plants a soft kiss on my shoulder. My neck. My cheek. My mouth. He sucks on my lower lip. It sends a pang straight to my core.

My hands go to his shoulders. I slide them around his neck, pulling him closer, bringing the kiss deeper.

His touch is tender. He runs his hands down my back and up again.

And again.

And again.

Every brush of his hands is magic. I kiss him harder. I shift my hips, so our crotches are aligned. All that fabric is in the way again, but I can still feel his erection through his jeans.

I break the kiss to pull my top over my head. Drew's eyes go wide.

He pulls his shirt over his head. My breath picks up. My heart races a little faster. He's so damn beautiful. I trace the lines of his body from his shoulders to his belly button. Then below his belly button.

I undo his jeans. He lifts his ass to help me get them down his hips. Then the boxers. Then it's just Drew on that seat.

He drags his fingertips up my thigh. It's slow enough to make me dizzy. My body is so desperate to be pressed against his. I press my eyes closed to contain the sensation.

There's this ache between my legs and there's only one way to satisfy it.

He's the only thing that satisfies me.

It occurs to me that I have a problem. That I really am addicted to him. But the second our eyes meet I don't care. It's like I can see all the way to his soul. It's like I can see all the things he can't manage to say.

His palm presses against my panties. He tugs them to my knees. I shift so he can get them off my feet.

Drew grabs my hips and brings my body onto his. No teasing. He enters me. His grip around me tightens. He pulls me closer.

I hold onto his shoulders and use them for leverage.

I shift up and down, driving him as deep as he'll go. He holds my gaze, watching me with fascination. Then he pulls me into a deep kiss.

We stay like that, lips locked, him shifting deeper and deeper inside me. My body is pressed against his—my chest, my stomach, my hands, my thighs—and the skin-to-skin contact is enough to make me sizzle. It's all so sweet, so agonizingly slow.

I keep my eyes closed and my lips pressed against his. The pleasure in my core builds with every thrust. That's agonizingly slow too.

Just when I'm sure I can't take it anymore, Drew moves faster. He plants kisses down my neck and chest, stopping to suck on my nipples, then kissing his way back to my mouth.

I slide my hands around his neck. An orgasm rises up inside me. I do everything to keep my lips on his. I dig my nails into his back. I squeeze my thighs against his.

I'm so close to the edge. One more thrust and I'm straight into free fall. Pleasure radiates to every single finger and toe. I moan into Drew's mouth as I come. I squeeze him as hard as I can.

He feels so fucking good.

Drew breaks our kiss to press his lips against my neck. His movements get faster, harder, more desperate. He digs his hands into my ass, pulling me closer.

He's almost there and it's a beautiful thing to watch. His eyelids press together. His lips part. There's so much pleasure on his face, like he's here and somewhere else all at once.

I'm greedy. I want him here.

"Open your eyes," I say. "I want to watch."

He does. He holds my gaze as he thrusts into me. He digs his fingers into my hips like it's the only way he can contain himself.

I can see the orgasm building in his expression. He can't bring himself to keep his eyes open. He can't bring himself to do anything but groan. He pulls me closer. He sucks on my earlobe.

With one more heavy groan, he comes. His cock is pulsing inside me. His nails are sharp against my skin. It's such an amazing sensation, knowing I'm bringing him this bliss.

We stay in the passenger seat with our bodies pressed together for a long time. It's the closest I've ever been to him. I'm terrified to move away. What if everything changes and he goes back to being utterly unable to articulate his feelings?

Finally, his eyes open. He runs his hand through my hair, still soft and sweet.

"I want to take you somewhere," he says.

I nod. Wherever it is, I want to be there.

Chapter Twenty-Five

The drive is dark and quiet. Somewhere around Malibu, Drew turns away from the main road. After ten minutes of twists and turns, we stop on a mountain top.

Drew gets out of the car. He pulls a hoodie from the backseat, unzips it and slings it around my shoulders.

"This is where I came the other day. When I was trying to think." He takes my hand and walks me toward the canyon. "Didn't help. I was still going out of my mind."

I take a look around. We're on top of one of the canyons in Malibu. The only light is from the moon and the stars. It's enough to make out the rocky scenery.

"About what?" I ask.

"About how I should have been there." He squeezes my hand. "How if I had been around more, you wouldn't have had to hurt yourself."

"That's not true.' I pull my hand back to my chest and pull the hoodie a little tighter. "And I don't want to hear you saying things like that. I don't need to add your guilty conscience to the list of shit I have to deal with."

It's dark, but I can still make out his eyes. They're serious, intense.

"Okay." He shifts his weight. "You sure you want to know every ugly thing about me?"

"Positive."

"It happened when I was about seventeen. After my parents got divorced. I was relieved. Finally, I wouldn't have to see them pretend to like each other. But Willow took it so hard. She was miserable and she ran off with—" He lets out a sharp exhale. His hands curl into fists. "The asshole was no good. He hurt her. Hit her. And worse."

His eyes are on fire. His posture is defensive. I slide my arms around his waist.

He stiffens. "She couldn't see it. Thought it didn't mean anything. That he loved her. She was only fifteen. She couldn't help it. But I hated myself for letting her run off with him. I found the guy and beat him within an inch of his life. Broke my hand. Couldn't play the guitar for two months." His voice drops. "Almost killed him. I will if I ever see him again."

"You defended your sister. There's nothing ugly about that."

"It wasn't defense. She was safe. I wanted to make him hurt."

I stare back at Drew. I'm not too keen on violence, but it's hard to fault him for beating the guy who abused his sister.

I run my hand through his hair. "Why did you stop?"

"I don't know. He was a big guy and should have had the upper hand, but he went limp. Stopped fighting back."

"You couldn't do it?"

"Maybe. Or maybe my hand hurt too fucking bad. Or maybe I had enough sense to realize someone was gonna call the cops. It wasn't mercy. Sure as shit wasn't my conscience." His hand slides into my hair, tilting me so we're eye to eye again. "If anyone ever hurt you like that I'd kill him."

"You threatened to kill a guy for grabbing my ass. I can only imagine what you'd do if someone actually hurt me."

"Anytime someone causes you pain, not just that way —I want to kill them." His gaze goes to the ground. "I keep hurting you. I hate myself for it."

"Drew-"

"Let me finish." His expression gets intense. "I know you think I'm overprotective. Maybe I am. The last six months or so, I've been trying to protect you from me. I wanted you all this time, Kara. For so long. But I was sure I'd only hurt you."

I swallow hard.

"I've hurt you a lot already."

Tension builds between my shoulder blades. I don't know what he's saying. I don't know how to respond. So I lean closer. I hold him tighter. With my head against his chest, I can hear his heartbeat. It's steady and strong.

"I mean it every time I say it. I don't want to hurt you." He holds me tighter. "But it's going to take a while for me to figure this relationship thing out."

"Okay."

"I'm gonna try, but you'll have to be patient."

"Okay."

"Make me a promise." He looks me dead in the eyes. "Promise you won't let me fuck this up."

"Promise you won't let *yourself* fuck this up."

He leans down to press his forehead against mine. "Deal."

"Deal," I agree.

———

It's well past midnight when we get home. Now that my lust is sated, my stomach is growling. I haven't eaten a proper meal since breakfast.

Drew stands behind me, sliding his arms around my waist and resting his chin against my shoulder. I lean into the comfort of his body against mine.

"You hungry?" He asks.

"Starving."

"I'll make something." He kisses me on the cheek and moves to the kitchen.

I plant myself on the table, watching him chop and dice. "When did you learn to cook?"

"Last few years. Miles taught me."

"That's so cute."

He looks at me as if to say *watch yourself, Kendrick.* "I wanted to eat homemade food. We don't tour as much as when we started, but it's still five months this year." He sets a pan on the stove. "If I never eat fast food again, it will be too soon."

"You don't crave burgers and fries?"

He sticks his tongue out in distaste. "Never. Tastes like screaming phone calls with my ex. Like drinking too much and wanting to start a fight but knowing Tom will kill me if I can't play."

"Is it really about playing?"

"Yeah, but—" Drew runs his hand through his hair. He turns toward me. "Tom cares more than he lets on."

"I'm telling him you said that."

Drew moves to my seat. He kneels next to me, so he's only barely looking up to me. "You won't." He grabs my shirt and pulls my lips into his.

I kiss him hard. "How do you know?"

"If you do, I'll tickle you until you pass out." He shifts

back to his feet. "Damn, Kendrick. You're distracting me from our dinner."

"You didn't eat with the guys?"

"Stomach was in knots."

"Really?"

He cocks an eyebrow. "I do have feelings."

"But you act like nothing could ever hurt you."

"When you hurt, I hurt. I felt sick knowing I was causing you pain. Kept going in circles, thinking you'd be better off if I backed off but wanting you too much to do it."

"I don't want you to back off. You're the only person I can be myself around."

"What about Meg?"

"It's not the same. Not as easy." I bite my lip. "I'm not good at relationships either. Jake loved me but it wasn't really me. It was the nice, normal girl I convinced him I was."

Smoke drifts from the pan on the stove. It's burning.

"Fuck." Drew moves to the kitchen and tends to the food.

"I won't be okay without you. Even if we don't work as a couple. I need you to be my friend."

He's quiet for a minute. When he speaks, his voice is low. "I always want to be your friend."

My stomach growls. I remind myself to be patient. "I was thinking... what if we slept together?"

"Pretty sure we crossed the bridge, Kendrick."

"Not sex. Sleeping in the same bed. I know a lot of guys don't like it—"

"How many guys you try this with?"

"Shut up."

"You can do better than 'shut up.'"

"I'm too hungry to think up good comebacks."

He laughs as he fiddles with the pot. He's cooking something and it smells good. Like garlic and parsley.

I settle into my seat, all my attention on the scent of the food. Eggs. Red peppers. Some green vegetable. Spinach or maybe kale. If it's kale I'm teasing him mercilessly for being so LA.

Drew turns off the stove, scoops the food onto plates, and joins me at the table.

Damn. Spinach. So much for proving my comeback prowess. "Thanks."

He makes eye contact. "I'd love to sleep with you."

"You sure?"

"But I usually practice for a while before bed."

"I like hearing you play."

"You won't like hearing 'No Way in Hell' for the three hundredth time. How about I join you in your room when I'm done?"

A warmth spreads through my belly. "Okay."

He smiles. "You sleep naked, right?"

"No."

"Fuck. Thought that was part of the deal."

I pluck a pepper from my eggs and throw it at him. Victory! It smacks his cheek.

He peels it off and pops it in his mouth. "I will if you will."

"We'll never actually sleep."

"So?"

"I can sleep commando."

His teeth sink into his lip. "Go on..."

"You have to wait for that."

Chapter Twenty-Six

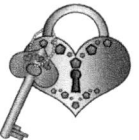

I sleep without underwear all the time, but it's different doing it knowing Drew is going to be pressed against me. Knowing his hands—

I'm getting ahead of myself. I take a quick shower, brush my teeth, and change into my normal pajamas: a tank top and cotton drawstring pants. Not the sexiest thing, but they're comfortable.

Drew joins me a few minutes later. He's wet and warm, fresh from the shower. And he's shirtless, wearing only a pair of cotton pajama pants.

"You really sleep like that?" I ask.

"Unless it's cold." He scoots next to me, so he's spooning me. His hand traces the neckline of my tank top as if feeling for a bra.

"Drew," I groan, shifting my body against his. He smells like soap. "What are you doing?"

"Keeping you honest." His fingers trace the edges of my pajama pants. They dip inside lower and lower.

Almost there.

Then his fingertips skim my clit.

Damn.

"I want to ask you something." He presses his body against mine.

"Right now?"

"You want me to stop?" He pulls his hand back to my belly button.

"I didn't say that."

He chuckles. "It's relevant to the subject at hand."

"You're trying to kill me."

"Yeah." He scrapes his teeth against my neck. "Do you ever fantasize about me?"

"So not going there."

"That's a yes."

Obviously it's a yes. I turn so I'm facing him. "Do you ever fantasize about me?"

"All the time." His hand goes to my hip. "I go out of my mind."

"Do you..." I take a deep breath. I want an answer to this so badly. I've never thought about another guy like this. Never wondered how he thought of me or if he— "Do you touch yourself?"

"You're kidding right?"

"No." I stammer. "What's funny about that?"

"A million times."

My sex clenches. Drew really thinks of me that much? He wants me that much? "Really?"

"Fuck yeah. You have any idea how sexy you are?" He yanks the strap of my tank top off my shoulders as if he's proving his point.

I relax into his touch, groaning as he toys with my nipple. He sucks on my neck, shifting his crotch against mine so I can feel his erection.

Drew shifts me so I'm lying on my back. He leans on

his elbow. His eyes meet mine. "You ever touch yourself thinking about me?"

"Not a million times."

"A hundred thousand?"

"No."

"A thousand?"

My cheeks burn. I avert my gaze to the ceiling.

"Fuck. I have a lot of catching up to do." He presses his lips to mine. "You have to show me sometime."

"Is it really that interesting?"

"Fuck yes." He pulls my other strap off my shoulder and rolls my tank to my stomach. He drags his hand to my other nipple, teasing me. "What do you think about when you touch yourself?"

"You mean when it's about you?"

"You thinking about other guys?"

I shake my head. "Not for a long time." I look up at Drew. His eyes are fixed on me like he's hanging on every word. This is a whole other level of intimacy, but I want that with him. I take a deep breath. "You touching me or inside of me." My cheeks burn. "Or things I want to do to you."

"Like what?"

I can't say this aloud. It's too much. But it's not like he's going to complain.

I make eye contact. "You're making this difficult."

He smiles. "Chose those words carefully, didn't you?"

I shift, straddling him so I'm on top, looking down at him. Here goes nothing. "I want to suck you off."

His eyes go wide. "I want to watch you touch yourself after."

"You're not in a position to make demands."

He brings his hand to the back of my head and presses me into a deep kiss. "Not a demand. A request. After."

"After." I grind against him.

I drag my hands over his chest and stomach. His body is so hard and defined and there's something so pleasing about the way it feels against my palm, like it was meant for it.

My hands brush the soft hairs below his belly button. He shudders, his hips rocking against me. I go lower, lower, until I'm at his waistband.

Lower. I rub him over his pajamas.

Drew groans into my mouth. He digs his fingers into my chest, squeezing my nipples.

I pull off his bottoms. Drew lifts his hips to help me. Then they're at his knees and off his feet. Then it's just him.

Something in Drew turns on, something animal. His pupils dilate. His breath gets heavy. He pulls the top over my head and tosses it on the floor in one desperate movement.

I press my lips against his neck then work my way down. I draw an outline around his chest piece with my tongue. His skin tastes good. Like soap and like Drew.

His hand goes to my hair. It presses gently against the back of my head, ready to guide me to just the right spot.

I drag my hands down his defined stomach. They rest on his hips, and I hold on tight as I position myself.

The muscles of his stomach tense. I flick my tongue against them. Then a little lower. I nibble on skin just below his belly button.

He lets out a desperate groan. Grabs onto my hair a little tighter. He's shaking. He wants me that badly.

He's at my mercy.

I press one hand against the bed to hold myself up. The other, I wrap around him. He's so thick and warm and hard.

I brush my lips against his tip. He shudders, his hand digging into my hair. I do it again and again, until he groans.

I slide my tongue over him, tasting him, testing his reactions.

His eyes close.

I flick my tongue against the underside of his tip. His fingers dig into my hair. That's it. That's the spot.

"Kara," he groans quietly. "Fuck, Kara."

My nipples harden. My sex clenches. The way he says my name—it's magic, it's poetry.

I do it again and again, until he's panting and shaking, until he brings his other hand to my hair. His fingers press against my head, a gentle nudge.

I take him into my mouth. Sucking on his tip at first, then going deeper. He's big. Too big for me to take completely. I wrap my hand around him, using it like an extension of my mouth, so I have all of him under my control.

Drew groans. It's such a great sound—his pleasure—and it's all because of me.

He guides me over him, digging his hands into my hair. I run my tongue over his base as I suck on him.

The ache between my legs tightens. There's something about having Drew in my mouth. It makes me all the more needy, all the more desperate.

I take him deeper.

"Kara," he says my name like it's his favorite thing in the world. "You're so fucking amazing."

He bites his lip. He groans.

I slide my hand from his hip to his ass, digging my fingers into his firm flesh, relaxing the muscles in my throat to push him deeper. Yes. There. I have almost all of him and he feels so good. He tastes so good.

His grip tightens in my hair.

He thrusts into my mouth. I grip him harder. I'm so keyed up, and the sounds escaping his lips are perfect.

"Fuck," he groans. "I'm gonna come."

The muscles of his stomach and thighs clench.

"Kara."

And then he's coming, tugging at my hair, gnawing at his skin.

I press my palm against his stomach to hold myself in place as he fills my mouth. When he's done, I swallow. It's not even a consideration. It's Drew.

He reaches for my hands and pulls me next to him. There's the calmest look on his face, like he can barely remember his own name.

His fingertips slide over my cheek. He stares at me with a mix of appreciation and need. "How the hell did you get so good at that?" His finger hooks on my lower lip, pulling my mouth open a centimeter or so. "Don't tell me if it's anything besides blind intuition."

"I'm not, I... thanks."

His lips close over mine. He kisses me hard, more desperate than he ever has. When he releases me, he's breathless. "You fantasize about that?"

"Only with you." I hold eye contact, attempting to maintain my confidence. He's gooey with post-orgasm affection. There's no reason to be shy. "I think about anything two people can do together."

"You're fucking amazing." He pulls me into another hard, desperate kiss.

"You can have any woman you want. Must be a line of fans ready to drop to their knees. Who would beg you—"

"I only want you." He teases my nipples until I groan. "I fucking love that sound." He pulls my pajamas to my feet. "You still game?"

"You really want to watch?"

He nods, his eyes wide with enthusiasm.

"I've never had an audience before."

He rolls back to his elbow. His fingertips trail over my breasts. "If you get too self-conscious, I can take over." He pinches my nipple. "But I hope you don't. I fucking love watching you come."

"Okay." I settle into the bed, positioning myself like I would if Drew wasn't here. But he is here. There's no sense in pretending I'm alone, masturbating while I think of him.

I touched myself while we were fucking, but this is different. This is a show.

Nervous energy passes through me. It fades away the second our eyes connect. He's lost in anticipation. He's still at my mercy.

I hold his gaze as I slide my hand down my stomach. I spread my legs wider to give him a better view. It's dark in here. He won't see my scars in high-def.

I go slow, teasing myself with light, long strokes over my outer lips. I stare into his eyes. His attention is on my movements, his mouth hanging open like he's watching his favorite movie.

It's magic. It makes it impossible to go slow. I forget about teasing and bring my fingers to my clit. I need to come. I need to show him how much I want him.

I rub myself. Soft then harder. Then just right. Drew sighs with pleasure. He brings his hands to my cheek and presses his thumb over my lower lip. I groan. Him touching me makes this better. I thrust my chest toward him. It's enough direction. He brings his hand to my breast and toys with my nipple.

Fuck yes.

Pressure builds between my legs. I've done this plenty. I know how to make myself come quickly. But with his eyes glued to me, with his hands on my body, I want to revel in how good it feels.

Every brush of his fingertips sends a pang straight to my sex. The knot pulls tighter and tighter, until it's too much to take. I find just the right spot and keep my pressure steady. There. Almost. My eyelids press together. I groan, arching my back and shifting my hips.

The orgasm is intense. Bliss spreads through my pelvis then my torso then all the way to my fingers.

When I blink my eyes open, Drew is still staring at me with rapt attention.

"Better than I imagined." He presses his lips to mine.

"You imagined that?"

He copies my words. "Not a million times." He pulls my body into his. "But pretty fucking close."

―――

The light falling over the bed casts Drew in a dreamy glow. It's bright enough that it must be well into mid-morning. I brush my teeth, fix a bowl of cereal and a cup of tea, and sit down with my textbook. There's a lot of weekend left and I want to spend it without schoolwork hanging over my head.

By the time Drew joins me at the table, I'm done with my finance homework.

He kisses me good morning. There's something normal about it. Like we're a regular couple who goes around using the words boyfriend and girlfriend.

He unlocks his phone and shows off his *15 Missed Texts* notification.

I read the one in the notification.

Tom: Let me know if you killed anyone. I'll need to start early to keep that out of the news.

Drew shakes his head and taps a few replies. I find my phone and check the damage. Just a few texts from Meg.

Meg: You're gone. Take it things went well? Let me know when you're done fucking Drew.

I keep my reply short and sweet.

Kara: Very well. Will let you know if I'm ever done. I have lots of plans for the weekend. Brunch Sunday?

Meg: Only if we're actually studying. I'm way behind.

Kara: Deal.

I take the last sip of my tea. "Anything bad?"

"Wish they'd mind their own business." He shoves his phone to the other side of the table. His lip corners turn down. He shifts like he's shaking off his funk. "I want to take you to the beach. It's supposed to be ninety today. I know you—"

"I don't go to the beach."

"What if you got a swimsuit that covered your thighs? Not that you should. I recommend one of those Brazilian thongs."

"You'd punch every guy who looked at me."

"I can control myself."

My voice drops. "No. I can't... not yet."

"We don't have to do it today. But if you visit on tour, I always want to get away. We're stopping at a lot of cities near the ocean."

"I don't know."

"I'll go shopping with you."

"You're volunteering to shop?"

"If I get to see you try on swimsuits, fuck yes."

I do miss swimming, and there are options. Long board shorts or swim skirts or somehow channeling all the don't-give-a-fuck in the world and wearing a regular, scar-revealing bikini.

But I'm caught on something else. Drew wants me to

visit on tour? He can't deal with talking to his friends about our relationship status and he wants me to visit him on tour. No fucking way.

"When are we telling *our* friends that we're together?" I ask. "We don't need a label for it. Just... hey, this is a thing. It's not like they don't know."

His eyes go to the floor. "I don't want to invite their commentary. It will only fuck things up."

"You need to tell them before the tour." I press my palm against the table. "It's about a month away, right?"

"Yeah."

"You do realize that everyone knows what's going on, right?"

He shrugs like he finds it plausible that Miles, Tom, or Pete has no clue that Drew and I are more than friends.

Maybe he's right. I'm sure everyone knows we're fucking. But that could be it. It's not like rock stars avoid no-strings-attached sex.

"I put them through hell with Vivian. I don't want them thinking it will be the same with you." He shifts, his expression softening. "After your midterms. That's two weeks, right?"

I nod.

He scoots closer. Runs his fingers over the inside of my wrist, tracing the faint scars. "You don't have to hide these, you know. They're not that noticeable."

"I'm not interested in your opinion on how I should cover or not cover my body."

Drew's lips curl into a smile. "How can you make telling me to fuck off sound so charming?"

"Practice."

He makes eye contact. "I do want to be with you. For a long time."

I push off the table and find my purse. "You don't have

to say the word boyfriend. You have two weeks." I slide into my canvas sneakers. "After that, I'm not going to be patient."

"Deal." He shifts to his feet with a nod and follows me out the door.

Chapter Twenty-Seven

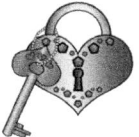

For some bizarre reason, Drew parks in the corner of the empty fourth floor of the garage.

The thought of heading to the beach in a bikini is enough to send me into full blown panic. I push everything else aside so I can focus on staying calm. I'm not committing to anything. I'm just trying on swimsuits.

The tile floor squeaks under my rubber soles. There are two department stores with swimwear sections, but I head straight for the specialty shop on the first floor. The woman at the counter is in her forties. She looks at me maternally, like she's going to warn me to wear sunblock.

She studies Drew as if she's trying to place him, then turns back to me. "Are you looking for something in particular, Miss?"

"Do you have anything with a skirt?"

She looks at me funny, like it's strange for someone my age to want a swim skirt. Thankfully, she makes no commentary, instead pointing me to a section in the corner.

It narrows my options considerably. There's one style and the skirt is only barely long enough. It's a lot of fabric, sure to cause enough drag to make swimming difficult. I allow myself a minute to imagine the possibility of wearing a regular swimsuit. Is there any world where I can care so little about the angry red marks that line my thighs?

Drew gives me space, hanging out by the register and making conversation with the saleswoman. She smiles at him, charmed by his personality, his looks, or his potential for commission.

I pick out a reasonably cute purple halter top swim skirt combo and motion to the dressing rooms.

She waves me over. "You sure you don't want to try anything else?"

"How about that one?" Drew points to a tiny black bikini. "Unless you'd rather skinny dip at our place?" He smirks.

The saleswoman plays a strong poker face.

"That would never hold my boobs." I turn back to the dressing room.

"You could try it. See if you like it." He pulls it off the rack and hands it to me.

"No."

His expression softens. "Are you going to hide forever?"

A crick develops in my neck. "You don't get a say in what I wear."

"Maybe something more supportive." The saleswoman points to a not so T&A-revealing black-and-white polka-dot bikini. "This brand has a few different cuts you can try." She pulls a huge handful of tops and bottoms from the rack and leads me to the dressing room.

In the locked stall, I strip to my underwear. Drew is too fucking pushy. He's always like this. It's usually more endearing than it is frustrating, but right now I can't deal with the extra stress.

The purple swim skirt is just long enough to keep me covered. The waist is too high and the top sits funny on my shoulders. It's not the most flattering and it's certainly not the most youthful, but it's a swimsuit I can wear without a panic attack.

That's something.

The mirror in here is too small for a really good look. I fight a sigh as I step into the main area. It's right at the back of the store, in view of Drew, the saleswoman, and anyone walking past us.

Drew makes eye contact immediately. "You look great." He shoves his hands into his pockets like he's on his best behavior.

I don't look great. The bottoms gap at the waist and pull at the hips. The top is too big and too tight all at once. The only good thing about this swimsuit, besides the color, is its ability to cover my upper thighs.

Drew comes closer. He's still a few feet away.

I turn back to him so the mirror is out of my eyeline. "I look like an old lady."

"Like a MILF."

I laugh despite the sense of dread in my gut. "It's exhausting hiding this all the time."

He moves closer. Much closer than is appropriate in the middle of a store with the saleswoman glancing in our direction.

"She's going to ask us to leave." I lean into his body anyway.

He wraps his arms around me. "Then I'll buy everything you've got in the dressing room and you can try 'em on at home."

"Would you really?"

"Last I heard, I don't get a say in what you wear."

"I didn't mean to be so—"

"I know." He kisses my forehead and steps back to an appropriate distance for the middle of a store. "I love how strong you are, Kara. I love that you tell me to back off when I'm being an ass."

The words *I love you, Kara* were in that sentence in that order. There were other words between them, but my body is ignoring those other words in favor of going into overdrive.

It's warm in here. Really warm. I lift my hair to fan the back of my neck. Better. I'm breathing okay.

"I'll try that other bikini, but there's no way I'm wearing it in public. Understand?" I put my hand on my hip in my most confident posture.

"Kendrick, you can say or do whatever you want if you're modeling swimwear for me."

In the dressing room, I change into the skimpiest of all the polka dot options. The triangle top tugs at my neck. So not happening with my bust size. The bikini bottoms are low rise. They barely cover my thong.

My gaze goes straight to the raised red scars on my thighs. They aren't as bad as they are in my mind, but they're noticeable.

I step back until I'm pressed against the wall. I try to look at myself like I'm taking in the whole picture, but I can't see anything but the scars.

Maybe it's better in the mirror outside.

With a deep breath, I step out of the dressing room. I block out everything but my reflection. First above the waist. The cut is a lot more flattering. My boobs look enormous in the tiny top. My eyes travel down. This bottom fits better. It's not digging into my hips.

And then the thighs.

Under the harsh fluorescent lights, the scars stand out like black tattoos on white skin.

That crick in my neck spreads to my upper back.

Drew comes closer. He looks in the mirror like he's studying my reflection it in. "You okay?"

I shake my head.

"You look hot as fuck, you know."

"Maybe waist up."

"Every inch of you looks hot as fuck." He leans closer. "I'd drag you to the dressing room and rip that bikini off if I didn't know it would get us arrested." He groans. "Even so. Might do it if you stay out here too long."

My cheeks flush. He really does make me feel *hot as fuck*.

I nod a thank you and return to the dressing room. One of the polka-dot bottoms is a swim skirt with ruffles. It's a lot shorter than the other skirt. It will probably draw attention to my scars as much as it hides them.

I change into it and a bra-style top. The latter fits like a charm. But the skirted bottoms—

They're feminine and adorable and absolutely ineffective at covering the parts I want hidden.

Outside, Drew clears his throat like he's waiting. Okay, fine, I did promise to model for him. I step into the main area and twirl like I really don't give a fuck that my thighs are visible to everyone who walks by the store.

Drew looks me up and down. His eyes go wide. "Your tits look amazing."

"You're a poet."

"Your ass too."

I check my reflection to assess the veracity of his claims. Scar issues aside, the swimsuit is flattering. It plays up my curves without any unfortunate pinching.

"For the record, you see anything you like, it's on me."

He shifts, his gaze glued to my ass. "Even if you want everything in the store."

"I'm not sure I like you buying me so much stuff."

"Trust me, Kendrick. This is not for you. It's for me."

He's panting like he can't stand that we're in public and not alone. I bite my lip to keep my mind out of the gutter. There's time for that when this is over.

"Okay." I move back to the dressing room and change into my normal clothes. My muscles are tight and my nerves are shot. The purple suit isn't quite right, but it works for the beach. This black-and-white polka-dot thing is just for us, alone, so I can see that needy look spread over his face again.

I fix my hair and bring my new swimsuits to the register. Drew whips out his credit card and pays without even looking at the total.

ONCE WE'RE INSIDE THE CAR, DREW TURNS TO ME, HIS expression dead serious. "For the record, Kara, your thighs are divine. I'm happy to prove it."

"How would you do that?"

His expression flares with something mischievous. "Bury my face between them."

My cheeks flush. "I'm not sure that proves anything."

"How about I do it anyway?" He reaches over and runs his hand over the inside of my thigh.

Heat courses through my body.

I want to feel normal. As normal as it's possible to feel stripping naked in a parking garage in the middle of the day.

I nod.

He leans over me, unbuckling my seatbelt then pushing my seat back until it's nearly flat.

"This might be uncomfortable for a minute." He shifts into the passenger seat next to me, pressing me against the window. "Bear with me."

He slides his hand up my t-shirt and unhooks my bra. His hands traces its outline. He keeps my shirt on, but pushes my bra up and out of the way.

He slides his hand over my breast. "Your tits are also divine." He pushes my shirt up to my neck. Then the bra.

He palms my breasts, teasing my nipples with his fingertips. I try to forget we're in a car in a parking garage in the middle of the day.

Drew kisses me hard. His tongue dances with mine. His hands work their magic on my chest.

Our kiss releases and he brings his mouth to my ear. "Do me a favor and take those jeans off."

"A favor?"

"You'll like the results."

He looks up at me with a shit-eating grin. Can't say that I'm opposed to the view. There's enough light in here that I can see every line of definition in Drew's chest, shoulders, and stomach. I can make out every brush of ink in his tattoos. My gaze is drawn to a glass heart on his shoulder. It's broken, bleeding.

I trace its outline. "Your ex?"

"That relationship wasn't something I'd want on my body."

"Then what's it for?"

"You want me to use my mouth to explain or you want me to use it to make you come?"

"First one then the other."

He shakes his head like he finds me ridiculous. "I got it with my sister."

"You did not."

He nods. "After all that shit happened. She has a matching one."

"Wasn't she fifteen?"

"I knew a guy."

"What's it supposed to mean?"

He drags his fingertips over my stomach, settling on my jeans then unbuttoning them. "It's a statement on my feelings at the time."

His heart was broken over his sister getting hurt. I swoon. Drew can be fucking sweet sometimes.

He pulls my panties to my thighs. He runs his fingertips over the scars on my hips. "I'd die buried in those thighs if I could." Drew looks up at me. "You still want to talk?"

"I kind of like what you're saying."

He runs his fingers over another half-dozen scars. "We could get matching tattoos."

I study his reaction for some sarcasm, but there isn't a hint of it. The guy can't say the word "girlfriend" but he has no problem offering to permanently mark his skin for me.

Rock stars—they make no sense at all.

He pushes my panties and jeans to my knees. Motions for me to take them off. "You're making it awfully hard to eat you out."

"I like this conversation."

"Take off the jeans if you want another word."

I do as I'm asked.

Drew looks at me like I'm crazy to want to hear more about this, but dammit, I really do like what he's saying.

"What kind of tattoo would we get?" I ask.

"Whatever you want." Drew pats the space on the seat right outside his chest. "Knees here."

I press my hands against his shoulders and drag my knees up the seat.

This little crick develops in my neck. He's had his face between my thighs before and it was amazing as all hell, but that was at night in the dark. This is the middle of the day in bright light.

I brace myself for the worst possible reaction.

Drew runs his fingertips up my inner thighs, tracing one scar after another. It's gentle, attentive.

"You okay?" he asks.

"Yeah, just..."

One of his hands slides around my leg, trailing up my hamstring and resting on my ass. He looks up at me. "Your thighs are amazing."

"But, they're so..."

"Sexy." He kneads the flesh of my ass. "Now sit on my face." He brings his hands to my hips, pulling me closer.

The seat doesn't go quite flat and the car isn't all that tall. I shift, moving closer, spreading my legs. My head bumps into the roof of the car.

Drew slides down the seat, bringing his mouth inches from my sex. His exhale wakes up all the nerves in my body, sending any doubts away.

When I'm with him, I really do feel divine.

He holds onto my hips, pulling me closer. His tongue slides over my clit. It's a long, luxurious lick. He goes slowly. Really slowly.

My head bumps into the roof of the car again. If only the damn thing was a convertible. We'd be getting arrested but there would be nothing limiting his range of motion.

Drew slides one hand up my torso. His fingers draw circles over my nipples. The same long, luxurious movements. Then his hand goes to my side. He squeezes me like he's telling me to stay in place.

I shift so I'm not quite pressed against the roof and I hold damn steady.

Drew guides me over his mouth, licking me from top to bottom. It's slow. So, so slow. Pleasure whirs inside me. I pant. I claw at the roof of the car. It's not fast enough. I need more. I need to be there, at the edge, pleasure spilling through my body.

"Drew," I whine.

"Hmm?" he mumbles into my inner thigh then sucks on the flesh.

"Make me come."

He moves his mouth a little higher, presses his lips into my thigh. "Hmm?"

"Pretty please."

That pleasure whirls, a little faster, a little higher, but still not nearly enough.

He moves his mouth a little closer, sucking on my flesh again. Then it's closer and he's sucking on my outer lips with the softest, lightest touch.

I struggle to keep track of my breath.

This is more, so, so much more. I close my eyes and dig my hands into the passenger seat.

Drew nibbles on my outer lips. I can't help but gasp. I lose track of everything except that pleasure whirring inside me.

His mouth moves over my sex, licking and sucking and biting.

His speed picks up and my breath picks up with it. I'm panting. I tug at his hair, holding his mouth against me like I'll die if he stops.

He explores me. Soft, hard, slow, fast, zig zag, side to side, front to back. And then his tongue hits just the right spot.

I gasp. "Drew..."

There. He tries out different speeds. Different pressure. It's not enough. Then it's too much. And then it's perfect.

I dig hard into his hair. "Don't stop."

He doesn't.

He licks me right there, perfect rhythm, perfect pressure.

Every flick of his tongue pushes me higher Closer. My sex clenches. Pleasure spreads through my thighs and stomach. It's like I'm so full I'm about to tip over and spill.

It's so much to take.

Almost.

I buck against his mouth, but he holds me steady. He licks me with care and attention.

There. An orgasm rises up in me. The muscles in my sex clench. They're so tight, so desperate it hurts. And then he licks me one more time, and I fill up completely.

I come, my sex throbbing with pleasure.

He sucks on my lips, just soft enough I don't overload completely. Once I catch my breath, he nibbles on my inner thigh.

His eyes turn toward mine. "Another?"

Damn, this man is insatiable. Not that I'm complaining. I nod.

"That's not very polite."

"Pretty please."

"Better." He sucks on my inner thighs. Then my lips.

My clit.

He's not wasting any time. His tongue laps at me with hard, steady strokes. Different than before but just as good.

I'm already halfway there. I have to press my hands against the roof of the car to contain the sensation.

Drew brings a finger to my sex, teasing me with it.

Whoa.

It's a whole new sensation and I want it so badly.

No waiting, I beg. "Please."

He slides his finger inside me. My sex clenches. Drew groans into my inner thigh. He can feel my pulsing and he fucking likes it.

His tongue goes back to my clit. He slides another finger inside me, teasing at first, then going harder, like he's fucking me with his fingers.

My sex clenches. Again. Again. The pressure is intense. He licks me again, strokes me again, and it only gets tighter.

Tighter.

Tighter.

I moan. "Drew."

He goes a little harder.

"Drew."

He groans against me.

"Drew." I nearly scream it. Almost there. It's so strong I can barely stand it.

He licks me. Strokes me.

Again.

And again.

And then I'm there. The tension inside me rises to a fever pitch, so much stronger and harder and tighter than before. And then it releases.

An orgasm rocks through me. My sex pulses like it's never going to stop.

I catch my breath, shifting so I'm sitting on Drew's lap instead of his face.

He's hard.

He presses his hands against my back, brings his lips to my ear. "You have another one in you?"

Hell yes.

I nod, shifting onto my knees so I can unzip his jeans and shove them to his knees.

He runs his hand through my hair. "This'll be fast. It was torture not fucking you in that store."

"Good. I want to feel you come inside me."

"Fuck." He groans as his cock brushes against me.

I'm in a completely awkward position, not quite sitting up, not quite lying down, but I make it work. Hands on Drew's shoulders, I tease him until I can't stand it anymore. Then I shift, lowering myself onto him so he fills me.

God, that feels good.

I shift my hips, rocking against him with a steady rhythm. My attention stays on Drew, on the delicious expression in his eyes. Pleasure looks damn good on him.

He stares back at me. It's not slow today. It's fast and needy. His hands go to my ass, guiding my movements so I'm going deeper, harder.

He groans. His eyelids press together. My body is spent, but his sounds are enough to push me back to the edge. I surrender to what feels good, closing my eyes and rocking against him. His nails dig into the flesh of my ass. His teeth nip at the skin on my shoulders. His groans reverberate over my chest.

My sex clenches.

Almost.

I lean into it, holding him tighter as I move faster and deeper. It's erratic and animal and I forget about everything that isn't him inside me.

The tension builds to a fever pitch. It hurts so good. And then my sex is pulsing around him, drawing him closer. I sink my teeth into his neck as I come, groaning loudly enough for anyone on the floor to hear.

Drew sinks his fingers into my skin. He pulls me closer, rocking his hips against mine to thrust into me. I can feel his orgasm in the tensing of his chest and shoulders. I blink my eyes open to watch him come.

It's fucking beautiful. He throws his head back, his lips part to make way for a groan. His whole body shudders as he fills me.

He wraps his arms around me, resting his chin on the top of my head. We stay like that for minutes. Eventually, we get back to our clothes and Drew shifts to the driver's seat.

Chapter Twenty-Eight

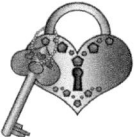

We spend half of the day in the pool, naked. The rest we spend in the living room, curled up on the couch or making food in the kitchen.

I have to devote Sunday to studying. Drew promises to give me the day for my schoolwork, and he sticks to it. He's still not home when it's time for bed. I get ready and curl up with my current reading-for-fun novel.

My eyes drift closed. Just a few minutes...

I wake up to the feeling of weight shifting on the mattress. I turn to see Drew, sitting next to me in his boxers, hands curled around a glass of water.

"Hey." He takes a long sip then hands the glass to me. "You finish?"

I nod, down half the glass, and set it on the bedside table.

"I'll give you room to study for the next two weeks." He shifts closer. "But I'm here if you need a break."

"A break?"

He smirks and lies next to me. His arm curls around my waist. He lifts himself up, so he's looking down at me.

His fingertips go to my wrist and he traces the faint scars. "These really weigh on you, huh?"

"Yeah."

His voice is low. "I know I freaked when you first told me. I wanted to protect you—"

"But there was no one to punch in the face?"

"Kendrick, don't be rude to people who are trying to open up to you." He moves closer. "I don't ever want you to hurt like that again. Not alone."

"You can't stop me from experiencing pain."

"But this—it's so much to hide. How do you manage that?"

"I'm used to it."

"You sure you're okay living like that?"

"Not forever." I shift onto my elbow. "But I'm not ready to face the kind of scrutiny I'll get when people see."

He nods like he understands. "If there's any way I can help—"

"Let me handle it. Please."

Drew turns off the lights and slides next to me. He turns me around so we're face to face. "Let's play a game. Truth or truth."

It's dark, but I can just make out his eyes.

"One question each," he says. "You can start."

I nod. I'm awake enough for one question. There's one burning a hole in my brain.

"You never want me to hurt again," I say.

"Yeah. But that's not a question."

I meet his gaze. "You're human. There must be times you hurt. Not someone you loved hurt, but you hurt."

"I hurt when the people I love hurt." He squeezes my hand. "I hurt when you hurt."

"When did you hurt because *you* hurt?"

"When Willow ran off with that asshole." His eyes turn down. "I didn't hear from her for days. I thought she was gone, forever, dead or ran away. I couldn't breathe. Couldn't think. Couldn't even play my guitar. I only went looking for her boyfriend so I could make sure he hurt as bad as I did."

I close my eyes to picture teenage Drew in a fit of rage and agony. I never saw him feel anything like that, but I can still picture it so easily.

"When else?" I ask.

"When I got my first C."

"You got a C?"

"Yeah." He shifts away like he's embarrassed. "This algorithms class in college. I studied my ass off, but it did me no good."

"But you're a rock star."

"Back then, I was just a guy who killed it on the guitar." He turns back. Makes eye contact. "Still cared what my parents thought of me. Still had this idea I'd end up some Silicon Valley programmer who only played as a hobby."

"I can't picture that."

"Me either. That's why I've been so pushy about this teaching thing. Because I know how it feels to try to fit into a life someone else made for you."

"Do you ever doubt your ability to play?"

"You already had your question. But no. Not since I was a teenager." His gaze drifts to the pillows. "That hurt. When my mom stopped talking to me."

"What happened?"

"She said that if I took a year off from school to pursue the band, that she couldn't support me. For my own good supposedly. Of course, I dared her to follow through. Dared her to stop talking to me. I figured I'd give it a couple weeks and she'd realize how wrong she was. But she never did. Six months went by and nothing. Wasn't until my sister called to tell me I wasn't invited home for Christmas that I realized there was no turning back. I fucking lost it. Cried even."

"Really?"

"Really."

"But you always act so tough not being in touch with your parents," I say.

"It's better not to think about it. I can't change her mind. Dropping out officially sealed it. She's never talking to me again."

"But you're... you make a lot of money. Don't you?"

He laughs. "I have six figures in my bank account and seven invested in mutual funds. That's rock and roll, huh, mutual funds?"

God, he says it so effortlessly. I have seven figures. I'm a millionaire. No big deal.

"Did you ever tell your mom that?"

"Nah. She wouldn't care. Willow tried for a while to change her mind, but only thing she decided was that she'd kick Willow out if the subject stayed in the conversation." He pulls me closer. "Maybe she'll forgive me one day. Maybe not. Either way, I'm not apologizing for doing what I love."

"You could see her while we're in San Francisco."

"I'm not sure that I want to," Drew says.

I nestle into his body. "I'm sorry you went through that."

"Thanks." He runs his fingertips over my shoulders.

We're quiet for a long time.

Drew shifts. He runs his fingers through my hair. "Why didn't you tell me about your cutting sooner?"

"Same reason you didn't talk to me about your ex or your family."

He tilts me so our gaze meets. He's staring at me like he's demanding an explanation.

"Because it's ugly." My gaze goes to the ceiling. "Because I was tired of people worrying about me, or looking at me like I was damaged. Because my ex-boyfriend dumped me the day after he saw those scars. But mostly because I wasn't ready to tell anyone."

It's hard to breathe.

I pull the blanket over my head. I can't think those words. Not yet.

"Let's go to bed. I'm exhausted." I shift into my pillow.

"You okay?"

"Yeah, fine. Goodnight."

"You sure?"

"Just tired." I turn and press my eyelids together.

"I'm gonna play for a while." He shifts off the bed. "Sweet dreams."

He stands in the doorway, eyes on me, for a few moments. Then he turns and he's gone.

And I'm stuck alone with the words I still can't admit.

———

We fall into a comfortable rhythm.

We have breakfast together. I go to school, study for hours in the library, come home and collapse on the couch. Drew holds me and strokes my hair and teases me mercilessly about how cute I look when I'm tired. He puts me to bed, forcing me to shower and dress and brush my teeth and making it very worth my while.

I push away my anxiety about the trip. I'm going to tell my mom and I'm going to survive it.

I'm going to let Drew help me.

I'm going to be okay.

The days of my tests are a blur. I'm in class or in the library or asleep in my bed. I walk out of my last final at two p.m. utterly exhausted. I'm about to crash on a concrete bench when I see a crowd forming on campus.

A dozen girls are milling around something. Or someone. I move closer. There's nervous shrieking laughter from the girls.

"Thank you, but I'm taken."

That's Drew.

He spots me through the girls and motions *come here*. I push past them to rush into his arms. He squeezes me tightly.

"What are you doing here?" I squeeze him back. He's warm and he smells fucking good.

"I have a surprise for you." He kisses me like he's oblivious to the crowd we're drawing. "We don't have long. We're meeting the band for karaoke tonight."

"You sing karaoke?"

"No, but for you, I might make an exception."

Chapter Twenty-Nine

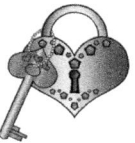

I follow Drew to his car. Thank goodness for my love of walking. If I had to deal with taking my car home before I get my arms around him, I think I'd go insane.

He opens the passenger door for me, bowing gentlemanly.

"Thank you." I offer him my hand in a ladylike gesture.

He plants a kiss on the back of my hand then turns my arm and plants a kiss on the inside of my wrist. It tickles. I giggle, kicking my feet against the seat so I won't squeal.

He catches the skin of my inner wrist between his teeth. "You're distracting me, Kendrick. It's not time for that yet.'

"Then get in. I want my surprise."

He smiles as he slides into the driver's seat. "You trust me?"

I nod. I do.

He pulls out of the parking garage, rolls the windows down, blasts The Beach Boys. The song fits the weather.

The sky is blue. The sun is shining. It's hot, especially for this time of year.

We take the curves of Sunset all the way to Pacific Coast Highway. Drew has one hand intertwined with mine, the other on the wheel. Mostly, he looks at the road. There's something about his expression when he looks at me.

Almost like he's nervous.

But that can't be possible. I've never seen him nervous.

The ocean sparkles under the bright sun. If it was a poster it would be called *Freedom* or *Serenity* or even *Paradise*.

We drive for an hour. Until we're way into Malibu, way past where Miles lives. We turn left, toward a side street. There are mansions here. All of them open onto the sand. Lucky owners live on the beach in Malibu. They probably spend two hours a day commuting but they live on the fucking sand.

Drew parks into the driveway of a two-story white-and-blue house. He pulls a keychain from the pocket of his jeans and nods to the house. "It's ours for the day."

"What?"

"I rented it." He gets out of the car and pulls an overnight bag from the backseat. "Technically, it's ours until tomorrow afternoon, though we'll probably be halfway to San Francisco by then."

"But why?"

He motions for me to follow him. We go straight to the backyard. It's enclosed by a tall gate on two sides. The last, the one that looks out on the ocean, is glass.

It's on the sand. The backyard is on the sand. There are lounge chairs and umbrellas. There's even a cabana.

He drops the overnight bag inside the cabana and pulls the curtain closed. We're as good as alone.

The air smells like salt. The waves are crashing in the distance. There's no mistaking that we're at the beach.

Drew's eyes find mine. "I brought both your swimsuits. I brought half your clothes. Enough that you can pick out what you wear." He pulls the curtain to peek out at the ocean. "There are no private beaches in Southern California. This is as close as it gets."

The beach *is* quiet. There are surfers about half a mile south, but there's no one close enough to see us in detail.

In theory, I can wear whatever the fuck I want without worrying about anyone seeing my scars.

In theory.

He kneels down to unzip the bag. "This is for you, Kara. You don't want to swim, we won't swim. You only want to swim in your clothes, then I'm going to be next to you getting my fucking jeans drenched. You want to stay right here and come on my face..." He unzips my jeans. "More than happy to oblige."

"The water must be freezing."

"Probably." He shifts back to his feet. "I got you something. Technically, it's for me, but I think you'll like it."

He pulls off his t-shirt, kicks off his shoes, and slides out of his jeans.

He's wearing a low-rise Speedo.

I fucking love it.

His eyes find mine. "What do you think?"

"I'm not sure. I can't see your ass."

He smiles and spins as if modeling for me. "Guess fair is fair. I got my show, now it's your turn."

"You call this a show?"

"I have a strip tease planned to "Hot For Teacher" but that's not until you get your credential."

My cheeks flush. That's quite the motivation.

"You brought the polka dot bikini?"

His tongue slides over his lips. In a flash he grabs it from the bag. "Yes, Ma'am."

His eyes stay on me as I strip out of my clothes. T-shirt, shoes, socks, jeans, underwear, bra. It's just me, standing in a cabana in Malibu, naked in front of him.

He looks at me like it's the first time he's seen me naked.

I take the bikini from his hands and slide it on.

"You look fucking amazing." He groans.

"You have sunscreen?"

He grabs a tube and takes his sweet, sweet time applying it to my chest, stomach, quads. Studying has kept me busy. It's been days since he's touched me properly.

I turn so he can get my back. His hands graze the top of my bikini bottoms them dip inside them. God yes.

His fingers trail up my back. "Your turn."

I take the sunscreen from Drew and apply it to every inch of exposed skin on his body—his muscular thighs, his ripped torso, his strong shoulders. I finish at his face, rubbing lotion into his cheeks and nose.

He leans down and kisses me hard. "You as desperate as I am?"

I nod. It's a good distraction.

I pull open the curtain and step into the backyard. The sun beats down on the concrete. It's bright. I look down at my thighs and trace my scars. No one is here right now. What if that changes? What if an MTV tour bus shows up the second we get in the water?

Drew's expression is soft, caring. "You ready?"

I nod. Ready as I'll ever be.

We leave the security of the backyard.

The sand is warm and rough between my toes. It's been years since I've been on a beach. I've lived in Los

Angeles four years and I've avoided the beach for every one of them.

It's about five hundred feet to the water. Still just us. We're still alone. I focus on the dark blue hue of the ocean. The way the salt and sunscreen mix into a familiar smell. The feel of the sun and the breeze on my bare skin.

Wet sand smooshes under my feet. A wave crashes and breaks. Water splashes my feet. It's cold.

I didn't come this far to back out now. I wade to my waist.

"Come on." Drew slides his arms around my waist. He pulls me under a wave with him.

Fuck. It's freezing.

I surface with a gasp. Drew's wet hair sticks to his skin His lips curl into a smile, his cheeks crinkling, his eyes lighting up.

Once again, the words form in my throat. I want to say it so badly. I want to hear it back.

But I can't.

The two weeks are up. The ball is in his court.

This might be over.

I might have to walk.

I try to push the thought out of my mind, but it won't go. Even when his arms slide around my waist. Even when his laugh rings in my ear. Even when his lips sink into mine.

This might be the last day we get together. I want to enjoy every moment I have with him, whatever this is.

After another ten minutes of swimming, I'm freezing. Not just my body but my heart.

I whisper in Drew's ear. "Let's go inside."

"Thought you'd never ask."

It's amazing how easy it is to forget all about your scar-induced anxiety when your stomach is in knots and your throat is ragged.

The beach is empty as we run back to the house. Drew leads me into three different rooms before he finds the master bathroom. It's huge—marble tile, wide glass shower, windows letting in the late afternoon light.

He slides his hands around my ass and presses me against the wall, sucking on my lower lip. He pushes my bikini bottoms to my knees. They fall to my feet with a wet thud.

His hands go right between my legs. No waiting, no teasing, he slides his fingers over my clit. It's too wet for proper friction. I grab a towel from the rack and wipe my skin and his hands.

"How long has it been?" he reaches around to unhook my bikini top.

"About five days?"

"Worst five days of my life." He pulls the bikini top off my shoulders. His eyes go wide. "How the fuck am I going to be away from you all May?"

"And most of April and June."

"Don't remind me."

He presses his fingers to my clit. There's enough friction now to send heat through my body. I press my lids together. I want to feel this moment, not a vague sense of dread over how wrong this might go.

"Come on." He presses his hand into my lower back.

I open my eyes and follow him into the shower. He slides off his swimsuit and kicks it aside. He's already hard.

My breath hitches.

He turns the water on, holding his hand under the showerhead to test the temperature. He wraps his hand around it and pulls it away from the wall.

It's detachable.

His eyes meet mine. He smiles mischievously. "I always wanted to try this." He slides his arm around my waist and pulls my body into his.

Our lips connect in a wet, messy kiss. My feelings rise up in my throat. They want out. They want into the space, into his ears, but it's not happening. Not verbally.

Instead, I channel my feelings into my kiss. Into the way my hips shift against him. He brings the faucet over our heads. It rains down with a steady stream, making our bodies slick and frictionless.

He moves me toward the wall and turns me around so my back is pressed against his chest.

Drew sinks his teeth into my neck. My earlobe. My shoulder. He toys with my nipples until I'm panting.

I'm still thinking.

I don't want to be thinking.

I bring my hand behind my back and rake it over his torso. Lower and lower until it's wrapped around his cock. I pump him with steady strokes.

"Kara." His nails sink into my hip. He lifts my leg, positioning me so his cock brushes against my sex.

I arch my back so he enters me.

A gasp escapes my lips. His low groan echoes against the glass walls.

He brings the showerhead over my chest. Then my stomach. Then beneath it.

The water streams over my clit. It's light and warm, a soft pressure. Not enough to consume my thoughts.

"More." I arch to take him deeper.

Drew groans as he thrusts into me. He moves the showerhead closer. Closer.

There.

"Yes," I breathe. "Fuck me."

"Put your hands on the wall so you can keep your balance."

I press my hands against the wall. It's rough concrete, easy to grip.

With one hand, Drew points the showerhead at my clit. The stream of water hits me with a warm, steady pressure. It's different than his hand or his tongue or even a vibrator. More intense, wetter, warmer.

My sex clenches. I arch my back as if to beckon him to fuck me, but he stays put.

His other arm holds my body against his at the chest, angled so his fingers brush against my nipple. He toys with me, teasing me, pinching me.

It feels good, but I'm not getting there. Those damn words are in my throat. Those damn words are ruining this.

I whisper them as softly as I can. *I love you.*

There.

The damn words are in the space. Too quiet for him to hear over the water, but at least they're not trying to suffocate me anymore.

He brings his mouth to my ear. "Shower's not working for you?"

I'm close to an orgasm but it doesn't feel good. Not the way it's supposed to.

Drew pulls out. He turns me around and stares into my eyes. I swallow hard. I can't stand the intensity of it.

"Come on." He returns the showerhead to its usual spot, pulls me out of the shower, and then towel-dries me himself.

I follow him to a plush, king-sized bed. Drew lifts me by the ass and throws me onto the bed. He climbs on after me and pins my knees to the bed.

He plants kisses up my inner thighs. Then his mouth is

on me, licking and sucking and biting like he's desperate to feel my release.

What if this is the last time? It can't be like this.

I take a deep breath, trying to clear my head. Drew is eating me out. It's good as ever. I should be enjoying it.

I focus on the feeling of his soft, wet tongue. I bring my hands to the back of his head, to lead him to the right spot. It's better. A few more licks and pleasure spreads through me. Not as intense as normal, but enough to command my attention.

He groans into my thigh between his movements. That sound feels better than anything else his mouth can do. As long as I'm stuck with the weight of these damn feelings, I need to focus on something besides my release.

His.

I tug at Drew's hair. "I want to try something."

"Anything." He groans into my thigh.

"Sixty-nine. I've never done it before."

He pokes his head up to look at me. "Fuck yeah. Might take some adjusting." He presses his lips to my stomach. "With our height difference."

He kisses his way to my chest. My neck. My lips. I kiss him harder, plunging my tongue into his mouth. I need this kind of intensity. I need to be in control of something, because I'm sure as shit not in control of my feelings.

I release him. "I want on top."

"Yes Ma'am." He brings his body next to mine, propping his head and neck up with a few pillows. He pats his shoulders. "Knees here."

I turn my body and plant my knees near his shoulders. His hands go to my hips and he pulls me onto his mouth. His tongue plunges inside me. He's not wasting any time.

I have an amazing view of his body, from his chest to his toes. I spend a long moment taking it in. The details pull me back into the moment. I trace the lines of his chest piece. The lines of his stomach. I shift lower, wrapping my hands around his cock.

It takes a few tries to get into position. I brush my lips against his cock, teasing him until his nails sink into my hips. I'm merciless. I flick my tongue against his tip again and again, until he groans against me.

Yes. That's what I need. I take him into my mouth and slide my tongue around him. He gets more aggressive with his movements, licking harder, sliding two fingers into my sex and rubbing against my g-spot. I respond with equal enthusiasm, sucking hard, taking him as deep as I can.

There's something amazing about the position, giving and receiving at once. He's making me feel good, and I'm making him feel good. It's like an endless cycle of pleasure, better and better and better.

I love the feel of him in my mouth. The taste. The way his thighs shudder and his nails sink into my skin.

He moves faster. Harder. An orgasm rises up inside me. This time, it's not just pressure. It's pleasure too. We're so good together here. It's possible we can be good together when our clothes are on.

I suck as hard as I can. I dig my fingers into his thighs. I moan against him.

The next flick of his tongue sends me over the edge. My sex pulses as I come. It's intense, unrelenting. I channel the feelings into my movements.

Drew groans into my thigh. He grabs my hips, shifting me. "I want to come inside you."

I flick my tongue against him one more time, then shift. I don't give Drew time to get on top. I turn around, plant my knees outside his hips, and bring my body onto his.

His cock slides inside me. I'm already throbbing. The

depth is intense. But I'm in control of this. I rock my hips, riding him.

He grabs onto my hips, thrusting into me with the same rhythm.

"You're so fucking sexy." He stares up at me like he's lost in how much he loves my body.

I move faster. Until I'm out of breath. Until my thighs are burning.

Drew's groans spur me on. Pleasure spills into his expression. His eyes close. His teeth sink into his lips.

"Fuck, Kara." He digs his nails into my skin. "I'm gonna come."

He thrusts violently, forcefully. I press my hands against his chest, widening my knees so he can go deeper.

And then he's there, his thighs shaking, his stomach tightening, his cock pulsing inside me as he comes.

I collapse onto his chest and hold him as close as I can.

No thinking.

No feeling.

Just his body against mine.

Chapter Thirty

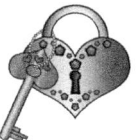

We drive to a luxe karaoke joint in Korea Town. The place is lit in soft shades of blue and gold. A twenty-something dude in a button-up black shirt points us to a room at the end of a long hallway. He doesn't look at us funny, like it's strange a rock band is congregating in a private karaoke room.

Not strange at all.

Drew runs his hands over my inner thighs. He takes his time to trace three of my scars. It's careful, like he finds them fascinating instead of off-putting, like they only make him want me more.

It's funny. When I'm with him, I forget all about the scars.

I'm not a poor, damaged girl. Maybe a girl driven mad with lust and some other l-word she can't admit.

But not poor, damaged Kara.

He removes his hand, tragically, to push the door open. Meg jumps to her feet and rushes to me.

"Thank God. I thought I'd have to hear Tom and Pete

do another duet." She throws her arms around me. "Your brain working yet?"

"If I never see another Scantron again, it will be way too soon."

"Ditto." She turns to Miles. "Only one more quarter of college."

"And then four years of med school," he says.

"You're no fun." She sticks her tongue out at him then looks to me. "Miles refuses to sing, which means—" She points to Pete and Tom and shakes her head.

"You don't sing?" I ask.

"Not for free." He turns to Meg. "Except maybe for you, babe."

"Uh-huh."

"But it wouldn't be fair to get you dripping wet then make you wait all night to fuck me." He slaps her ass. "Now would it?"

"I could live with it," Meg says.

He picks her up and spins her. They fall onto the couch, Meg landing perfectly in Miles's lap.

Tom flips through the karaoke book. He points something out to Pete. They share a look of glee.

And then Pete nods. "Okay, okay. I'm more than happy to rise to this particular occasion." He winks at me and Meg. "And many others."

"He and the girlfriend are on a break," Tom says.

"Why don't you shut the fuck up," Pete says.

"Tom, why are you so obsessed with other people's relationships?" Meg asks. "Like first you pulled that shit with me and Miles. And now you're meddling with Pete. And I'm sure you—" She looks at me, then clears her throat like she didn't say anything. "You're a manwhore. What do you care if other people are settling down?"

"I want what's best for my friends," Tom says.

"Yeah, what you think is best," Meg says.

Miles pulls her closer. "Babe, Tom is as stubborn as you are. This is not an argument you're gonna settle." He kisses her neck. "How about you let him work himself into a fit?"

"You happy with how things turned out or not?" Tom asks.

She nods like he has a point. I guess he does. Whatever Tom did to fuck things up between Meg and Miles, they're happy now. They're gooey, madly in love.

Tom opens a bottle of whiskey and pours shots for everyone except Miles. He passes them around the table. Each slides, smoothly stopping near the intended shot taker.

It's impressive, really.

Meg pushes hers back. "I'm not drinking."

"It's not like your pussy is going to get Miles tipsy." Tom slides the shot back to her. "You gotta celebrate properly."

"Haven't you heard of solidarity?" she asks.

"Heard? I spent an entire tour sober because of your boyfriend and spent another tour celibate because of her—" He points at Drew. "Because."

Meg shakes her head. "You fucked like eighteen girls in Japan alone. No way you spent more than three days celibate."

"He did," Pete says. "Shocked us all."

Tom looks to Meg. "You drinking or not?"

"I don't need my girlfriend dry." Miles smirks.

Just in case we all missed his double entendre, he slides his hands up her thighs. She groans like she can hardly pull herself off him. Thankfully, she manages.

"Okay." She holds up her shot as a toast. "To our last quarter of college!"

I hold up my drink. And then, all at once, we all—well,

everyone but Miles—slam our shots. It burns my throat, but there's a certain pleasant richness to the whiskey.

Pete taps something into the karaoke machine. "If you'll excuse me."

The name of the band and song flashes onscreen. "No Way in Hell" - Sinful Serenade.

Miles groans in agony. "You're so bad at doing me."

Pete clears his throat. He rises to his feet then stands on the table in his best Miles impersonation. "Hey baby." He scans the imaginary crowd, landing on Miles. "This one is for you."

He blows a kiss.

The song starts. Pete does his best imitation of Miles's breathy, throaty singing. He's way off-key, but he brings the energy.

The song gets to the guitar solo—a polyphonic version of it. Pete scans his audience. He blows us all kisses.

"It's just, ugh, I hurt so bad deep inside that I can't even bear to wear a shirt. There's too much paiiiiiiiiiin in my chest." He plops his mic into one hand, pulls his shirt over his head, and tosses it to the ground. "That's better."

Tom and Drew crack up.

Miles pouts and crosses his arms over his chest. "I am not like that."

Pete claws at his chest. "Yeah, baby, look at my hot tattoos."

Meg stifles a laugh.

He growls. "Oh, you think this is funny?"

"Hilarious." She paws at him.

The verse picks up. Pete ups the breathy factor of his singing, stopping every syllable and a half to grunt into the mic.

It *is* hilarious. I fall onto the couch next to Drew and revel in the imitation. It's quite the performance.

When the song ends, Miles is beet red and everyone else is dying of laughter.

Tom taps something into the karaoke machine.

Another Sinful Serenade song.

He grabs the mic and blows Miles a kiss. "This is too much fun."

"Don't make me leave," Miles says.

"Check the book." Pete motions to the book of songs by artist. "We've got about six more to go."

"You can't leave." Meg draws a line over his chest. "I need you to serenade me."

"My impressionists aren't getting you there?"

She shakes her head. "Only the real thing will do."

The song intro plays. Tom grabs the other mic and jumps onto the table next to Pete. "This one is going out to my biggest fans, Mr. Miles Webb and Mr. Drew Denton."

The song is a ballad, very much about love and affection. Pete and Tom take turns singing one line at a time in their best throaty, breathy voices.

Miles is red and huffy. Meg whispers something in his ear. It must be pretty good because his frown turns upside down.

Drew moves a little closer. He runs his fingers over my lower back. We're positioned across from everyone. No one can see him touching me.

How can he still be so hot and cold?

Is he ashamed to be with me?

I shake off the thought in favor of watching the performance. The song ends. Pete collapses on the couch in hysterical laughter. Tom pours another round of shots and passes them out.

Everyone except Miles drinks.

That shit burns.

My head spins just enough to make me dizzy. I hang

back while everyone takes turns singing. Tom serenades us with a Disney song. Pete performs some Aerosmith. Meg does her best Britney Spears.

When it's Miles's turn, he shakes his head but obliges. He pulls Meg onto his lap and he sings "I Want Your Sex" while staring into her eyes. She blushes like a tomato.

Everyone else groans.

Then it's my turn, supposedly. I shake my head. "I don't sing."

There must be a song that goes something like, *What the hell are we doing, why are you afraid of the word "girlfriend?"*

It doesn't really have a good ring to it, but it's an honest sentiment.

Drew nudges me. "You sing very well."

"Um, no, you sing very well," I say.

Tom laughs. "Drew doesn't sing. He won't even sing backup."

I fold my arms over my chest. "Shows what you know."

"Damn, I guess there are certain perks to—" Tom clears his throat. "Whatever you two are."

Drew shoots Tom a death glare. I sigh. Whatever. Been there, done that, couldn't find a song to describe it accurately.

I grab the mic and pick my favorite No Doubt song, "Don't Speak." I'm way off-key, but I do my best to sell the enthusiasm.

I stare at Drew as I sing. He watches me closely, like he's looking for some meaning in my eyes. Truth is, I don't know what I'm thinking except *Your two weeks are over. Time to put up or shut up.*

After I finish the song, I do a little bow and set the mic back on the table. Drew pats the spot next to him, inviting me to sit with him.

I make eye contact. "Can I talk to you outside?"

"Is it important?"

I bite my lip. "Tom, repeat that last thing you said."

"What thing?" He plays dumb.

I shoot Tom a death glare.

He shakes his head like he finds it a bad idea. "This is not the time, kid."

"Kara, what are you doing?" Drew asks.

I shake my head. 'How about another round of shots?'

"That I can do." Tom passes out another round of shots. One for everyone but Miles. "Anything more, and I suggest you actually take it outside."

I slam my shot back. Beautiful liquid courage. No more shyness. I slide onto Drew's lap and kiss him.

My chest heaves against his.

He kisses me back for a second. Then he's pushing me away, pushing me off, staring at me with this look that says *What the fuck?*

Behind me, someone clears his throat. Someone else.

Drew just stares at me.

All this hurt in his eyes.

Like I've betrayed his secret.

I slide off his lap and plant my ass on the bench seat. My arms fold over my chest. Everyone is staring at me. At us.

Pete breaks the silence. "Am I really the only one with the balls to say something?"

"You're going to make it worse," Tom says.

"How could it get worse?" Pete looks at me. "Drew good in bed?"

"Yeah," I reply.

"As good with his hands as he always says?" Pete asks.

"Better."

Drew snaps at no one in particular. "What are you doing?"

Pete waves him away. "The better question is what are *you* doing?"

Meg looks to me. *Are you okay?* I nod. I'm not, but I need to hear this.

"I'm not even going to ask if you're with Kara, because we all know you are." Pete takes his shot. He stares at Drew. "And I'm not going to ask if you're in love with her, because we all know you are."

The room is dead silent.

"What the fuck is wrong with you?" Pete asks. "Why are you trying so hard to throw away the only person you've been able to tolerate in years?"

Drew takes his shot, like that will somehow absolve him of answering the question.

Tom shakes his head. "Jesus, fuck this. Drew, answer the fucking question. Your girlfriend is about to cry. Are you fucking stupid or just desperate to be as miserable as possible?"

Drew scowls.

Tom shakes his head. "I'll give you five seconds. Five, four, three—"

Drew presses his palms into the seat.

"Two, one."

Nothing.

"Fuck me." Tom sighs like he's about to commit ritual suicide. He pushes off his seat. It's fast, a flash, and he grabs me and kisses me.

Tom is kissing me.

What the hell?

And then he's not. And there's this loud thud of flesh pounding into flesh. And a scream. Meg's scream.

Someone lands on the floor. Tom. And Drew is standing there shaking his fist, his expression the picture of embarrassment.

Drew punched Tom.

"I told you not to touch her." Drew's eyes turn to the floor, like he's confused by his reaction.

He turns. His eyes catch mine. It's a split second and then he pushes past me. Pushes out the door.

And he's gone.

Chapter Thirty-One

Three splashes of cool water on my face and I'm still this awful mix of hot and cold. There are two other girls in this little bathroom. They teeter over the sink with their stripper heels, adding another round of lipstick to their already made-up lips.

One of them, the younger, blonder one, looks at me with pity in her eyes.

"Boy troubles?" she pouts.

Can't blame her for asking. Mascara is running down my cheeks. Eyeliner smudged beyond meaningful description. My lipstick isn't doing much better.

I grab a paper towel and wipe my face as clean as I can. "I'm fine, thanks." The most obvious lie in the history of lies, but it's not like blondie cares.

I hide out in the handicapped stall, resting my ass against the metal bar. There's a plentiful supply of toilet paper for wiping the smudged makeup from my eyes. I can't see it, but I'm sure it still looks like shit.

The main door open and all the noise—half a dozen

different songs being sung off key—fills the room. The party girls teeter out and someone else comes in.

"Kara."

It's Meg.

She knocks on the stall door. "You want to talk about this?"

"Not really, no."

"You want to get blind drunk?"

It's a tempting offer. Certainly would help me forget that word that starts with a D and rhymes with screw.

But it will feel worse in the morning.

"No thank you," I say. "If it's all right with you, I'd like to find some way to disappear and never have to think about him again." I toss a mascara-stained piece of toilet paper into the trash can. "I'll take a cab... somewhere."

"You can spend the night at my place," she says. "Or we can go to the Malibu pad. Plenty of room and Miles always has a fridge full of food."

"No Miles right now," I say. "Your boyfriend is nice and all, but—"

"I get it." She taps the door. "Want to open up?"

"Not really, no."

"I've got your purse. We can leave right now and call a cab. You don't have to talk to anyone but me."

I go to open the door. "You swear no one else is in here?"

"On my love of sashimi."

A tiny laugh breaks up the tension in my throat. So it's possible to feel something good besides the desperate need Drew stirs inside me. That's a start.

I open the door. Meg steps inside. She squeezes me with a very tight hug.

"I blame myself," she says. "If I hadn't been in relationship land, you wouldn't be forced to spend so much time with Drew."

"Yeah, I really dreaded all that time with him." I tear a piece of toilet paper in half. "It was all awful. Not like I was desperate to be around him constantly."

"Still. I haven't been around as much as I should be. You've always been the world's best friend." She steps back and looks me in the eyes sympathetically. "I'm sorry. This sucks."

"You can say that again."

"This sucks."

I laugh and cry at the same time. "I was doomed from the start. He's so..."

"Oh, yeah, he's so... possessive and overprotective and unable to communicate."

"And caring."

"I'll take your word on it."

"And hot as the sun."

"Can't object to that one." She grabs a few sheets of toilet paper and wipes the messy makeup from my eyes. "I think I made it worse."

"Eyeliner was never your strong suit."

She leans down as if she's examining my face. "You want me to make sure Tom gets another black eye?"

"He was trying to help."

"Funny way of doing it."

"Same plan as you," I say. "Make Drew jealous. Pray that gets him talking."

"It worked a lot better when I did it."

"Yeah. He said he wanted to try."

She points me to the mirror. My makeup is mostly tamed. Still messy but not *I've been crying over my not-boyfriend in the bathroom* messy.

Meg hands me my purse. "We can sneak out now."

"Please."

Fuck my life. Tom is sitting in the lounge, checking his black eye with his cell phone camera.

And of course, Miles and Pete are next to him. An audience. Just what I need to shred whatever is left of my dignity.

Everyone looks at me like I am a poor, unfortunate creature. *Poor, damaged Kara. What can we do to help her?*

As crazy as Drew drives me, he never looks at me like I might break.

Meg points her finger at Tom. "If I don't hear an explanation or an apology in the next thirty seconds, I'm going to disembowel you with one of your drumsticks."

"How the hell would you?" He shakes his head. "Don't tell me. I'll have nightmares."

"You have about twenty seconds left," she says.

"Babe, I like this side of you but, maybe give him a chance to explain," Miles says.

"Forget it. Kara and I are going home by ourselves. We have had enough Sinful trouble for the night," she says.

Tom looks to Pete. "You think we'll ever find another guitarist as good as Drew?"

"No." Pete shakes his head. "Better hope he forgives you."

"Fuck that asshole. He better hope I forgive *him*." Tom's attention turns to me. "You all right?"

"Not really," I say.

Tom frowns. "He'll come around."

Pete stares at Tom with incredulity. "You wanted to help Kara."

"No way," Tom says. "Just don't like seeing women get jerked around."

Pete's jaw drops. "You cared more about her feelings than about the band. This has never happened."

Miles nods. "Never."

Tom looks away like he's embarrassed.

"I appreciate the sentiment," I say. "But please don't help me anymore."

Miles waves Tom away. He looks at Meg. "You need a cab?"

"I've got it." She kisses him goodbye. "If you do kill Tom, call me. I want to hear him scream for mercy."

———

THE CAB RIDE TO MEG'S PLACE IS FAST AND MERCIFULLY silent. Her building still smells vaguely like sushi, but hey, there's no one here to interrogate me or kiss me or drive me out of my damn mind.

I look to the bed and its soft, inviting comforter. "Are your sheets clean?"

"Changed them this morning."

I flop onto the mattress with a tiny thud. Not as soft as it looks.

Meg sits next to me. She pokes my shoulder. When I roll over, she points to a can of green tea like it's supposed to tempt me. Fine. I take it and pop the top open.

"You hungry?" she asks.

"No."

"I have Frosted Flakes."

"I'm not a monster."

She gets up, pours a bowl of cereal, and hands it to me.

"I sent Miles to your place," she says. "To get your stuff, tell Drew he's an asshole. That kind of thing."

"I doubt he's there." I crunch my cereal loudly. "Probably driving around trying to think because it's just so hard for him." I focus my attention on my snack. "Are Miles and Drew close?"

"As far as I can tell." She steals a flake. "But I don't have any intel. I don't think Drew talks to anyone except you."

"It doesn't matter." I make eye contact with Meg. "Drew and I are supposed to drive to the bay tomorrow."

"Not on my watch, sweet pea. I'll drive you before I let you do that."

"I'll manage."

"Screw that. If our roles were reversed, you'd drive me to the airport and watch while I went through security. You're such a good friend, Kara. Way better than what Drew deserves. I don't care how awful his ex was. I don't care how massive his cock is or how good he is with his hands. You deserve better than the shit he pulled tonight."

She's right. But it doesn't do anything to change the way I feel about him.

"I know that look."

"Yeah?" I ask.

"Only thing you want is for him to realize he's an asshole and try to make it up to you."

I nod.

Her phone buzzes. She looks at the screen, her brow furrowing.

"What?"

"Tom bought you a ticket from LAX to SFO. For tomorrow afternoon. It's first class."

"What's the catch?"

"He wants to take you to the airport." She stares at her phone like she's looking for some hidden meaning. "He didn't phrase it like an offer."

There goes any potential that this won't be hanging over my head all week. A first-class ticket is a decent way to travel. If things weren't all fucked, I'd prefer being in the car with Drew, even for eight hours.

But they are fucked.

First class is worth thirty minutes in Tom's car.

"Okay," I say. "What time?"

"Two. He'll pick you up at noon and buy you lunch. There's nothing to eat here and Miles and I are leaving first thing for Hawaii." She presses her fingers into her phone. "Unless... we can go in a few days."

"No way. You're not delaying your trip for me. I'll feel a million times worse."

"You sure? You'd probably do it for me."

"Not if Drew looked at me the way Miles looks at you."

"He does. He's just stupid. Miles is stupid too. It takes guys time to pull their heads out of their asses. Especially when they're used to being idolized."

"I want to leave tomorrow." I leave the cereal on Meg's desk. Then it's back to the bed that's not quite as soft as it looks. "I need to see my mom and get this whole telling her I'm not working for her company thing over with."

She looks down at her phone. "You want anything specific in your suitcase?"

"A coat, I guess. It's probably fifty degrees in San Francisco."

"Condoms?"

"Why would you ask that?"

"Miles asked." She squints. "Why did he ask?" She taps a reply. A moment later she's laughing and shaking her head. "That's how you know an ex-player."

"Yeah?"

"He says the best way to get over someone is to get under someone else "

"He's probably right."

"I'll tell him you'd rather be on top." She taps a reply. "He says Pete could use the rebound fuck. But you need to be *really* into dirty talk."

"Is he serious?"

She looks closely at the phone. "I'm ninety percent sure he's not. Pete's pretty cute. Has that dark hair. Also good with his hands—"

"Are *you* serious?"

She shakes her head. "Do you want the condoms?"

"I want Drew."

She taps a reply and tosses her phone on her desk. "How about an action movie to drown your thoughts?"

"One with really loud explosions, please."

Chapter Thirty-Two

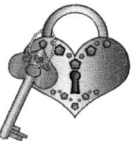

I wake up to the sound of my cell phone alarm. According to the clock, it's eleven thirty. There's a key on the desk and a note under it.

Kara,

Feel free to stay as long as you want if you decide to bail on the flight. Lock up when you leave.

Call me if you need to talk. Anytime. I'll keep my phone on all night every night.

Love you,

Meg

My suitcase is sitting next to the door. I find a change of clothes in it. I shower, brush my teeth, get dressed.

I gather my stuff together and wait for Tom on the curb. There are fifteen minutes until noon. I occupy the time by making a playlist of breakup songs angry enough to fit my mood. "You Oughta Know," "These Boots Were Made for Walking," "I Hate Myself For Loving You." I'm up to thirty-five songs when a loud voice grabs my attention.

"You're gonna get mugged staring at your phone like

that." Tom is leaning against the door of a red sports car convertible, sunglasses covering his black eye.

It's a nice car. A few years old. Flashy but well built. Very Tom.

He's holding two Starbucks cups. He offers one to me. "Earl Grey, right?"

I nod and take the drink. It's a little oversteeped but still better than anything else I've felt all day.

He pops the trunk of the car and tosses my suitcase inside. "I brought you a sandwich. In case you're not willing to sit down for lunch."

"What kind of sandwich?"

"Caprese."

"I'll take it."

He examines my expression. "All right. Get in." He opens the passenger door for me then slides into the driver's seat.

I buckle my seatbelt and focus my attention on my tea. I need the energy.

Tom turns on the car. "Shoulda started with 'I'm sorry about all this.'"

"Thanks." I find the paper bag-wrapped sandwich sitting in a cup holder. It smells good. "Can we put the top up?"

"Yeah.

He pushes a button. With a whir, the convertible roof slides over us, blocking out the rest of the world.

Now, I'm only one person's pity project. It's almost tolerable.

Tom slips his drink into the cup holder. "Drew asked me to make sure you got to San Francisco okay."

"You already bought me a ticket. You don't have to act as my chaperone."

"Yeah, but what if you suddenly realize you're over him

and you're desperate for rebound sex? I'd hate to miss that chance."

"Tom, are you flirting with me?"

"A little." He winks. "It could be our secret.'

"Really?"

He shakes his head. "No. I respect you too much to rebound-fuck you."

"Is that a compliment or an insult?"

"A compliment."

I unwrap the sandwich and take a bite. It's good. Fresh, thick tomatoes, crisp basil, soft mozzarella. "I guess it's not good for the band if Drew is in jail."

"Fuck Drew." He shrugs. "You probably want to fuck Drew. He must be pretty good for you to put up with so much shit."

My cheeks flush. 'He is. But that's not why I like him."

"Why do you like him? He's an asshole."

"Not as much as you are."

He pulls onto the freeway. "About as much."

"He makes me laugh. He's sweet. Pushy but sweet. I can be myself with him. Or I could... I thought I could trust him with anything. I thought a lot of things."

"Don't talk like that. He's mad for you Not that he deserves you. Or anyone with such great tits."

"Uh... thanks?"

"He's happy when he's around you."

"How is the black eye doing? The one Drew gave you because he was so *happy* around me."

"Good." He takes off the sunglasses and turns to me. "Makes me look tough."

It does. I turn my attention back to the sandwich. I haven't eaten any real food since last night.

"He's in love with you, Kara. It's obvious to everyone but him. And maybe you."

I examine Tom's expression. He can't believe that. If Drew was in love with me, he wouldn't run away.

Tom makes eye contact. "Drew's a fucking idiot. But that move we pulled, I pulled, that wasn't gonna help shit. Drew hates attention. And after everything with Vivian—"

"Was it really that bad?"

"Worse. You should have seen the shit Pete gave him after that. Fucker is such a romantic. Couldn't deal with Drew pinning the whole thing on relationships sucking ass. They got into these stupid fights. And everybody on that tour—not just me—everybody kept one eye on Drew. It drove him batshit."

"He drives himself batshit."

"I'm not making excuses for him. If you don't think he deserves a chance to apologize, then fuck him. I'll find you a nice boy toy to help you get over it."

"No thanks."

"But there's no doubt in my mind that he loves you."

"What the fuck do you know about love?"

"Everybody can see it. The way he looks at you. He's fucking crazy about you. And you love him too, right?"

I finish my sandwich.

"Okay. Not my business." Tom's voice softens. "I know you asked me to stop helping, but I lined up a show in San Francisco. It's Wednesday night. We have a stand-in for Miles—"

"Don't you have a manager to do this stuff for you?"

"Aidan? I tried to get him fired when he wouldn't stop offering Miles coke, but he's some VIP's nephew. I only let him do any actual managing if it's strictly necessary."

"You did that for Miles?"

"I did it 'cause I fucking hate Aidan."

"You did it for Miles."

Tom runs his hand through his hair like he's embarrassed.

"Drew was right. You care more than you let on."

"Drew said that?"

"Yeah."

Tom crushes his empty cup and shoves it into his seat-back pocket. 'Come to the show. If he doesn't make this up to you, I'll buy you a trip anywhere you want. All expenses paid. Eat, drink, and fuck strange men until you're over it. You can leave the second the show ends. Go to Japan or Ireland or the Bahamas on my dime."

"Maybe."

"Just do me one favor."

"Yeah?"

"Make him earn it."

Chapter Thirty-Three

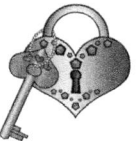

First class is nice—big seats, soft blankets, overly friendly flight attendants who constantly push the free champagne. I say no every time. I need my head clear and staring at the puffy white clouds outside the window is helping.

After we land, I kill time at the airport. Damn San Francisco. My salad and smoothie snack sets me back twenty dollars. When there's no excuse left to stay at the terminal, I take the BART into the city and take a bus into Richmond.

My mom's place is a few blocks off the line. My suitcase hits every crack in the sidewalk, every pebble, every curb. She's working late tonight. After all, I'm supposed to arrive by car at some time well into the evening.

That leaves a solid three or four hours to work up the courage to tell my mom I'm not joining her company.

One more block. The sky is blue and bright. It's warm. It's like the city is mocking me. The second I feel like shit, the weather is nice. Where's the grey, cloudy, rainy place that had my feet wet every other day in high school?

There's someone sitting on the stoop we share with our next-door neighbor. Tall. Dark hair. Jeans and a wrinkled t-shirt. Black Converse.

No.

One more step and it's clear.

That's Drew sitting on my stoop. He has bags under his eyes and an overgrown five o'clock shadow. His skin is pale. His posture is hunched.

I come closer until I'm about three feet away.

He looks up at me. There's so much in his eyes. It makes my knees weak.

I dig my fingers into my suitcase handle. "Have you slept?"

"No." His voice is steady. "I have to talk to you."

"Where the fuck have you been?"

"Driving. Thought it would help me think. Once I hit San Luis Obispo, figured I might as well keep going. Tom get you here okay?"

"First class."

"Good."

I stare at him, trying to figure out what I can possibly say. The rubber soles of my shoes squeak against the concrete as I shift my weight. He looks like he's about to break and the only thing I want to do is wrap my arms around him and promise it will be okay.

Maybe it's better to do it quickly, like a Band-Aid. It hurts for a moment, then it's over.

"Can I buy you a cup of coffee or something?" He pushes himself to his feet. "I have some stuff I want to say to you."

"I don't think that's a good idea."

"Kara."

My eyes go to the concrete. I can't leave things like this. At the very least, I need to get my feelings off my chest.

"Want to tell me what you're thinking?" he asks.

I meet his gaze. "That there's no way the 'stuff' you have to say is enough." I walk past him to climb the steps.

He grabs my suitcase from my hands and carries it for me.

God, the look on his face is so desperate. He feels as shitty as I do. That's something.

"If you need time, I'll come back." His fingertips brush my shoulder. "I have nowhere else I want to be."

I shake my head.

"I can bring an acoustic guitar."

My neck tightens. There's too much swirling around my brain.

"I can't talk to you right now." I find my keys in my purse. "You embarrassed me in front of your friends. Our friends. You made me into the band's pity project."

I unlock the door and step inside.

He's still standing there, his eyes filled with pain. "I'm sorry."

"Go home, Drew."

My hands are shaking as I close and lock the door. I want so badly to open it. I want to talk to him. I want to drag him onto that couch and fuck him until I finally feel something good.

But I can't. Not yet. Not until I've made sense of my thoughts.

Chapter Thirty-Four

I spend thirty minutes in the shower with the water as loud, hot, and heavy as possible. My body is achy and exhausted.

After, I change into an outfit from my dresser and bury myself under the covers. Sleep doesn't come. It's late afternoon, still light out.

I go to the window to shut the blinds.

He's still there, sitting on the stoop with slumped posture.

There goes any chance of slumber.

I make my way downstairs. I'm going to open the door and ask him to leave. I'm not going to give in to how badly I want to wipe the misery from his expression with my lips.

Here goes nothing.

I open the door. He stands, turns to me. He's standing on the bottom step. For once, he's shorter.

Drew looks up at me. "I'm not leaving until I talk to you."

"What good could that possibly accomplish?"

"I…" He runs his hand through his hair. Shakes his

head like he's shaking away his thoughts. "Fine. Don't talk to me. I'm a fucking asshole for bailing last night, and I know I can't ever apologize enough. But I have to make sure you get through telling your mom okay."

"I've got it under control."

"Kara."

I step back inside. I can't be in here, not knowing he's on the other side with that look of unspeakable agony on his face. I find my purse, sling it over my shoulder, and step onto the stoop.

He's close enough that my body perks. It wants to feel good and it knows he can deliver. Not today, no matter how much better I'd feel if we were using our mouths for something besides conversation.

I lock the door and slide my key into my purse. I stare at him, at all the pain in his eyes. Is he really that desperate to talk to me? Do I really mean that much to him?

It's hard to believe, given how quickly he ran away last night.

He stares back. "I'm sorry. It's not that I don't feel that way about you. I panicked."

"Go home, Drew. I'll call you when I'm ready to talk to you." I push past him, onto the sidewalk, and I don't look back.

I walk around the neighborhood until I'm hungry enough for dinner. My phone buzzes a dozen times. I ignore it.

The sun sets with a streak of orange. The temperature cools. Clouds form, bringing that on and off drizzle I know all too well.

Figures the city waits until I'm wearing canvas sneakers and a cotton sweater to rain.

The rain isn't too bad. By the time I'm at my block, I'm wet but not drenched.

Drew's still here, sitting on the porch.

He's soaking wet.

"You found a way to get your shower in." I push past him to go for the door. "Congrats."

He grabs my wrist. "Tell me how to make this up to you."

"I'm done begging you to love me." I unlock the door and push it open. "Go home."

"You are my home, Kara. Wherever you are, that's home."

Fuck him and his sweet voice and the pain in his eyes and how pathetic he looks dripping wet. I'm too empathetic.

Drew deserves to wait, but I can't put myself through that.

"Fine. Come in." I unlock the door.

Drew follows me inside.

I keep myself busy in the kitchen. The house is clean but not overly so. There are dishes in the sink. The pantry and fridge are stocked. Mom is eating. Cooking even.

Drew's footsteps are behind me. They still make my heart race. I turn back to him. Suddenly, I see the house in a whole new light. A wall he can press me against. A table just the right height. A couch I can use to mount him.

His eyes meet mine. "You want me to do it?"

God yes. I clear my throat. "Do what?"

"Make coffee." He motions to the coffee maker then to the couch. "Sit down. I'll fix yours with extra cream and sugar."

I take a seat at the far end of the couch and play with

the fabric of my jeans to keep my thoughts from drifting to the gutter. How can my body be so utterly against me? It doesn't help that my heart is so fucking devoted to him.

He stays in the kitchen until the coffee's done. Then he fixes two cups and hands one to me.

It's decent even if coffee isn't my favorite. Plenty sweet. Exactly the way I like it.

He makes eye contact. "I'm sorry. I know I fucked up. I don't have an excuse." He moves closer. "I wish I could explain it. There was so much attention and I kept thinking about the way everyone treated me when I was with Vivian. And after. Like I was caustic. Like I was about to explode. I panicked. And then Tom kissed you and I lost it. I knew he was making a point, but I still wanted to kill him." His voice gets serious. "I had to get out of there so I wouldn't."

I hold his gaze. I want to call out his bullshit, but I can't. It's awful when everyone looks at you like you're going to break. "Okay."

He moves closer, sets his cup on the table, and offers me his hand. I want to hold it. I want it on my body. But that's only going to make this more difficult.

I down half my cup of coffee. I won't tell him until I finish my drink. A girl can't deal with heartbreak and caffeine deprivation at the same time.

He pushes a stray hair behind my ear. "Remember that game, truth or truth?"

Right. That super fun game where we ask each other questions we don't want to answer.

But we did answer them.

And honestly.

That has to count for something. I nod, okay, turning so we're eye to eye. Those are some gorgeous eyes. Deep and brown and full of life.

He stares back. "Is there any chance you'll back down to your mom and skip out on your teaching credential?"

I run through the options. There was a chance, a good chance, but now I'm too determined to do anything else. "No. I don't think I would have gotten here without you, but no. No chance I'll back down."

His smile breaks up the misery in his expression. His eyes light up. His cheeks crinkle. It's sweet and smug at once.

He cocks his eyebrow. "Say that part about how you couldn't do it without me again."

His voice wavers. Not his usual playful self.

"No. Your ego is already the size of the Golden Gate Bridge."

"My ego, huh?"

"Yes."

Drew brushes his hands over my wrist, tracing the outline of my watch. "Guess it's your turn."

My gaze goes to the floor. I swallow the last drop of my drink. Okay. No more excuses.

I make eye contact with Drew. I open my mouth to speak, but my tongue is sticky. Words aren't cooperating with me.

His expression is utter fascination. No concern, no apprehension, no clue what I'm about to say.

It's like pulling off a Band-Aid. It only hurts for a minute.

"Are you in love with me?" I ask.

His jaw drops. Confusion forms in his eyes. "Fuck. Didn't think you'd start with that."

"You don't have to tattoo it on your body or something."

His eyes go to the ceiling. His lips rub together. "I'm not sure. I'm not sure what that's supposed to feel like."

I shift to my feet. The door is that way. It's harder to ask him to leave than to storm off, but Drew knows when he really needs to back off.

I can do this.

I gaze into those deep, brown eyes. "Here's the thing, Drew. I've been running away from my feelings, but I can't anymore. I love you. I've loved you for a long time. I don't want to love you—you drive me out of my freaking mind—but I do. I love you like I love dancing, like I love chocolate, like I love breathing. Hell, I'd gladly give up breathing for you. I've already said 'fuck it' to sleeping and thinking and walking around with a settled stomach."

His expression is so damn intense. I have to look away to maintain my composure.

Like a Band-Aid.

It hurts for a minute and it's over.

Only this is going to hurt a lot longer than a minute.

"I love you too much to not be your everything."

"I do—"

I interrupt him. "I know you have *feelings* for me. You've been my best friend for a long time, and for a long time that was enough. But not anymore. I need to know you love me enough to hire someone to write 'Drew and Kara forever' in the sky. That you love me enough to give up breathing."

His eyes are wide, like he's hanging on every word.

Almost done. The pain is almost over. "And if you're not sure yet, or you're not ready to deal with it yet, fine. But that means you need to leave, because I have things to do."

"Let me hold your hand while you tell your mom."

I shake my head. "That's a boyfriend task."

His eyes turn down. He frowns. "I do... I just haven't worked this out yet."

"And it's nice you want to, but it's a bunch of bullshit. You either love me or you don't. You either want me or you don't. There's no middle ground." I walk to the door. It takes all my strength, but I pull it open. "Think about it. Figure it out. I'll be at that show Wednesday. But that's all you get, Drew. After Wednesday, I'm done."

He's silent. Still. Staring at me like I'm from another planet.

Seems a lot like a no, but there's still a chance of a yes.

He runs his fingertips over my wrist. "Do me a favor."

"Yeah?"

"Come here." He brings his hand to my cheek and pulls me into a slow, deep kiss.

My heartbeat picks up. Drew releases me. His eyes find mine. There's something in them, something deep and powerful.

But he doesn't say anything.

I fight a sigh, but it still comes.

He stares at me for a moment. Then he makes his way to the door.

Then he's gone.

Chapter Thirty-Five

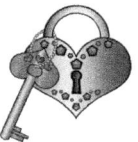

I wait on the couch, blanket up to my shoulders, eyes glued to the TV. Band-Aid number one still stings. I'm not so sure I'm ready for Band-Aid number two.

I flip through the channels unmoved. Eventually, I settle on a *Friends* rerun. My phone buzzes with a text but I can't bring myself to look at it. What if it's Drew, telling me he doesn't love me, and that he'll never love me? I can only take so much rejection in one twenty-four hour period.

The next rerun is *Seinfeld*. Then *How I Met Your Mother*. The laugh tracks are more grating with every minute. Fuck it. I find something dark and depressing on a cable channel —an independent film about miserable people who hate each other.

That's better.

Twenty minutes later, keys jangle in the door. My mom steps inside with a smile. She looks good. Her hair is fixed. Her makeup is neat. Her clothes fit perfectly.

She's taking care of herself.

She's okay.

It's possible she can handle this news.

"Sweetie." Mom steps into the main room. "When did you get in?"

"A few hours ago."

"Did you eat dinner?"

"I had a snack. I'm not that hungry."

She checks the time on her watch. "Too late for a cup of tea?"

"That sounds great."

She retreats to the kitchen and fiddles with the kettle. My tech-savvy, business-running mother still hasn't adopted an electric kettle.

I study my mom's posture. She's standing up straight. Not hunched or curled into herself the way she sometimes is. There are no hints of pain or sadness on her face.

I sit at the coffee table and play with my hands. My phone buzzes. A text from Drew, no doubt, but I'm not ready to hear whatever it is he's saying. Not until I deal with this.

I shove my phone into my purse and drop it on the ground.

Mom brings out a pot of tea, two cups, and a little plate of cookies. Double chocolate chip. My favorite.

Only the smell of chocolate brings me right back to that day in the kitchen with Drew. To his hands, his lips, his—

Not the time. I shake off my lust and pour myself a cup of tea.

Mom smiles. "I'm so glad you're here. I missed you over New Year's."

"Me too."

She fixes her cup and takes a sip. A satisfied look spreads across her face. She's enjoying something.

Another good sign.

"How is work?" I take a sip.

"Busy. Always busy."

"And you're good?"

"Yeah, sweetie. I am."

"Really? Really good and not like you were after Dad died?"

She frowns. Her posture stays the same. Shoulders back, head straight. Confident. "Your father was everything to me. There's always going to be something missing."

"I miss him too."

Mom pats my hand. "I don't know how I got so lucky to raise such a sweet daughter, but it wasn't okay what happened after your father died. You did more than your share."

That stiff feeling in my neck softens. "Thank you."

Mom takes a deep breath. "I'll never be the same person I was before Dad died, but I'll be okay."

"Are you sure?"

"Yes, sweetie. I'm sure."

Deep breath. Here goes nothing. "I don't want to work at your company."

Mom is looking at me with confusion. She presses her hands into her cup and takes a sip. Her eyes go to her drink.

I exhale slowly. Band-Aid, off. The sting lessens. The tension in my back and shoulders lessens. The tightness in my chest lessens.

It's okay.

It's going to be okay.

"It's not because of you," I say. "It's just that I hate finance. I hate business. I hate that internship, and I know I shouldn't because it's such a great opportunity. But I hate it so much." I play with my jeans. "I got into UCLA's teaching program. To start in the fall."

"Sweetie, that's great."

"It is?"

"Of course." She presses her hands together. "What you love comes first."

"Really?"

"Really."

I relax into the couch. "I've been so worried you'd hate me for going against your plan."

"I wish you'd told me sooner. I would have taken the week off."

"It's okay. I have a lot of thinking to do."

"Something you want to talk about?"

This conversation is going okay. No reason why I can't continue that.

"It's this guy," I say. "Drew."

"That boy from down the street? His family must have moved in about ten years ago."

"Yeah. I'm in love with him."

"Let's talk about it."

We spend the whole night poring over all the messy details. In the end, I don't have the answers, but I feel better.

Like it's not so bad trusting someone.

Even someone who hurt me once upon a time.

Before I go to bed, I check my phone. I have new messages from Tom, Meg, and even Pete and old messages from my mom updating me on her ETA.

Nothing from Drew.

I send an "I'm fine" text to the potentially concerned parties.

I'm not ready to talk to Drew, but I'm sure he's going out of his mind worrying about me telling my mom.

I can't bring myself to make him suffer. Even if he fucking deserves it.

I send him a short message.

Kara: I told my mom. Don't call or reply or anything. I'm still not ready for a no.

Chapter Thirty-Six

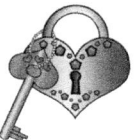

I keep my phone off. Mom and I hit my favorite San Francisco spots. She calls in sick on Monday and Tuesday so we can keep acting like tourists.

Then it's Wednesday, and I can't eat, sleep, think, or breathe. About par for the course, really.

I have no easy way to occupy myself with Mom at work. I fill out my UCLA paperwork online. I check the Sinful Serenade show information on Tom's Twitter account. There are half a dozen pictures of him posing with pretty fans.

Drew isn't in any of the pictures.

Not that I'm checking.

Not that the only thing on my mind is what Drew is going to say to me tonight, if he's going to say anything at all.

I change into a sweater dress, tights, and boots and keep myself busy by walking around the city in the general direction of the concert venue. It's four miles away or so. By show time, I'm within ten blocks. I grab a bagel and a cup of tea to calm my stomach.

It only helps so much.

The line for the venue curves onto Market Street. There must be a hundred people waiting on the concrete. Most are in their teens or twenties, in ripped jeans and colorful sneakers. I should feel out of place given my not at all rock and roll outfit, but I don't.

Even when I cut to the front of the line to give my name to the bouncer. He looks at me like he can't believe that I am on the list. But I am.

"Backstage is there, honey." He nods to a door in the corner. "Nice girl like you—hope you're not one of these guys' girlfriends."

"We'll see." I ignore the direction of backstage and go straight to the main area. I'm not ready to see Drew yet. And I'm really not in the mood to see Tom sucking face with his groupie of the night. Or worse, getting sucked off by his groupie of the night.

The venue is close to full. I find the bar and order a grapefruit and tequila. It burns in a pleasant way that promises to calm the nerves in my stomach.

My mind is going in circles. What if he doesn't love me? How the fuck am I going to deal with that? I talk myself out of leaving twenty times.

The lights cut out. The room is pitch black and everyone is screaming. Screaming out of their fucking minds.

A spotlight turns on. It's focused on a single figure on the stage. A tall guy in a black v-neck and dark jeans, with an acoustic-electric guitar around his shoulders.

Drew.

He steps up to a microphone. His cheeks flush. He's actually nervous.

"You guys realize I'm not Mr. Webb, right?" He waves

at the crowd. "Not sure I can promise to strip the way he does."

A few dozen girls scream in a mix of agony and ecstasy.

"It's nice to be in San Francisco. It's my hometown."

There's way more screaming. Drew smiles like he's regaining confidence. He scans the crowd, but there's no way it's anything but a sea of darkness from his view. And even if it's not, I'm way in the back. I can barely make out his expression.

" I talked my bandmates into letting me have a set with just me and the guitar. Tom tried to argue you all wouldn't be excited by this private show, just me and my guitar. Is that so?" He smiles over the sounds of screams. "I promised this girl—"

The screams drown out everything else in the room. Drew melts under the attention. It takes him a moment to regain his confident posture.

He steps up to the mic. "Let's just say this is a special occasion."

He plays the opening of "No Way in Hell," the songs Miles wrote about falling in love with Meg. Then he's singing. His voice is beautiful. It's not polished. It's not hitting every note. It's not as showy or as energetic as when Miles sings, but it's raw and it's real and it's dripping with feeling.

The crowd is fucking insane. The reserved guitarist is suddenly in the spotlight. He's even singing.

He's singing for me.

He plays "Be Brave, Love." He sings every single word.

Drew shifts, grabs the mic. He looks out to the crowd. "Let's not let Miles know how much you all prefer me, huh?" He smiles over the laughter and cheering. ' I have one more song to sing—a cover. You'll like it. But first, I need your help. I need to find someone very important to me." Drew looks out at the crowd. "Kara Kendrick, where the fuck are you?"

Girls are screaming, cheering, swooning. There's a name for Drew's rumored girlfriend. I admit it. I read celebrity gossip.

Someone in the crowd screams something that sounds a lot like, "Is she your girlfriend?"

Drew blushes. He scans the crowd. "If she'll have me, she's my girlfriend."

The fangirl squeals.

He wants me to be his girlfriend.

There must be six, seven hundred people here, and he's telling all of them he wants me to be his girlfriend.

"Do me a favor." He motions for the crowd to part. "Make room for her."

It takes a minute but the crowd parts. There's an empty space going down the middle of the room. Must be three hundred people on each side of it and they're all waiting for me.

Drew motions to someone backstage. The spotlight cuts and something behind it flashes.

It's there in lights.

Drew and Kara Forever.

I melt.

I don't really have a choice. I move to the center of the room, to the line that's there just for me. One of the spotlights finds me. People gasp. It's like you can hear jaws dropping.

Drew's eyes find mine. I'm about ten feet from the stage, plus the five it's raised above the floor. I stare up at him. He stares back at me.

"Kara, come up here. Before the crowd gets restless and demands I strip to nothing."

The cheers are deafening. Drew makes a better frontman than I'd guess. But then offering to take off his clothes is a pretty powerful card to play.

The crowd chants. "Take it off! Take it off! Take it off!"

He blushes as he screams back. "Let's make a deal. You get her up here, and I will."

Someone pushes me forward. Then I'm being lifted and passed around. Weightless, hands on my back, moving me toward Drew. I'm stage diving from the damn floor.

There. I'm pushed onto the stage. My boots make contact with the ground.

His eyes find mine. "Where should I start?" He shrugs his guitar off his shoulders and hands it to me.

I hold tight.

He pulls his t-shirt over his head and tosses it on the ground.

The crowd screams.

Drew speaks into the mic. "The rest is only if this goes well." He winks at the crowd then looks back to me. "Kara, this is for you."

I hand back his guitar. He slings it over his shoulders. His eyes on mine, he strums.

The intro starts. It's a ballad. And it's familiar. Really familiar.

Holy shit, it's "Maybe I'm Amazed," by Paul McCartney. The song that pretty much screams *I Love You*.

He sings. His eyes close. His heart is in every line. His voice is dripping with feeling. It's sweet and clear and perfect.

My body goes into overdrive. Heart racing. Lungs stalling. Knees buckling.

His voice washes over me, mixing me up and making me warm all over.

I have nothing to hold onto, no way to steady myself.

Drew is on a stage, singing for me. It shouldn't be this novel, what with him being a rock star. But he doesn't sing. He never sings. And he's interrupting his fucking concert to sing for me.

Drew's voice picks up, louder, dripping with even more feeling. He sounds good. Not like a professional singer. Rawer. Realer.

He plays the outro. His eyes blink open. He sets his guitar on the ground and grabs the mic.

He's five feet away.

His eyes are glued to mine. "Kara, I'm sorry this took me so long. I was terrified of ruining things. Terrified I'd lose you. Once I worked it out, it was obvious."

I take a deep breath.

"I'm sure this isn't the best place to profess my feelings for you. But that's too bad because these words have been burning a fucking hole in my gut the last few days."

He takes a step, so he's two feet away.

"I love you. I'm madly in love with you." His voice is sweet. "You are my everything. You mean more to me than anything in the fucking world. Hell, I'd give up the guitar before I'd give up you."

There's a mix of *aww* and *no fucking way* from the crowd.

Drew blushes. He turns to the audience. "Let's hope it doesn't come to that." His eyes connect with mine. "I want you to be my girlfriend. I want the whole fucking world to know how much I love you."

There's an *aww* from the crowd. People are clapping and cheering, but the only thing I can see is Drew.

The sincerity in his eyes.

The smile on his lips.

Drew. My Drew.

I take a step toward him. "Say it again."

"Answer first," he says. "I know it's high school and it's cheesy, but I want everything official. Will you be my girlfriend?"

"Yes. Of course.'

He smiles. "I love you."

"I love you too."

He slings the mic over his shoulder. Then his arms are around me, pulling me close.

His lips press into mine.

He's mine.

All mine.

Always.

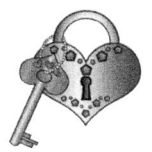

Epilogue

"Drew, I can't leave my graduation party."

This does not stop Drew. He squeezes my hand and sneaks me out the side door.

God, he looks good in a suit, cleaned up like the nice boy next door.

"We have a very important appointment." He presses his lips to mine. "And only an hour to catch up for the last two weeks."

"Why did your flight have to get in late? It's been torture seeing you in that suit all day."

"You like it?"

I nod, licking my lips like a puppy waiting for a treat.

"Not as much as I like that dress."

He holds me against the wall. His hands skim the neckline of my dress then dip below it. Oh God. The brush of his fingers against my nipples is enough to make my sex clench. Has it really only been two weeks? Feels like it's been two years.

He sucks on my neck. "Better stop before I fuck you right here."

"Where are we going?"

"That's a surprise before the surprise."

"And you're still not going to tell me?"

He nods with this mischievous smile. What am I getting myself into?

Drew's car is parked around the corner. Far enough away that no one will hear us leave. The man thinks of everything.

"You want to give me a hint?" I ask.

"It's for us."

"A better hint."

"It might hurt."

I stare at him, but there are no clues in his expression.

He squeezes my hand as he drives.

Actually being boyfriend/girlfriend is amazing. He's been on tour the last month and a half, but we haven't been apart for more than two weeks at a time. He visits or sends me a ticket to come for the weekend.

On other days, we make do with our cell phones and web cams. Drew can put on quite the show when he wants to.

And now that I'm officially done with my undergraduate degree, I'm coming on tour with him. Two months on the road with my rock star boyfriend.

"You have everything packed to leave in the morning?" He pulls onto Wilshire and drives twenty miles over the speed limit.

"Everything."

"I better find your suitcase and toss all the underwear."

"You really want me going without panties at a bunch of sweaty rock concerts?"

He nods. "My hands deserve a reward for all their hard work."

Dammit, he still makes me blush. He still makes my

body go into overdrive. It's better now that I know he's really mine.

We drive for ten minutes and park at a hotel valet. Drew grabs an overnight backpack from the backseat and rushes out of the car. I nod to the valet as I step out. Between my royal blue commencement dress and his black suit, we stand out. At least no one will recognize Drew like this.

Nothing to delay our reunion.

He squeezes my hand all the way to the registration counter. He gives his assumed name—Bruce Wayne—and checks in. The clerk slides us two keys. We don't wait for the details. We go straight to the elevator.

The second the doors close, my hands are on him. I kiss him hard, sucking on his lip, plunging my tongue into his mouth. God, he tastes good. Familiar. Like Drew. Like home.

He slides his hands under my ass, lifting me and pressing me against the wall of the elevator. I wrap my legs around him, slide my arms around his shoulders.

"There's a camera in the ceiling." I press my neck against his lips.

"And?" He sinks his teeth into my skin. His hands get lost in the fabric of my tea-length dress. "Tell me you're not wearing panties."

"Only one way to find out."

The elevator dings at our floor. Drew groans. He shifts so I can feel his erection, then sets me down on my feet.

"Fuck, Kara. I missed you. I can barely walk."

I smile and look at the room information. "The room is only twenty feet away. You'll make it."

I find our suite and open the door with the electronic key. Drew whisks me inside, immediately pressing me against the door. He tugs at the skirt of my dress, still lost in the fabric.

"Well fuck this." He drops to his knees and ducks under the skirt. His fingers trail up my thighs. His mouth follows their path.

Then his mouth is on me. I'm *not* wearing any panties. He flicks his tongue against my clit. I'm so keyed up that it pushes me to the edge.

I find the dress's zipper, undo it, and pull the whole thing over my head.

Drew looks up at me. His eyes go wide. His hand trails up my stomach to my chest and toys with my nipples.

"You taste so fucking good." He flicks his tongue against my clit. "Better than I remembered."

I tug at his hair. It's a shame. This is the only time his hair has ever been neat and I'm making a mess of it. Somehow, I'm sure he doesn't mind.

Pleasure builds quickly. A few more flicks of his tongue and I'm there. I tumble into an orgasm. All that pressure releases in wave after wave of bliss.

"Drew," I groan. "Get the fuck out of those clothes."

He scoops me up and brings me to the bed. I undo the knot of his tie as he shifts his jacket off his shoulders. The shirt comes off one button at a time. There's a black belt holding up the black slacks. I unbuckle it then pull the pants to his feet.

He kicks off his shoes. Then the pants. He's wearing nothing but boxers and black dress socks.

"Sexy look?" He pats his crotch like he's telling me to sit.

"Yeah." I slide his boxers off his hips and bring my body into his. "But white socks would be better."

"How about Argyle?"

"I'm already wet, baby. You don't have to try harder to get me there."

He smiles. He grabs my hips and wrestles me onto my back. With one violent thrust, he enters me.

"Oh God." I wrap my legs around him, shifting my hips to meet his movements. "I missed you."

"I missed you more."

His lips close over mine. I slide my hands into his hair and hold his mouth against mine, exploring his mouth like it's been years instead of weeks. His tongue dances with mine, playful and aggressive.

He thrusts into me. I match his rhythm, pushing him deeper. He groans into my mouth. I groan back. I've already made a mess of his hair, so I go crazy.

We stay locked together, rocking into each other's bodies, need pouring back and forth. Pleasure builds inside me. I resist. I want to come with him. It's been too long.

I bring my mouth to his neck and suck on his skin. Until he's groaning. Until his hands squeeze the sheets. There. He's close. I let go of control, moving faster and harder.

An orgasm rises up inside me. I groan. I pull one hand free and intertwine it with his.

I stare deep into Drew's eyes, at all the love and affection and desire in them. He stares back and I know we'll be locked like this until we're there.

A few more thrusts and we're coming together. My sex clenches around him. His cock pulses inside me. Pleasure spreads to my fingers and toes as he fills me.

Fuck yes.

I collapse on the bed.

He lies next to me, bringing my body into his, wrapping his arms around me. "I love you."

"I love you too." I turn my neck to press my lips to his. "How long do we have?"

"About ten minutes until we need to get dressed."

"Can I have a clue yet?"

"No." He slides his hand below my waist. "You can have an orgasm."

His fingers graze my clit.

It would be silly to waste ten perfectly good minutes.

"I accept your offer."

I press my body into his. He strokes me until I'm there, moaning his name as I come.

WE WASH UP, DRESS, AND MAKE OUR WAY TO THE STREET. Drew leads the way on a walk of unspecified length.

He stops at the corner. "Close your eyes."

"We have to cross the street!"

"You trust me?"

I do. I press my lids together. It amplifies the sound of traffic. The heat of the sun. The softness of his lips on my neck.

The light changes. We cross the street, walk straight for one block, turn right.

"Open your eyes." Drew points to the shop in the middle of a strip mall.

It's a tattoo parlor.

"Our appointment starts in ten minutes," he says.

"What kind of appointment?"

"The couple's tattoo. You think I'd joke about that?" He slides his arm around my waist. "You can back out if you're scared. It does hurt."

I slide my arms around his neck and look him dead in the eyes. "Makes sense, because loving you hurts."

"A good hurt?"

"Very good."

He presses his lips into mine. "Do you want to do it?"

A tattoo with Drew? It's terrifying and exhilarating all at once. So much more permanent than anything else, even marriage. He'll never be able to unmark his body. I'll never be able to unmark mine. But then, it's not like there's anything I could do to convince my body it's not addicted to Drew.

"Let's do it," I say.

"I have a design picked out." He leads me into the shop and waves at one of the artists. "You'll like it."

The tattoo artist, an inked-up man in a black t-shirt and skinny jeans, introduces himself. "You must be Kara. I'm Ed. I've heard a lot about you."

"That so?" I ask.

Ed nods. He pulls out a sketchbook and flips to a page. There's a drawing of a matching set of tattoos—an ornate key and a heart shaped lock. "Drew wants the lock."

I turn to Drew. "You do realize the phallic implications of the key?"

He plays dumb. "You should explain them to me. Preferably with a demonstration." He looks to Ed. "You guys have a bathroom, right?"

"No way in hell," Ed says.

"That's one of our songs. About another girl though." Drew turns to me. "I figured I'd get it on my other shoulder. Instead of a broken heart, I have one that can only be unlocked by you.'

I swear to God, I melt. I have the key to Drew's heart. It's cheesy, but it's perfect. "I want mine on the opposite shoulder."

He slides his hands into my hair. "You sure?"

"Positive." I kiss him so hard I can't breathe. It doesn't

help the nervous feeling in my stomach, but it still feels so damn good.

A tattoo. This *is* going to hurt.

"I can go first," Drew says. "In case you chicken out."

"I want to go first."

Drew winks at Ed. "She always does."

"Shut the fuck up, Denton. You come first plenty."

Ed smiles. He points to a smooth leather chair. It looks like something out of a dentist's office.

"Make yourself comfortable," he says.

I do. Drew sits next to me, squeezing my hand hard enough to cut off circulation to my fingers. His eyes find mine. Those brown eyes are wide with excitement and wonder.

"You don't have to do this," he says.

"I want to."

"Good." His smile gets wider.

Ed returns. He rubs my arm with some kind of antiseptic and shaves the area with a safety razor. Then he sprays water on my arm, then slaps something there and peels it off.

It's a stencil of the design.

He does the same to Drew.

I check our reflections in the mirror. I'm the key and he's the lock. There's no doubt they're matching, that they're for us.

"You have any ink, Kara?" Ed asks.

"None."

He grabs a tattoo gun and prepares the different colors of ink, separating them into small, individual cups. "It hurts, but it's not too bad. Like a shot at the doctor. Let me know when you're ready."

"I'm ready," I say.

The tattoo gun turns on with a rhythmic buzz. Drew offers his hand. I take it.

Ow. That hurts like a bitch. I close my eyes, focusing on the pain. It's familiar, good and bad all at once. I squeeze Drew's hand a little tighter. I open my eyes and stare into his.

It's enough to get me through this.

It's about thirty minutes, on and off. The shading hurts the most, but it's nothing compared to how exhilarated I feel when I look at my new tattoo in the mirror.

Drew presses his lips against my forehead. "You were right. We should get back to the party. Your mom is probably missing us."

"Your sister is probably flirting with Tom."

"Not if he wants to live through the tour."

"She wants his bod."

"Better stop that from happening." Drew smiles. "You're not buying this bluff, are you?"

"Not a chance."

Drew goes next. His tattoo takes longer. An hour maybe. The whole time, he holds my hand. No squeezing necessary. He doesn't seem to mind the pain.

When we're finished, Ed wraps our new ink and gives us instructions on how to take care of it. He looks at Drew with a serious expression. "Make sure she follows procedure."

"He thinks you're trouble," Drew says.

"Because he knows you're trouble."

Drew smiles. This flush spreads across his cheeks. Almost like he's nervous. He checks something on his phone then turns back to me.

"Meet me outside," he says.

I raise my eyebrow as if to ask why.

"It's a surprise," Drew says. "And I have to settle up with Ed. Go."

Okay. I like the surprises so far. I make my way back to the car. Our graduation ceremony was early. It's still light out. Another hour or two to sunset even. I bring my gaze to the sky.

Oh my God. There in tiny little clouds, it says "Kara, will you marry me?"

I rub my eyes again to make sure I'm not dreaming.

I'm not.

The door to the tattoo shop opens and Drew steps outside. "They wouldn't give me enough letters to write 'Kara Kendrick, I love you more than life itself, will you marry me?'"

He makes his way to me. Right here, in the parking lot, he drops to one knee.

My mouth goes sticky. I can't talk. I can't think. Drew is proposing to me. He's really mine.

"Isn't Miles going to hate you for stealing his thunder?" I ask.

"You want to do this or you want to talk about Miles?" Drew pulls a ring box from his jeans. "I asked for his blessing. He said Meg won't discuss it until after her first year of med school."

"Oh."

"I asked for your mom's blessing too." He looks up at me. "She said that we're too young, but you should do whatever makes you happy."

Drew pops open the ring box. It takes great effort, but I manage to breathe.

"You're really doing this?" I ask.

He nods. "I don't have any doubts about wanting to spend the rest of my life with you. I love you now. I'm going to love you forever." His eyes meet mine. "Kara Kendrick, will you marry me?"

"Yes." I barely manage to get the word out, but there it is. My body is light again. It's so much more exhilarating than the tattoo. It's the best thing I've ever felt.

He slides the ring—a completely enormous but completely perfect ring—onto my finger and rises to his feet. His lips meet mine. Once again, I melt.

"I love you," he says.

"I love you too."

The End

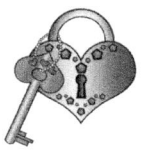

Want More Sinful Serenade?

Sign up for the Crystal Kaswell mailing list to get exclusive alternate POV scenes from *Sing Your Heart Out*, *Strum Your Heart Out*, and *Rock Your Heart Out*. You'll also get exclusive teasers and news on new releases and sales.

Turn the page for an excerpt from *Rock Your Heart Out*, Tom and Willow's story, available now.

Sinful Serenade
Sing Your Heart Out - Miles
Strum Your Heart Out - Drew
Rock Your Heart Out - Tom
Play Your Heart Out - Pete
Sinful Ever After – series sequel
Just a Taste - Miles's POV

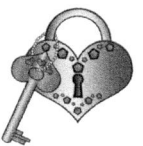

Rock Your Heart Out Teaser

<u>Get *Rock Your Heart Out* Now</u>

The room is dark except for the yellow light streaming from under the closed bathroom door. Quiet except for the *tap-tap-tap* of the shower.

Then there's no more *tap-tap-tap*. The shower is off.

I grope the wall for the light switch. Nothing. Still dark.

Okay. No big deal. My brother knows I'm coming. I knock just in case my ETA text messages didn't get through. "Drew. It's me. Take your time."

No response. Maybe he didn't hear me. I go to knock again but the handle turns.

The bathroom door pulls open. Light pours into the main room. It surrounds a muscular man in a soft, yellow glow.

That's not Drew.

Thank God, because he's naked.

Completely and totally naked.

There's a strange naked man in Drew's hotel room, and he's between me and the exit.

I take a step backwards. There's nowhere to go. I'm against the wall. My heart beat speeds up. This guy doesn't look menacing but that's not enough to convince the nerves in my stomach to settle.

"Hey. Didn't think you were coming," he says.

His voice is calm. Not threatening.

I take a deep breath. This must be an innocent mistake. The guy at the front desk gave me the wrong key.

Please let it be an innocent mistake.

"Alice?" he asks.

I shake my head. I'm not Alice. Given the way he's standing, tall and proud and utterly naked, she must be a sexual partner.

He reaches for something and the room illuminates. He's no longer highlights on hard muscles. Actually, he's really familiar. Green eyes. Dark blond hair hanging wet around his face. Soft lips curled into a welcoming smile.

I know him. Know who he is.

Relief floods my limbs as I exhale. That's him. Tom Steele, the drummer in my guitarist brother's alternative rock band, Sinful Serenade.

He's not dangerous. He's my brother's best friend.

Give or take. Drew isn't really the friendly type.

"Did you change your hair?" he asks. "Your nose maybe? Don't get me wrong. You look good. Just different."

I shake my head. My mouth is too sticky to form words.

He's naked.

My eyes won't co-operate with me. They trace a line down his body. Strong jaw, soft lips, broad shoulders, sculpted torso.

I've seen plenty of men naked in photography classes, but none of them made me feel sweaty and flushed.

My gaze goes lower.

To his happy trail

Lower.

Holy shit.

He's pierced. There's a barbell stud going through the top to the bottom of his tip.

My jaw drops. "Is that a..."

"Prince Albert?'

It's impossible to speak. I nod.

"It's an apadravya. Like a Prince Albert but on both sides."

"Oh."

"It's new," he says. "Real new, actually. I'm out of commission for another three weeks. But I still have a mouth and two hands, so hop on the bed."

Me... on the bed... with Tom.

He steps closer. "You're not Alice, are you?"

Finally, I collect some hint of my senses. "No, I'm sorry." I press my back against the wall. Nerves collect in my stomach. Not fear but embarrassment. "Isn't this Drew's room?"

"We switched." His eyes fix on mine. "How did you get a key?"

It is an honest mistake. That's a relief. How did I get this key? At the desk. Asking for Bruce Wayne. It's hard to think given the circumstances. I say the first thing that makes it to my lips. "You're naked."

He laughs. "You're observant."

I can't drag my gaze away from his piercing. "Didn't that hurt?"

"Not as much as you'd think."

"What's the point?"

He studies my expression. "If you don't like it stop staring."

I press my eyelids together. "Sorry."

"You want to tell me what you're doing in my hotel room?"

"I thought this was Drew's room."

Somehow, I manage to look him in the eyes. That's definitely Tom. We've never met—I was in boarding school when the band was forming—but I've seen him in music videos and on the cover of *Rolling Stone*.

Tom pulls a towel around his waist. That makes it easier to think.

"I'm Drew's sister. Willow." I dig into my purse and pull out my driver's license. "Here. See."

Tom glances at the ID then returns it. "You shoulda told me before I let you gawk." He goes to the bed, digs through an open suitcase, and pulls on a pair of boxers. "I don't mind. I'm not shy. But your brother will kill me if he finds out you saw me naked."

There's a tattoo of a lion on his chest. Thick black lines. The pattern continues down his arm, all the way to his wrist.

"I know I'm sexy as hell, but you should probably stop staring."

God, he's right. I'm being all kinds of rude. There's no excuse. "I'm sorry. It's just—"

"Been a while?"

"Something like that." My cheeks flush. It's been six years since I've had sex. Six years since I've felt a hint of desire.

"I feel you, kid. I'm under strict orders from my piercer: no sex for six weeks." He looks back to me with a playful smile. "Can't even fuck myself."

He's casual with that information. *Hi, I'm Tom, my cock is pierced, I can't fuck anyone for three more weeks. Not even myself.*

Tom gets dressed like it doesn't bother him that I'm

gawking. Skinny jeans. Converse. V-neck. Tight cotton hoodie.

Picture perfect, effortlessly cool rock star.

I press my hands against my sides and force myself to stare at the wall. Okay. We've got this mix up settled. Now I have to figure out what the hell I'm going to say to Drew about why I'm here. The truth isn't an option.

Tom's voice pulls me out of my thoughts.

"Hope I didn't scare you." He smirks and motions to his now clothed crotch. "I know it's a monster."

I clear my throat. "I wasn't expecting a naked man in my hotel room."

"You look rattled."

"Surprised."

"Intrigued?" He raises a brow.

My cheeks flush. "I've never seen a, uh, piercing like that before." I press my lips together before I shove my foot into my mouth. "I have a lot on my mind. That's all."

His eyes pass over me. "If you need something—money a place to stay—I can arrange that."

I study his expression for a clue to his intentions. He seems earnest but I don't trust my instincts when it comes to men. "No thanks. It's a family thing."

Tom raises an eyebrow. "As you wish." He taps a few numbers into the hotel phone's keypad and brings it to his ear. "Hey. You two finished? I ran into your sister at the front desk. You want me to bring her over?" Tom laughs at whatever Drew says. "I know. I wouldn't. I'm too beautiful to die." He sets the phone back in the receiver. His eyes meet mine. "He's ready. Room 417."

I nod. "Thank you. And sorry."

"I don't mind." Tom shrugs. "Just keep this between us."

"Sure." It's too mortifying to tell anyone. "Good night."

I grab my bag, sling it over my shoulder, and reach for the door.

"Willow—"

"Yeah?"

"There are leaked pics of me online. If you need to take another look."

<u>Get *Rock Your Heart Out* Now</u>

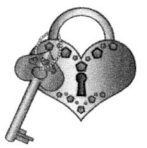

Author's Note

Thank you so much for reading *Strum Your Heart Out*. I hope you loved Kara and Drew's story as much as I did.

If you or someone you know struggles with self-harm, you can find more information about coping and resources at SIOS or SAFE.

If you enjoyed the story, please help other readers find it by leaving an honest review.

Want news about new releases and sales before anyone else? How about exclusive sneak peeks and bonus scenes? Sign up for the Crystal Kaswell mailing list.

Want to talk books? Awesome! I love hearing from my readers. Join my Facebook Fan Group here or contact me through Facebook, Twitter, or Instagram.

You can find more of my books here.

Acknowledgments

My first thanks goes to my husband, who not only tolerates but loves all my weird quirks (even my rants about grammar). Kevin, I couldn't do it without you. And the second goes to my father for always encouraging me to follow my dreams and especially for taking me to the book store when I was supposed to me grounded.

My beta readers--there are too many to name--I appreciate your feedback more than you'll ever realize. To my editors, thank you so much for your prompt responses and your amazing edits.

As always, my biggest thanks goes to my readers. Thank you for taking a chance on Sinful Serenade. I hope you'll be back for _Rock Your Heart Out_.

Printed in Great Britain
by Amazon